Discover other titles by Karen Pomerantz:

Trapping Honey

The Cost of Living

Published by Karen Pomerantz

ISBN: 978-1-9160367-1-0

Cover design by Dawn Bevins Design

Credit for burning city element of cover art:
fotorince/Shutterstock.com
Credit for alleyway element of cover art:
1000 Words/Shutterstock.com

BRING THE THUNDER

Karen Pomerantz

For Paul.

Now binge-watching TV shows need never take as
long as Sons of Anarchy again. x

CHAPTER ONE

The blazing inferno across the river wasn't usually a feature of the view from the man's high-rise office.

He was used to the red and orange tones of the sun setting across the city skyline, but they were never normally accompanied by the dense black smoke that currently belched from the fires raging below.

Here and there throughout his panoramic view of the city, more buildings were also ablaze, six in all.

A ringing sound cut through the pensive moment, followed by brief mumbling before a mobile phone was offered to the man. He held it to his ear.

'It's done,' said a voice.

'So I can see.'

'What's next?'

'Nothing. We shouldn't be in touch for a while.' He hovered his thumb over the "call end" button on the burner phone when a thought suddenly occurred to him. 'Does anyone else know the reason?'

'No. You said to keep that between us, so I did. All involved just think the operation was privately funded by a wealthy anonymous donor who was a big supporter of the cause.'

'Good. Keep it that way.' With that, he clicked off.

He handed the phone back to its owner then swivelled his office chair around to face the window. 'What of Pendleton Tower?'

'Technical problem with the detonators apparently, although I expect there may have been some user-error involved. Regardless, the guys on the ground thought it prudent to abandon that one rather than stick around once the first blast had gone off.'

'It wasn't integral to the plan anyway.' The man paused then, his mind elsewhere, planning.

'Join me,' he said suddenly, offering a crystal glass to the other man. He raised his own glass out in front of him and toasted, 'to power and money.'

'Power and money.'

They both sipped quietly at the forty-year-old scotch the man had been saving for a special occasion.

'That'll be all for tonight,' he said.

As the office door closed gently, he turned his attention back to the view outside the window. Settling down into the plush leather, he cradled his scotch and watched the neighbouring palaces burn.

CHAPTER TWO

Sam pulled her foot out of the way rapidly. A young woman had hit the floor at speed with a thud of knee pads on wood and was sliding towards Sam and her boyfriend. The impressive skid caused the fallen roller derby player to clear most of the ten-foot buffer between the track edge and the couple's trackside seats on the spectators' front row. She panted a brief 'sorry!' at them both before quickly jumping back up onto her skates and sprinting off to try to regain her position in the game.

The referee that she had collided with on her way off the track picked himself - and a little dignity - back up, adjusted one of his wrist-guards, then turned back to monitor the action on the oval track.

Loud dance music pumped out of the gym hall's P.A. system and it became accompanied by a sound like ocean waves breaking onto a beach. The aural illusion got increasingly louder as the skater who was the home team's appointed jammer came drifting smoothly around the track bend. Gracefully, she crossed one leg over in front of the other, then power-fully drove the floor away from her with her skate wheels, each rhythmical push sounding like a new wave as she whooshed past the watching couple.

The opposition jammer - on the visiting team - soon followed, her sparkly shorts revealing every muscle movement as she chased her adversary down.

Ahead of both jammers, a tight pack of eight blockers lay in wait, their team loyalties equally spread, and with polar intentions towards helping or hindering the progress of each jammer around the track.

'INSIDE!' the leading jammer screamed ahead to her team-mates. A stout blocker with "Thora Hurts" on the back of her home team shirt instantly responded to her jammer's request. She deftly slid her skate into a small space next to the inside track boundary tape that had been left unguarded by the opposing players. The opposition blocker nearest to her was the first to realise her team's mistake, as a mighty force made contact with her hip and propelled her sideways and into the rest of her teammates.

'A huge body check there from Thora Hurts has left the inside of the track wiiiiide open,' the announcer cried. The leading jammer sailed past with a 'Thanks Thora!' and continued her fast laps of the track as cheers went up from the audience. The gap was then engulfed by the purple shirts of Thora and the rest of the home team blockers as suddenly as they had created it. With an audible "oof," of forced exhalation, the trailing jammer slammed straight into a solid wall of bodies.

Sam's boyfriend's brow was furrowed in concentration.

'Don't worry, Chris,' Sam said, smiling at the clear focus on his face as four short, sharp whistle blasts signalled the end of that jam. 'I've been playing this game for months now and I still struggle with some of the rules.'

'Rules? I haven't even got my head around the basic gameplay.' Chris said as the skaters that had been on the track returned to their respective benches and a new group of women from each team lined-up on-track in their chosen starting positions. 'And I thought it used a ball,' he mumbled.

Sam couldn't help but roll her eyes. 'Well, you wouldn't be the first to think that,' she said kindly, hiding her hurt, *I thought he'd taken a little more interest when I'd explained the game last night.* 'Okay, so, think of it more like a race on roller skates, only with people physically trying to stop the racers from getting past and onto another lap.'

'So, if it's a race… and there's no ball… how do points get scored?'

'Okay, see the players with the stars on their helmets?' Sam pointed to two women positioned behind all the other players. One tall and athletically built, the other short and stout, both of them poised ready to launch themselves forward when the whistle blew. 'They are the jammers, and they score points when they overtake members of the opposite team.'

'And the other players are all blockers?'

The Non-Skating Official who was jam timing blew his whistle and the jammers lunged forward into the mass of bodies that were doing their best to seal up any gaps between themselves and their team-mates.

'Yep, they try to stop the other team's jammer from scoring points whilst helping their own jammer get through the pack and past the other blockers.'

'Okay,' he paused. 'Trust you to pick something over-complicated like this as a hobby.'

Sam punched Chris jokingly in the shoulder and he reached up a muscular arm over her head to encircle her, pulling her close as they continued to watch Sam's league, Stormy City, holding their own against the visiting North Valley Roller Girls.

'How come I'd not heard of roller derby before you discovered it?' asked Chris incredulously a few minutes later. 'A full contact sport, played by women, on roller skates, mostly wearing hot pants. This is awesome!'

'Erm, do remember that the hot pants are for the players to keep cool and sometimes to express their individuality, not for your objectification.'

'Hey,' he turned to look at her, 'I'm just winding you up, you know I'm not one of those guys.'

'I know,' she met his eyes for a moment. 'Anyway, don't be fooled. It's not all hot pants, fishnet tights and glitter. Some of us rollergirls prefer plain old sports capris. We're serious athletes you know!' Sam added with a mock stern face.

Chris laughed, 'serious athletes? I know some of the girls hit the gym pretty hard outside of training, but surely this,' he nodded out towards the game in front of them, 'is mostly for entertainment value?'

Sam narrowed her eyes, hurt.

'Look, you know I'll support you in whatever you do, but you must get that roller derby is never going to be taken seriously?'

'It *is* taken seriously by a lot of people.' Another skater hit the floor near them, elbows first, having tripped over a fallen teammate. Sam saw Chris hastily retract the arm that he had thrust out in front of her, but she was more bothered by his words than any over-protective actions at the moment. She huffed and gestured to the fallen skater who rolled over and bounced back up, digging the toe-stops on the front of her skates into the floor to help her pounce forwards. 'You have to be pretty tough to take a battering like that for an hour and still get back up again at the end of it. I think you and your football team could learn a thing or two from these girls.'

'This is the exact thing I worry about though, these falls. Some look pretty serious, and at some point you're going to do yourself some real damage.' Chris angled Sam towards him. 'I love you and I want you to be safe, I never want you to get hurt.' He kissed her on the top of her head then relaxed his hold a little. 'I prefer you on this side of the track.'

Sam took his hand and spoke gently, knowing that he meant well. 'I won't do serious damage to myself, that's what all the protective gear is for - protection! Please don't make me feel bad about being a part of this; it's good exercise and it's been great for building my confidence.'

Chris smiled at her, changing the subject; 'be honest, you're in it for the glitter and glam side of it too, "Thunder Kiss",' he used his free hand to tap her garish new necklace which featured her roller derby alter-ego name in purple glitter. He put his arm around her shoulders once more, 'but seriously, please try not to get yourself hurt.'

Sam wriggled uncomfortably, lessening Chris's hold on her a little.

He took the hint and withdrew his arm as four whistle blasts came again and changed the subject back to the sport's basics. 'How long does each race last? They seem pretty short.'

Sam relaxed her tense muscles, 'we call them jams, and they may be short but they're exhausting! They last two minutes if the lead jammer doesn't call it off before that.'

'Five seconds!' came the warning call from the jam timer, drawing Sam's attention back to the track. All the players visibly tensed, muscles at the ready, the blockers braced for impact from the waiting jammers. Sam held her breath in anticipation.

Sam tuned into the announcer's commentary; 'Stormy City position themselves nearest the jammers with North Valley right in front.'

The starting whistle sounded, and the two jammers launched themselves side-by-side at the pack. 'Cantget Yourhandson is jamming for Stormy City. Eases past her own blockers for the North Valley wall... Both jammers now locked in against the opposition. Look at the strength and agility here! Both of these women are jumping, pushing, testing the blockers' links, trying to find a crack of daylight to squeeze through!'

Oh no.

'Oh, Stormy City's wall crumbles first! North Valley jammer took her chance there. Dived shoulder-first through an impossible gap. You couldn't have gotten a chihuahua through there! Shows you though, when you are in a wall you've got to work together, move together, be together. And you'd better be ready because these jammers are coming in hot!'

The North Valley jammer was a streak of green, sprinting past her teammates who were still managing to hold back Cantget, and the jammer referee blew two short, sharp whistle blasts.

'Damn it!' said Sam.

CHAPTER THREE

'What's up?' asked Chris, 'what was the whistle for?'

'North Valley's jammer got through the pack first, so she is considered lead jammer for the duration of the jam. She'll call it off early now, before we get any points.'

North Valley's supporters erupted in cheers, and this seemed to prompt Cantget into pushing herself. After a few hard hits from her at the same point on a weakening link between two Valley blockers, one of the women fell to her knees. Cantget tried to jump through the gap, but the fallen blocker had managed to land right in the way, tripping her up. Her skates left the ground and she seemed to hang airborne for a split second before crashing down, knees first onto the hard, wooden floor on the other side of the downed blocker. Cantget put her hands out and hit the floor with the palms of her wrist guards, managing to stop from slamming her face into the track as well.

Sam gasped at the spectacular fall along with the rest of the audience, and the nearby medics stood, ready to react. Her knee pads had done their job and, as the blockers who were still standing began closing in around her, Cantget pushed herself back onto her feet, spurring herself onwards to shouts from the crowd, and doing her best to chase the lead jammer down.

Sam leaned forwards to get a better view as the two jammers skated round the track and approached the pack of blockers again. 'Stormy City's blockers are at the rear of the pack as the jammers skate around the track, they're fumbling to get into place and reform that defensive wall in time for the North Valley jammer's fast approach. They're tracking her from side to side; will they anticipate which way she might go?'

'To the inside!' called one of the blockers and the whole group committed to a move in that direction together. The jammer took a sudden big jump towards the gap that they had created on the outside and sailed past them. As Sam had predicted, she then called the jam off with a few taps to her hips, scoring four points for North Valley, and leaving the trailing Cantget with none for the home team.

Chris exhaled dramatically, 'Well, that was tense.'

Sam responded with a playful elbow to the ribs. She had found it thrilling and she knew he had too, even if he wasn't ready to admit it yet.

She took the opportunity of a break in the action to check her watch. Craning her neck, she took a look around the hall, sad not to catch a glimpse of her best friend.

Jane paused in front of the double doors that led to the gym hall, flustered from trying to find her way through the endless corridors of the city's main leisure centre. Tucking a stray section of long, auburn hair behind her ear she took a deep breath. An exhalation later, she pushed a door open and was met with an assault on her senses. Loud dance music was competing against the echoing vocal cords of an excitable commentator describing the roller derby game's action, with appropriate reactions from the assembled crowd to accompany him.

The smell in the room, years of sweat and dirt ingrained into the wooden floor, brought memories of school sports sessions flooding back. She and Sammy would stand around, bored, staring at the floor and waiting to be picked for a team. Not being naturally sporty, they were always picked last, played badly, and were then persecuted by their peers afterwards.

Jane in particular was easy fodder for the bullies back then, and she often felt like not much had changed.

Scanning the back of the crowd's heads she remembered her friend's recent radical change in hairstyle. After that, she was relieved to spot Sammy and her brightly-coloured hair within seconds. Sammy looked relaxed, excitedly applauding her team now and then, with Chris next to her, absent-mindedly rubbing her back beneath her shirt. Jane felt awkward, *I can't go over there right now. I'll give them a minute before I intrude.*

She wandered past the stalls selling a large variety of goods. Each team playing had a merchandise stall selling t-shirts, keyrings and the like with the teams' logos on. One stall displayed skate wheels and other parts, with a rail of garish leggings and shorts alongside the table. There was also a few craft and handmade-style vendors displaying jewellery and greeting cards.

A-ha! There you are. At the corner of the hall furthest from the entrance, next to the table with all the raffle prizes on, she spotted a selection of homemade cakes, which Sammy had said was a staple at roller derby games.

The selection was a little overwhelming, with the league members clearly having put some serious effort in, with even gluten-free and vegan options on offer. Jane opted for something simple, 'A banana muffin please,' she said to the blue-haired woman that was standing behind the table, intently watching the game.

'Any particular one?' the woman asked.

Jane shook her head.

'Here you go, love, one vanilla muffin, one pound please.'

'Oh, I meant the banana,' Jane said gently.

'Sorry, I can't hear you very well over the music. Sultana?'

Jane didn't want to speak up. She waved the woman's concern away, 'it's fine, thanks.'

She hovered at the back of the crowd as out of the way as she could get from any passing foot traffic and licked at the glitter on top of her cake. With the sweet smell of vanilla tickling her nostrils and a mouthful of moist sponge, she looked out at the game being played in front of her.

It was an unlikely new hobby for her sport-allergic childhood friend, but Jane could see the appeal. The players were all so different, so unique in looks, size and age. The personality differences were apparent even in their choice of uniforms, with some people choosing to wear sports capris, and others relishing the cheeky length of tiny shorts by wearing fishnet tights under them, sometimes adding more individuality with brightly patterned socks or leg warmers.

The muffin was nice, but it was sweeter than she was in the mood for. She wrapped the remaining half of it up and discreetly deposited the package in the nearest bin.

Jane's gaze wandered back to Sammy and Chris. Chris was now leaning back, supporting himself on the palms of his hands, with Sammy leaning forward, craning past a nearby referee to see the action currently taking place on the other side of the track. *Looks like it's safe to approach now.* Jane wiped the last of the cupcake crumbs from her lips and began picking her way through the crowd seated haphazardly on gym mats on the floor. She mis-timed her final steps and tripped over a young girl who jumped up excitedly just as Jane was passing her.

'SO sorry!' Jane flushed, turning her face quickly away from whoever's lap she had almost landed in.

'Jane! You made it,' Sammy replied enthusiastically, hugging her friend.

'Oh, thank goodness it was you,' Jane said quietly, returning the hug.

'Hi, Jane,' Chris leaned past his girlfriend to greet Jane who smiled in response.

'Sit here,' Sammy gestured, wiggling up closer to Chris to make room.

Chris put his arm over Sammy's shoulder and began stroking her hair.

'They have banana muffins in the corner, your favourite!'

'Er, yeah, I already had a cake thanks.'

A scrum started up on-track near where they were sitting, and Jane winced at the sound of clashing elbow and knee pads. She felt a little on-edge sitting so close to the action but didn't want her friends to feel that they had to move. *You can brave it for a while at least*, she told herself. *If it gets to be too much, well, let's worry about that then.*

Jane directed her thoughts to something else as a distraction. 'I love the hair. It looks even better in real life than in the picture you sent.'

'Thanks,' Sammy grabbed at a few bright pink strands and pulled them in front of her face to examine them with crossed eyes, 'I still can't believe I've done it,' she laughed.

'It suits this bold, new you.'

'All I've done is taken up a new hobby, and I promise that I didn't feel very bold about it, I was downright terrified.'

Jane flinched at the sound of the jammer's wheels whooshing past them on the wooden floor.

'You should come with me to practice sometime, give it a go.'

'I'm really not fit enough.'

'Come on, Jane. I've said it before,' Sammy gestured to the ten women lining-up at their benches ready for the next jam, a rare occurrence, as there was nearly always someone in the penalty box. 'Look at them. Do they all look fit? No. This is a fully inclusive sport, and you don't need to be anything other than enthusiastic, and I really mean that.'

Jane sat back silently, *I'm not entirely convinced that roller derby is something that I can do, or if I even want to do it.*

CHAPTER FOUR

Four sudden whistle blasts signalled the end of the jam, causing Jane to whip her head back up and Sammy's attention also turned back to the track.

Both teams made efficient use of the thirty seconds between jams, getting players positioned on-track and psyching each other out, but they were very evenly matched, so it was making very little difference on the scoreboard where it mattered most.

Even the penalty box was balanced, with two blockers from each team sitting where they had been sent during the final few seconds of the last jam. 'Just two blockers per team out on-track for this next jam, a Jammer's delight,' the announcer informed them.

'Oh! That's Honey jamming!' Sammy shouted excitedly, and Jane looked over to see a bright pink plait hanging down beneath the bottom of the Stormy City jammer's helmet and a little honey bee patch on the back of her shorts.

'Oh, yes', Chris responded warily, 'the "Derby Wife".'

'Don't be jealous, silly!' said Sammy, 'it's just a term of endearment, it means we get on well and that we have each other's back on-track… when I finally make it there.'

'I bet that will be sooner than you think.' Jane said quietly into her ear. 'I have every faith in you.'

'Thank you.' Sammy gave her oldest friend an appreciative glance.

Jane relaxed a little. She let the surrounding sounds wash over her, not fully taking in the detail, just the dull, hollow, echo created by the walls of the gym hall.

'Oh my god, this is such a close game!' squealed a voice behind them, 'it's going to be pretty hard to watch! Hey, Pinky,' the woman greeted Sammy and waved at Chris. 'Cazz Kay,' she said, offering her hand first to Chris, then Jane, to shake in greeting. 'Do you mind if I join you guys? I've only just got here; I had a rugby thing this morning and then on the way over I got caught up at a roadblock. Seems some idiot had thrown a holdall out of their car window for some reason, so you can imagine the chaos with it being so soon after the attacks in the city centre. The bomb squad were called and everything.'

'Yeah, I saw armed guards again in the shopping centre last weekend. What was in the bag?' asked Sammy.

'No idea, I only know that much because I had nothing to do but browse Twitter while I was stuck in the jam. Can't have been anything too serious, as they let us all past eventually. What have I missed?'

'Nothing of note, no-one's fouled out or off injured. Score's 97-89,' she gestured to the score-board. 'How's your cousin doing?'

'Not too bad thanks, Sam; she's out of hospital and home with my Aunt and Uncle for now, they're fussing over her no-end. She's also cursing ever having taken a job in the city.'

'Cazz's cousin was caught up in the explosions a couple of weeks ago,' Sammy explained.

'Terrifying, isn't it?' said Cazz. 'Just going about your daily business and that happens. She was lucky; she was in an office across the street from one of the buildings that blew; the window imploded and furniture was thrown around. She got bashed about a bit but was out of the way of most of the flying glass. The problem was being impaled by the office stationery that had been sent flying! You couldn't make it up! I hope they catch the bastards soon.'

'They said on the news there was someone they wanted for questioning,' Chris said.

Jane sensed an unease to the silence that followed the serious topic of conversation.

It seemed that Chris noticed too. He changed the subject. 'So, Cazz, you play rugby?'

'Three times a week, well, two since taking up roller derby in the last couple of months, there's only so many hours in a day, you know?'

'And what brought you to roller derby?'

'A friend on my rugby team had started and said I should give it a try.'

Sammy beamed, 'I can't tell you how excited the Stormy City girls are to have you guys join us, people describe the sport as rugby on rollerskates for a reason, and you guys have come to us with half of the skills already!'

'I've been telling people that as a summary, but then they fixate on what happens to the ball!' Cazz laughed heartily. 'It'll still be a little while before I'm deemed safe enough on wheels to play competitively though I think. I'm not a natural like you.'

Sammy blushed. 'You'll pass all those minimum

skills in no time at the rate you practice, don't worry about it, and you're gonna feel right at home with the full contact training!'

Jane smiled at Sammy's reassuring nature, it was something she was frequently on the receiving end of herself.

'I've never actually seen live Roller Derby before, I've been looking forward to this! Did your parents not fancy coming along, Sam? I thought they were curious to see what this new hobby of yours involved.'

'They might have done, but they've got to pack for a cruise next week.'

'Nice. Oh look, Honey's up. I love watching her.'

'How long has she been skating?' Jane watched Honey Trap intently as she gracefully dodged around the blockers, completely unfazed by their efforts to hold her back.

'About four years,' Sammy said. She turned her attention to Jane, 'I really do think you'd enjoy it. They're a really friendly bunch, and you used to love skating when we were younger.'

Jane pondered the idea again, Cazz's enthusiasm having had an effect on her; 'You know, I think I could be tempted actually. It would be nice to get my skates on again but something new is always difficult for me. Plus roller derby seems quite brash and eccentric.'

Sam burst out laughing, 'Yes, there's a definite rebel-type vibe to it, but most of the derby community will tell you what outcasts they've always been, how they have anxiety or other mental health concerns, and how they were never any good at sport when they were at school. Remind you of anybody?' she asked pointedly.

Jane shrugged shyly, silently acknowledging that her friend was describing both of them.

Sam's tone turned more serious. 'They'd be great with you, you know. We've had it all already; Seasonal Affective Disorder, clinical depression, you name it. Will you give it a chance?'

Jane hesitated. She looked over at the Stormy City bench where the skaters were all hugging each other as the first half of the game drew to a close. 'Okay. I'll try.'

Sammy hugged her friend. 'I can't wait, but be prepared for people constantly asking you about where the ball fits in!'

Jane turned her focus back to the team bench. The purple huddle had broken apart as players dispersed in all directions to the toilets, the vending machines for snacks, and into the crowd to speak to family and friends.

'Honey seems pretty tough,' Jane said.

'She's had to be. A couple of years ago she was kidnapped by this creepy guy she used to know.'

Jane's mouth fell open.

'Obviously she managed to get away from him, broke a few of his bones, I'm told, but then she had to hike for three miles in the Peak District with this massive cut in her thigh before she found help.'

'How do you get over something like that?' Jane muttered.

'The girls on the team said that when she returned to roller derby she just sort of threw herself intensely into her training. She would just do things that she used to be reluctant to even try before, saying that basically, after running for your life from an obsessed psycho, being scared of anything less seemed rather silly.

'She told me that the fishnet tights she wears for bouts are the ones he made her wear. They keep the nerves away for her apparently, a reminder that nothing that happens to her during a game could be as bad as that experience.'

'What experience?' came Honey's voice from above them.

CHAPTER FIVE

'Samantha was just telling us how brutal you can be at practice, and how she struggles to play against you,' Chris told Honey who was standing behind them, a banana in one hand and a sports bottle in the other.

Sammy shot him a grateful smile.

Honey took a swig of her drink. 'No apologies, no holding back, no reason not to give it my all. That's how I play these days. Sam's being modest of course, aren't you wifey? Sam's our rising star, she just needs to get past this defeatist attitude, get over her fears, and get on with it,' she winked.

Jane and the others rose to their feet to have a proper conversation with the skater. Sammy was flushed with embarrassment at Honey's compliment, but no-one aside from Jane seemed to notice.

Honey's face was glistening with perspiration, and thin rivulets of pink were running down her neck where the sweat had taken some of her semi-permanent hair dye with it.

'So, take my mind off the four-point differential currently on the scoreboard. I know Cazz, obviously, but introduce me to your friends, Sam.'

'Oh of course, sorry! This is my boyfriend, Chris, and my best friend of many, many years, Jane.'

'Pleased to meet you both. Either of you two fancy joining the team? We have a new intake starting in a couple of weeks,' Honey directed her question to both Chris and Jane.

'Always recruiting!' said Sammy, 'shouldn't you have your mind on the game?'

'Hey, I'm on a break! And yes, I am always re-cruiting, it's how to keep a team alive and fresh.'

'I'll pass, thanks,' said Chris, 'I already have a sporting commitment.'

'Okay, suit yourself, but you're missing out. What about you, Jane?' Honey queried.

Jane gave a shy shrug in response.

'Seems like Jane could be persuaded, Sam,' Honey said with a sly smile. Jane smiled back then looked over to Sammy for help.

'I've already talked Jane into coming, somewhat apprehensively.'

'Ah, no worries,' said Honey knowingly, looking Jane in the eye. 'The whole league is used to dealing with people's nerves and anxieties about joining us! Come along, give us a go, take your time to adjust, and just gradually get comfortable,' she winked at Jane, 'you'll fit right in!'

Jane's smile broadened into a wide grin at Honey's considerate words. She had warmed to the rollergirl instantly and got the impression that it was easily done with Honey.

'Right, I'd better go to the loo before we have to regroup and talk tactics, I've drank loads this half!'

'I'll come with you,' said Cazz.

'Loving the new colour by the way, Sam, hope I

was your inspiration!' Honey called as she rolled away towards the hall doors, Cazz at her side.

'It is an awesome colour,' said Jane quietly as she admired Sammy's newly-dyed magenta bob, noting that it was actually a fair few shades darker than Honey's shocking pink, and had a slight purple hue to it too. *Whatever you think, Sammy, you ARE being bold and I can see you enjoying the more confident person that you've become over the last few months.*

'Hey, Sam!' a tall woman that Jane had seen playing with Stormy City before the break skated up and executed a noisy hockey stop as she reached them. 'Our line-up manager has been called away, sick offspring or something, would you be able to step-in for him? You know the players and their strengths better than anyone else here who doesn't already have skates on.' She paused for breath, watching Sammy expectantly. 'Pleeease?'

Sammy looked torn.

Chris shooed her away encouragingly. 'Hey, you go if you want to, I wasn't going to stay till the end anyway.'

Her face fell, 'You weren't?'

'One of our strikers wanted to get in some extra training so I said I'd help him out in goal. I mean, you said you only wanted me to get an idea of the sport anyway, didn't you?'

'I guess.' She turned to Jane, 'How would you feel about it?'

Jane felt a quick stab of anxiety, but regained her composure quickly, 'Don't worry about me, I'm here to watch the game as much as to see you,' she lied, 'so go, get involved!'

Sammy still seemed a little reluctant, but also looked anxious to go with the tall skater.

Go! Jane mouthed at her insistently.

Sammy gave her friend a hug, 'Thanks, I'll call you later,' she promised, before pulling away and turning to the skater. 'Okay, Jynx. Get me up to speed.'

Jynx looked relieved. 'Thanks so much, we're already a referee down because Travis didn't bother to turn up today, again. I don't want us to look completely disorganised.' Her wristguards became a blur with all her gesticulating as the pair departed, Jynx informing Sammy of the line-ups that had been working well for them so far.

Jane watched them go, Sammy's excitement clearly apparent in the bounce she had to her step.

'And then there were two,' said Chris to no-one in particular as they sat back down on the gym mats.

'Er… and me!' chimed in Cazz, who had just returned from the toilets.

Jane smiled gratefully, she still wasn't fully comfortable in Chris's company alone yet, having not had a real chance to get to know him. She chanced a look in his direction. He was looking out across the track, a small smile on his lips as he watched Sammy taking charge of the team of skaters around her, handing out helmet covers and arranging skaters onto different sides of the bench area.

'Do you two not get on so well?' Cazz queried quietly.

Jane rotated a flat hand side-to-side, *'so-so'*. Chris had been suitably patient so far and was always civil to Jane and accepting of her, but her inability to properly socialise with him was clearly a source of frustration for him.

'I don't suppose you'll be joining us at the after-party?' he asked Jane, whilst still looking straight ahead at Sam. Jane smiled at him and shook her head apologetically. He hadn't bothered looking her way, so she hoped he had seen her gesture out the corner of his eye and didn't just assume - as he had done in the past - that she was ignoring him completely.

A woman approached Cazz on her other side and after a quick hug they began talking to one another intently as they watched the game, Cazz clearly forgetting about Jane who sat silently beside her.

Jane was unsure as to whether the waves of tension that she could almost visualise coming from Chris were really there or just a figment of her imagination. She began to feel very alone in the midst of all the things going on around her.

She focussed her attention towards the track. Sam had recently explained to her a few of the key scenarios that often came up in games so that she would know what to look out for today.

As Jane allowed herself to be sucked into the gameplay, she saw Stormy City increase their lead over the next few jams. A later penalty for the Stormy City jammer meant that the visiting team were awarded a power jam in their favour. North Valley clawed back a massive twenty-four points for that jam, closing the gap on the scoreboard to 142-138, and back to the four-point differential that had been bothering Honey at half-time.

CHAPTER SIX

Stormy City suffered a setback about ten minutes later. Cantget was blocking, having jammed for much of the first half, when she took a particularly hard shoulder hit to her sternum and ribs. She stayed down when she fell. The medics were called over, and the referees whistled the jam dead. Everyone in the room with skates on their feet respectfully dropped to one knee and as Cantget was clearly hyperventilating and taking oxygen from the medical team, the seven referees all skated in front of her, each stopping and dropping down on one knee to form a human curtain, giving the small young woman some privacy from the two-hundred pairs of concerned eyes watching her whilst she was feeling her most vulnerable.

Sam nervously twiddled with strands of her hair. She wasn't used to the feel of it being so short yet, so it frequently slipped prematurely through her fingers.

'What happened there?' whispered Jynx, 'I couldn't quite see.'

It was the announcer who answered her question, 'Well, I think we're all agreed that Slaughtermelons has been an offensive powerhouse this afternoon! A huge impact in that hit taking her opponent clean out, *but...* completely legal! You're going to know all about this when it happens to you, as you can see. It's called the Can Opener folks, that's because when you do it, you are opening up a can of whoop-ass on your opponent. Signature Slaughtermelons.'

A couple of minutes later, with her skates removed and the help of the medics, Cantget stood. Her boyfriend, Zed, was one of the referees and had shown incredible restraint and professionalism in letting the medics get on with it whilst facing away from his injured girlfriend as part of her dignity curtain. He brushed the woman's hand gently as he returned to his impartial position on the outside track boundary and as she watched the exchange, Sam couldn't help but envy his belief that his partner would be okay without his intervention.

Sam joined the crowd in cheering and applauding the injured woman as the medics began to lead her back to the team bench to sit out the next few jams with an ice pack lodged firmly up her shirt. Before she had even taken two steps with the medical team, Slaughtermelons had stepped in to replace one of them, supporting Cantget on one side and escorting her back to the bench, apologising profusely for nearly breaking her ribs. 'All's fair in love and derby,' Cantget replied with a smile that turned into a grimace as she moved to sit down. 'Nice hit by the way.'

The referees had all returned to their posts and the next line-up that Sam had arranged all stood. 'Wait!' Sam called suddenly. *With one of our main jammers out of the picture, it won't be long before we fall behind.* She glanced up to see which players North Valley were fielding for that jam.

A Valley skater that had proven herself a more-than-capable jammer during the game's first half, a young woman who chose to skate under her given name of Phillips, was wearing the jammer star on her helmet.

Sam made her decision quickly. 'Honey, you okay to jam for me?'

'Always.'

'I'm going to hold the stronger blockers back for the next jam to support a relief jammer while Cantget sits out. You'll only be dealing with two of their blockers as the others are in the penalty box and I know you're more than a match for them without an assist.'

'Yep, no worries,' she hustled to the jam line to take up her starting position as Sam instructed her chosen four blockers to join Honey on-track.

'FIVE SECONDS!' came the shout from the jam timer, bringing Sam's full attention back to the track to watch her Derby Wife do her thing. The whistle blew, and Honey threw herself at the visiting team's reduced wall of two blockers. The opposing jammer, Phillips, moved at the same time, trying to trick the two Stormy blockers who were focussed on her by constantly moving her feet and changing direction. Sam found herself mesmerised by the strange dance that Phillips seemed to be doing on her toe-stops, the girl was a very agile skater.

The blockers moved with her, using each other for support, careful to stick together.

Rather than hop about as her adversary was doing, Honey had chosen a more offensive technique. 'Woah! You don't see that too often,' the announcer screamed over the PA system, drowning out Sam's loud cheers; 'Honey Trap for Stormy City getting super-low there and managing to down Slaughtermelons with a shoulder check to her *hip*! If she'd gotten much lower, Honey would've been wearing Melons like a backpack!'

This left one remaining North Valley blocker to hold Honey back by herself. Sam saw a one-sided smile appear on Honey's lips, aimed at the nervous-looking blocker who was now facing her to track her more easily.

Honey ducked down close to the blocker. She snapped herself forward and upwards, driving her shoulder into the sternum of the woman in front of her. The impact lifted the blocker off the ground for a fraction of a second, her legs coming up in front of her before she landed hard onto the polished floor surface.

By the time the sympathetic "oooch" sound had left Sam's lips, Honey had already propelled herself forwards and away from the falling North Valley blocker and was sprinting out of the first turn. It was then that Phillips slipped free. Honey was lead jammer and heading for the pack on her first scoring pass. As she hurtled around the second bend and down the straightway, Phillips was slowly closing the gap between them and also ready to start scoring points.

On the opposite side of the oval, Sam saw the blockers in the penalty box standing up to serve their final few seconds, hovering on the track edge, ready to rejoin play.

The Stormy bench coach signalled to Honey not to call off the jam yet and to go for some points, despite the opposing jammer hot on her heels. The penalised blockers returned to the track, and a pack of all eight blockers quickly formed into two separate walls in the path of the oncoming jammers.

Honey reached the back of the pack before Phillips, but only just. The Stormy City blockers anticipated her moves and parted their purple wall to let her past, quickly closing the gap back up before Phillips could follow her through.

Phillips used her fancy footwork again to try to bounce around and hit the wall of bodies in different places, but it was a solid one. It was going to take her some time to disrupt it without any of her North Valley teammates assisting her, but they were all too busy readying themselves for Honey's approach. They needn't have bothered.

The green-clad portion of the pack was now positioned on a bend of the oval track.

Honey faked a move to the right.

The Valley blockers committed to tracking her in that direction.

She quickly changed tack and went left.

Springing forward on the inside of the blocker that was protecting the inside line, Honey leapt upwards.

Both skates in the air.

The apex of the bend passed beneath her as her long pink plait trailed out behind.

She landed one foot then the other back onto the track, in front of the wall of four blockers.

Four points scored, she quickly tapped her hands to her hips and called off the jam to an appreciative roar from the watching crowd and screams and cheers from the announcer.

Sam squealed with excitement as she realised that the Stormy City blockers still had Phillips contained, and had not allowed her to pick up a single point for that jam.

Oh my god, Honey's amazing! I wish I could skate like that.

Phillips gave Honey a high five of admiration as they passed each other on the way back to their respective benches. At that moment Sam couldn't help but feel like there was no other sport like it in the world. *Jane is going to love it.*

She looked across the track to where her friends were sitting to give them a big thumbs up, wanting them to share in this moment of elation with her. Jane and Chris were gone.

CHAPTER SEVEN

Sam scoured the crowd and eventually spotted Jane, now sitting on a chair a couple of rows back from where they had previously sat together with Chris. Her friend looked a little distracted as she applauded Honey, but then looked across and saw Sam looking over and gave her a broad smile back with a double thumbs up.

She scanned the hall for Chris, finding him at the main entrance to the room, his phone in-hand as he pulled the door open and exited without a look back.

I know he said he wouldn't stay right till the end, but I didn't think he'd leave quite so soon. I can't believe he missed Honey's jam, that would have totally sold him on roller derby.

Jane must have spotted the change in Sam's expression, as she gave her an apologetic shrug across the hall.

Sam returned it with a wonky, "Oh, well," sort of smile. Her phone buzzed in her pocket and she pulled it out to see a message from Chris; "Pick you up at 7pm. x"

She scowled at the innocent object in her hand.

'Sam, who do you want as pivot on this one?' asked the woman that Sam had handed the jammer star to earlier.

'Oh, erm. You choose, whoever you work best with if you need to pass the star,' she replied, pocketing her phone and choosing not to let Chris's departure distract her for the time being.

'Thanks guys!' said a breathless Honey to her blockers on arrival back at the bench, 'no way I could have done that without you keeping hold of Phillips the way you did.'

'All part of the blocker service, madam,' Thora bowed theatrically.

They lost the bout with a respectable score of 163-181.

After the two teams had finished fist-bumping sweaty hands with the referees and other officials, they hugged all the opposition players. The audience all lined up on the track boundary with everyone extending a hand out over the track. Sam and Stormy City's bench coach ran behind the Stormy skaters as they did a lap of honour, high-fiving everyone at the track edge as they ran or skated past. As North Valley did the same, Sam watched a particularly excitable three-year-old squealing in delight when one player low-fived her as she skated by. 'Go Mummy!' she heard her shout, and the child's dad had to restrain her from running around the track after her smiling mum as the players continued round to high-five the waiting officials.

Jane caught Sam's eye, smiling and waving from across the hall, and gestured that they'd speak later on the phone. Sam fired her a thumbs-up before winding her way in-between the volunteers on their knees lifting the track boundary tape up off the wooden hall floor. Ahead of her, the Stormy skaters rolled gracefully towards the doors leading to the changing rooms as a flurry of clearing up took place around them.

The mood in the Stormy City changing room was upbeat despite their defeat. The air was thick with camaraderie and team spirit, with the women all complimenting each other on their performances. The gathered rollergirls cheered as Sam entered the room and she cheered back. 'Nice job out there, guys, that was a really close one for a while!' she declared.

'They did all do a fantastic job, I'm so proud I could cry!' said a young woman to Sam's right who was busy peeling endless lengths of hockey tape from her knee pads where it had been securing the velcro straps. She was tall and athletically built, with long, braided hair that she wore pulled across into a low ponytail on one side of her head.

'Nothing new there then Belle!' laughed her team-mate who was packing her own gear away into a large, wheeled holdall, 'it doesn't take much to set you off!'

Belle replied by blowing a raspberry at the offending teammate.

'Belle at the Brawl, is that any way for the bouting team captain, let alone the league's head coach to behave?' Sam laughed, earning herself a wink from the captain.

'Did you hear Belle's news, Sam?' Honey said.

Sam looked at Belle and raised her eyebrows expectantly.

'I made Team West Indies.'

'Oh my god, that's amazing! A national team, go you! What did your family say, they must be so proud of you representing like that?'

'Well, Dad was pleased I was embracing my heritage, but not sure why I'd bother as there's no money in it.'

Sam was momentarily taken aback and unsure of how to respond.

Belle laughed at her expression, 'Dad's not very driven, I get that from my mother's side. They were both proud though, we're having all the family over tomorrow for a celebratory meal.'

'That's great, Belle.' Sam sat on the floor next to her coach, doing her best to avoid the damp streaks of sweat on the surface all around her that seemed to emanate from various discarded knee and elbow pads. 'Hey, Belle, I've got a friend that's interested in joining—'

'Oh, get her to come to the after-party!' interrupted one of the others excitedly.

'Sure,' Belle replied, 'just stick her name down on the list for the next Newbie Intake.'

'Er, I will, thanks. But there's something else, she's sort of a special case.'

'Not like that one we had a while back who used to bring dog biscuits to snack on?' interjected the teammate that had previously been subject to Belle's raspberry-blowing.

'She had a name,' cut in Honey, sternly, 'and I'd better not find out that she left because you were bullying her!'

Sam hurriedly continued, easing the tension, 'Er, no, not that sort of special case, she suffers with a very specific anxiety-based dis—'

'Anxiety disorders we've done, that's no issue, just tell her to take it slowly, and let her know we're patient, and we'll be here for her,' said Belle genuinely.

'Guys! Let me finish,' said Sam, affectionately rolling her eyes at the caring but presumptuous nature of her peers. 'At times she physically struggles to speak. It's beyond a disorder really, it's pretty much a disability.'

'She's mute?' queried Belle.

'Not technically. She refers to it as SM, its official name is Selective Mutism, although that term sort of implies that she has a conscious choice in when and where she speaks and who to, but it's not actually like that.'

'Okay, well that's actually new, but as always, we'll work with it,' Belle said.

'Hang on,' Honey looked quizzical, 'I spoke with Jane earlier.'

'But did you *really*?' asked Sam, smiling knowingly. Her friend had become extremely adept over the years at letting people talk whilst acknowledging them with the right body language signals in the right places. They'd often part ways none the wiser about her condition.

Honey was tilting her head and mumbling to herself, obviously trying to recall her earlier conversation with Jane as she removed her helmet and replaced it with a glittery hairband.

'Are you coming to the after-party, Sam?' Jynx asked.

'Yeah, Chris and I are gonna come a bit later, he's taking me out for dinner first.'

'Aw, he's always looking after you, isn't he?' Jynx placed both hands on her heart as she spoke.

Sam couldn't help but bristle slightly at her words.

'It's not so much that you left early, it's that you never mentioned beforehand that that was your intention,' Sam stabbed at the lone garlic mushroom on her plate.

Chris swallowed the last of his own starter before replying, 'Well, I *was* going to stick around a little longer, but to be honest I was struggling to keep up with what was going on. I don't know the rules, and Jane obviously wasn't explaining it to me.' He looked down at his empty plate as he placed his cutlery onto it. 'It's rather an over-complicated game.'

'It's a sport, Chris. With rules. Don't get put off just because it doesn't involve kicking a ball into a net. Those rules allow us to use complex strategies to gain advantages. It's chess on skates, and it's challenging, yeah, but that's the fun of it!'

He smiled, 'Didn't you once share a meme saying it was like playing speed chess whilst having bricks thrown at you?'

Sam relaxed a little. 'Yeah, well that does about sum up the experience of playing.'

' "Playing" being the key word there, Samantha, it is only a sport, don't take criticism of it to heart so much.'

'But I take *everything* about that sport seriously. One day you'll understand what it's given to me.'

A waiter approached their table, checking their drinks for refill requirements and then removing both their plates. 'So it seems like maybe I shouldn't have gone off to join the bench crew then, guess you needed me more than they did!' Sam chuckled.

Chris stuck his tongue out at her in response.

'Alright, Chris?'

Sam looked around to see a tall, slender man was approaching their table.

CHAPTER EIGHT

'Hey, Scott,' Chris reached out and shook the man's hand. 'This is Samantha.'

'Ah, you weren't lying,' Scott said to Chris as he extended his hand towards Sam to shake, 'that *is* some crazy hair colour.'

Scott's smile as he said this was warm, and Sam chuckled along with the two men. 'Is that all he's told you about me?'

'On the contrary, he never shuts up about you actually.'

Chris gave him a friendly punch on the arm.

'It is my absolute pleasure to meet you, Samantha. I won't intrude for long.' He turned his attention more towards Chris, 'I just wanted to pop over to say that I heard the news, and a huge congratulations on your promotion.'

'What?' Sam said.

'I was planning to tell you about it over dinner, we just hadn't quite got that far yet,' Chris laughed.

'I'm so sorry, I assumed Samantha would know!' Scott looked mortified.

'It's not a problem, Scott,' reassured Chris, 'I only

found out yesterday and we've both been busy all day, so this is the first chance we've had to talk.'

Sam couldn't help but laugh at Scott's awkward expression. 'Really, Scott, it's okay. So, tell me all about it.'

'Er… I'm not sure if I can,' Scott looked questioningly at Chris.

'It's fine, Samantha was security cleared once we'd been going out for a year. We can talk in front of her.'

Sam leaned in conspiratorially, 'Is this that possible contract that had been hanging around for a while? The city-wide database thingy you've been working on, "CONNECTED:"? Have you finally sold it?'

'Yes, here!' said Scott excitedly, 'the council ran a pilot with it and loved it, but as always with them it was a case of not wanting to spend the money. They spent months on the fence, then I guess the attacks last month pushed them into action, because we got a call and they want to adopt the full system, with plans to expand it over the next few years to add in all the extra modules like the CCTV and airport monitoring and all the other features.'

'And the promotion comes in where?'

'I'm being given a small team to manage to work on an area of the "CONNECTED:" installation in the city. It will mean pulling some extra hours and being on-call to support the team in any issues that come up whilst it's all being put in place.'

'Well, after all those years you've put in to Dixon Defences, it's great to see you get something back, and it's brilliant for your career progression.'

'What do you do, Samantha?' Scott asked, 'Chris has said you have a degree in Psychology, where has that led you to?'

'I'm a carer at a nursing home for the elderly.'

'What made you choose that path?'

Sam thought for a moment. 'I think it chose me in a way. I volunteered there during my free time between studying when I was an undergraduate, and they offered me a full-time place when I'd finished my studies.'

'You're not tempted with a graduate place at Dixon Defences? Their training programmes are excellent, there's loads of graduate opportunities to either build on what you've already studied or try something completely different. You'll get a wage *and* they'll pay back your student loan whilst you're training with them.'

'You sound like an advert for the place.'

'I don't really need to be,' Scott said matter-of-factly, 'the programme sells itself.'

'Scott heads up recruitment and staff training at the site I work at,' Chris explained, 'he's a big believer in investing in the people, but doesn't always know when to quit, right Scott?'

'Sorry, I do get carried away sometimes! Anyway, again, lovely to meet you finally, Samantha. You take care of yourself and you know where to find me if you want to consider a change in career.' He nodded them both a farewell and returned to his own table, leaving them both thinking about what he had said.

Chris spoke first. 'You can't really want to work at the home and pub forever, Samantha; doing that rather than a graduate job does seem a bit like a wasted opportunity. Think about the courses at Dixon Defences, okay? Just think about them.'

Sam smiled with one side of her mouth. She was keen to move the conversation on. 'So, promotion huh? Congratulations. I can't believe you'll be in charge of people!' she laughed.

'Oi!' Chris chuckled back. 'Yeah, it's a great opportunity! And at the end of phase one I'll get a bonus, and then another bonus plus a pay rise once all the user training has been done and the handover to the customer is complete. The bonuses are expected to be pretty sizeable,' he looked intently at her face, 'I'd be able to look after us both,' he finished pointedly.

'You mean marriage again, don't you?' Sam smiled, only mildly irritated as she sensed that this latest attempt to bring up the subject was simply over-enthusiasm on Chris's part due to the excitement of his career news. 'Chris, I'm pleased for you that you'll be better off financially and professionally, but I don't need looking after in that way.'

Just then the waiter returned, carrying two large pasta bowls which he deposited expertly in front of the couple. He took their orders for more drinks before leaving them to their main courses. Sam silently took the slice of garlic bread that was perched on the top of Chris's bowl, took a bite, then placed it on the side of her own bowl as he simultaneously reached over to remove the tomatoes from the salad that adorned her side plate.

They ate silently for a couple of minutes, until Sam noticed that Chris kept glancing across at a man a couple of tables over. 'What's up, Chris? Is he from work too?'

'He keeps looking over at you.'

'And?'

'And it's strange, I don't like it.'

'Well, I'm alright, I can handle that kind of thing

nowadays. Don't invent a problem to step in and save me from. Just eat your carbs and fuel up for training tomorrow.'

'You didn't have a problem with me stepping in when we met and those uni lads were giving you grief across the bar,' he mumbled, 'you asked me for my help, I didn't offer.'

Sam remained patient, 'I did, but that was years ago.' A smile spread across her face as she remembered something, 'As I recall, I then spent the next week trying to get you to stop asking me out!' She laughed and gave his hand a gentle squeeze before taking hers back to reach for her glass.

'Lucky me, I'd still be chasing if you hadn't changed since then.'

'Exactly,' Sam said, 'I have indeed, changed.' She took a sip of her drink, and a thought suddenly occurred to her. 'Is that why you don't like me working at the pub still? In case I end up in that situation again?'

'No,' said Chris, straightening up and becoming more animated at the subject, 'you just don't need to. I get you working there whilst you were at uni, but you don't need to now that you have a degree.'

'But I like working there, I like the people.'

'People like Travis?'

'Well that's rather specific, but yes. Why do you bring him up specifically?'

'How well do you know him?'

'We're not best mates or anything, but he's okay.'

'You need to be careful around him, Samantha.'

'Where is this coming from?' Sam tilted her head enquiringly.

'My teammate mentioned him today when I said I'd been to your game. He knows him from school.

Apparently, he's heavily into drugs and often gets caught up with some dodgy people as a result. Just… be aware, okay?'

'Okay,' Sam said softly, 'thanks for letting me know.'

'S'okay,' Chris mumbled, looking down at his food and prodding the pasta around with his fork.

'Look,' Sam sighed, 'when you met me, I needed to be looked after, and I still need that on occasion. However, overall… I've changed… but how you see me hasn't. Sometimes the way you speak about our future, and the possibility of marriage, it can be really suffocating. I won't suddenly become yours for you to take care of how you see fit. I can think for myself you know; you don't own me.

'I met you, and it's been you and roller derby - the sport *and* the people - that have helped me move forward. You need to recognise that and move forward yourself. Let me breathe a little.'

Chris stopped eating for a moment, giving her his undivided attention and a sincere look. 'Okay. I'll try to back off a bit and give you some space. You'll have to be patient with me though, it's not in my nature to stand by.'

The waiter arrived with their drinks at this point, leaving Chris's words hanging between them as he wished the couple "buon appetito".

The party was in full swing by the time they arrived at The Tin Whistle, the pub playing host to the start of the evening's debauchery. The couple walked in the door to be met with a view of ten team backsides directly in front of them as Sam's league mates partook in their after-party tradition of building human pyramids until the staff asked them to stop.

The pub was a typical student haunt, dimly lit in a vain attempt to hide the grime. Here and there chalkboards were scattered on the walls, announcing different cheap drinks specials for every day of the week. Two pool tables were situated at the back of the long room near a large projector screen which was currently showing sports highlights.

Drunken squeals of delight announcing Sam's arrival emanated from the women who were facing the door watching the pyramid. Consequently, the pyramid collapsed into a pile of giggly rollergirls as those supporting the middle had tried to turn around to see who was there.

Chris led Sam towards the bar, stopping every few feet so she could be hugged by people. The place was busy, as was usual at this time on a Saturday night, so it took them a couple of minutes to make it through the crowds of chatting friends and dancing bodies and actually reach the bar.

The barman came over to them quickly despite the queuing hordes of people. 'Hey, Sam.'

'Hiya, Travis.'

CHAPTER NINE

'I take it you're off duty tonight?' Travis asked.

'Yeah, the boss let me swap with Tilly for Thursday so I could party with the team tonight.' She waved at the petite redhead serving at the other end of the long bar and mouthed a thank-you to her. Tilly waved back with a smile then got back to pulling pints.

'What can I get you then?' asked Travis, eyes moving back and forth between Chris and Sam, both hands wide on the bar in a stereotypical barman pose.

'One of those berry ciders for me please,' Sam said quickly, seeing the unimpressed look that Chris was firing Travis's way.

'What was the fourth award today?' Travis asked as he reached into the fridge, and Chris's expression switched to one of confusion.

'We have Best Jammer and Blocker awards, and Most Valuable Player - like Man of the Match - all chosen by the opposition,' Sam explained briefly for Chris's benefit, 'the fourth one is left blank and the other team think up their own award that they want to give, today they went for Best Comeback, and gave it to Cantget,' Sam turned back to Travis, 'she came back on to jam some more after a pretty hard hit to the ribs.'

'How come you weren't at the game?' Chris blurted out, 'I heard you usually referee.'

Sam shot Chris a look.

'Yeah, I do ref, but I wasn't feeling so hot this afternoon, so I had to pass.'

'You look well now, speedy recovery?' Chris asked, unconvinced.

'Yes, it's good to see that you got over it quickly,' Sam interjected, 'what was it you wanted to drink, Chris?'

Chris told Travis his order and stayed to pay whilst Sam was pulled away to dance by Thora Hurts.

A couple of drinks later, Sam realised that she'd been so caught up in dancing around with her team-mates that she'd not spent any time with Chris. Her eyes searched the room for him, but there were so many people that it was difficult to see beyond their little corner of the pub. Fuelled by alcohol, she began to worry that he had taken her comments earlier about him backing off a bit too literally and decided to just leave her to it and go home.

Her eyes still scanning the crowd as these thoughts took hold, she suddenly spotted him, in an animated conversation with the husband of one of the players. From the looks of the arm movements, they were discussing guitars. Relief washed over Sam, and she chastised herself for being so silly. At that moment, Chris looked directly at her, like he could sense her gaze. For all she was not aware of where he had been for the past half hour, he had clearly been keeping those piercing blue eyes on her, as usual, but had at least given her some breathing room. He gave her a questioning thumbs-up, which she returned with a smile, and Chris resumed his conversation.

'LEG WRESTLING TIME!' hollered Belle at the Brawl, her personal favourite pastime for team nights out.

'YEEEESSSSS!' came the guttural response from Thora Hurts who was the reigning champion. *This is my cue to go and sit elsewhere before I'm expected to participate*, thought Sam.

She headed towards a long table where Chris had just sat down to continue his conversation and positioned herself in a space on the bench next to him. Across from a collection of teammates who were drunkenly discussing the merits of historic rules changes in Roller Derby compared to their predecessors, she caught a few phrases like "minor penalties"; "knee starts"; and "releasing the jammers", but none of it made much sense to her.

Honey sat down next to her and placed a fresh bottle of berry cider in front of her. 'Ah, thanks, Honey!'

'You're very welcome, wifey. Cheers!' The two clinked their bottles and drank the refreshing liquid greedily. It was hot in the pub with all those bodies around, and Sam had long ago discarded her Black Veil Brides band hoody and was sitting in her team t-shirt with her skate name, "Thunder Kiss" on the back. Honey had on a sparkly turquoise halter-neck top and glittery hairband to match.

Out of the corner of her eye, Sam saw a young man fist-bump his friends before heading over in their direction, eagerly watched by his friends. Honey had noticed him too and tensed up. He tapped Sam on the shoulder to politely get her attention. Honey must have caught Sam's uncomfortable expression, as she then turned to the man and abruptly said, 'No.'

'What? I haven't even said anything yet, don't you even want to hear me out?' he asked, pulling a mock pet lip and adorable puppy dog eyes at her.

Honey didn't even face him to see this, else her resolve may well have faltered. 'We're out on a girls' night, not out to pull. My friend here,' she gestured to Sam, 'is taken, and I am not interested. If you genuinely want to get to know me, or any other one of these girls, then wait till you're sober and we're not on a team bonding social.'

The young man's face dropped, and he attempted to hide his embarrassment with anger. 'You're a real bitch, you know that?' he said, turning to leave.

'I prefer to think of myself as feisty, but you tell your friends whatever you need to to save face, I'll understand.'

Sam laughed at her friend, impressed at how she had handled the situation and quietly grateful that she had not had to deal with it herself. 'He was cute! You so could have wrapped him round your finger!'

'Correction,' stated Honey, 'he *appeared* cute, but showed his true colours pretty quickly. Never trust a man who's been drinking and is being egged on by his friends. You're nothing but a conquest to those ones. I was serious, I'd have considered giving him the time of day under other circumstances, but I'm not taking any shit just so he can be top dog. If he goes home thinking I'm a bitch, then so be it… you only ever need to prove anything to yourself, not anyone else.' Honey's words trailed off and she changed tack then, as a roar of laughter could be heard from the group of lads that Honey's potential suitor had just returned to. 'So, tell me more about your friend, Jane. I can't stop thinking about her condition, it sounds fascinating.'

'What condition? Who's Jane?' shot one of the women from across the table, easily distracted away from the talk of Roller Derby rules of play.

Sam explained, 'My best friend, Jane, wants to join the league, or have a go at least, so will be coming on the next newbie intake,' she began. 'She has a… well, a disability. When she's feeling particularly anxious, or in certain situations, she can't speak.'

The women looked at Sam blankly. 'It's called Selective Mutism,' she continued, 'generally it's picked up early in young children, but Jane's wasn't diagnosed until much later, it's very much a part of her now.'

A bespectacled woman named River scoffed at this, 'That is no way a real thing, it's utter bollocks,' reminding Sam why she had never managed to click with her. 'If she can physically form words, then surely she must just be refusing to speak at the times she's mute.'

'It's not that simple, it's a psychological thing that stops her from speaking, like stage fright.'

'Ah no worries,' interjected Thora Hurts, panting from her last leg wrestle and "hydrating" with a vodka cocktail. 'She's bound to talk to me, I'm nice, the newbies always say so.'

'It's *anxiety*… not a choice, it doesn't matter how nice you are, until she feels extremely comfortable with you, and the environment you're in, and the people around you at the time, the whole package, then she won't be *able* to speak.'

A cheer erupted from the little crowd that had gathered around the leg wrestling rollergirls, distracting those who had been speaking to Sam.

The blonde woman sitting across from her was thoughtfully sipping an unidentifiable purple liquid through a straw from a fishbowl that was intended as a gimmick for four people to share. She suddenly stopped, 'Oh my god! We should all get team tattoos!' she squealed.

'Nicola! Not everyone wants to cover themselves in that crap like you do,' River scorned.

'Please don't call me that, you know I hate "Nicola", it's "Nikki".'

Honey, blocking out the ensuing argument, turned to Sam, 'She'll be okay with us,' she assured her friend.

Chris turned to them then. 'Honey, I hear that you're musically inclined?'

'I have been known to play a tune from time to time, yes.'

'Where do you go for decent gear?'

'Listen guys, I'm just gonna go to the toilet while you talk guitars,' announced Sam, and she stepped out over the bench where she had been sitting in-between them, letting them have a proper conversation without having to talk across her. She kissed Chris before heading towards the toilets at the back of the pub.

Away from her friends, her mood shifted. She felt like a dark cloud was hovering nearby, unseen to anyone but her. *This is supposed to be a cheerful evening*, she chastised herself, doing her best to shake the feeling off.

It wasn't working.

CHAPTER TEN

Sam exited the toilets and, rather than returning to Chris and her friends, she went through a door at the side of the bar marked "Employees Only".

She had been thinking about Jane, and whilst away from the clamour of the after-party she'd also struggled to get out of her head the idea that maybe she should be looking for another job. She decided to phone Jane, her friend would do an excellent job of listening, even if she had no actual advice.

Wanting somewhere quiet to make her phone call, she headed down a corridor that led to a fire escape at the rear of the building.

It was still incredibly loud in the back area once you combined the alcohol-fuelled voices, loud music, and the bank of dishwashers and glass cleaners trying their hardest to keep up with the revelry of the evening, so Sam carried on past.

Clumsily, she pushed down on the quick release bar on the fire escape door at the end of the corridor then, giggling to herself, she almost fell through it.

She had a full view of the little rundown alley that the pub backed on to from her position just outside the door. There wasn't a lot to see, lighting was limited to a couple of security lights on the backs of one or two buildings, with another couple whose bulbs had long since given up. Chain-link fences with pedestrian gates in them located at both ends of the short space ensured that no vehicles could enter the area.

It was always quiet out here in terms of people, Sam had never seen anyone else around, apart from a single occasion when one of the male workers at the gentleman's club across the alley had stopped for a quick spliff whilst bringing out the empty glass bottles to their recycling bins.

Tonight though, as usual, the alley was completely empty. The air outside was a comfortable summer evening's temperature, much cooler than the stuffy pub, but warm enough that Sam luckily wouldn't be missing the hoody that she had left inside. She took her phone out of her pocket and called Jane.

Jane didn't answer her call, which wasn't unusual, as she wasn't much of a talker on the phone either and was often likely to let it ring through to voicemail. *Of course*, Sam thought, *she could just be in the bath or otherwise unable to answer the phone*, that happened sometimes too. She left a message for her friend.

Just as Sam began to lower the phone away from her ear to hang up the call, the doors to the strip club across the alleyway burst open. A nervous-looking, skinny man was forced outside by a besuited man built like a bouncer. 'Brad, I— I'm sorry! C'mon, we've been working together for years, man!' the skinny guy pleaded with a third gentleman who joined them both in the alley. The doors to the club closed behind them, plunging the alley back into semi-darkness, the lone security light above the door struggling to make a dent in the dark.

Brad appeared to be of a whole different class to the other two; his suit was well-tailored, and the reflection of the security light in his glossy leather shoes seemed to enhance the alley's lighting. The edge of a cufflink was glinting beneath the sleeve of his suit jacket, adding to the air of power and authority that his posture somehow oozed.

He nodded impatiently towards the bouncer-looking guy who appeared to have been waiting for this signal. It was the bouncer's next move that had instantly cut the skinny man's pleading short, for he then proceeded to drive a knife deep into his stomach.

Sam's mouth opened in a tiny "o" of horror, but thankfully the minuscule noise that escaped was masked by the "oof" sound the skinny man made before his legs gave way, leaving him kneeling pathetically in the alley in between the other two men. Sam clamped her hands over her open mouth, and in the process her phone slipped. Heart pounding, she managed to catch it before giving herself away.

This whole scene had taken less than two seconds to play out in front of her, but it didn't matter, she was a part of it now. She knew that she couldn't allow herself to be seen, and that meant she couldn't risk opening the pub's fire door to go back inside the building, as it would flood the alleyway with light and she'd be instantly spotted. She opted instead for slowly, silently, shuffling backwards and sideways, away from the fire door, until she could press her back up against the wall and melt into the darkest shadows around her without alerting the men there to her presence. All that she could do now was wait it out.

The bouncer guy was standing solidly behind the man that he had just stabbed, arms folded loosely across his ample chest, his knife still lodged into his victim's stomach. It was Brad who spoke next, whilst inspecting what Sam imagined to be perfectly manicured finger nails. 'Do you know why I agreed to meet you tonight, David?' He didn't wait for an answer, 'The police want you in for questioning; it's all over the news.'

'I know, I fucked up, but I promise no-one knows about any of my dealings with you, I always kept your name out of everything, you're not at risk,' David managed to croak desperately, drawing ragged breaths between his words, each one laced with pain.

' "Fucked up"? You must have fucked up pretty fucking royally!' Brad spat, undoing his suit jacket. 'How dare you come here, asking me for money to help you lay low, when it's *your* fuck-ups that have endangered *me*!' As he spoke the final word, Brad lashed out with his shiny leather shoe and kicked hard at the blade that was still protruding from David's bloody belly. David howled in pain. 'I'm sorry!' he wailed.

Brad stepped backwards, away from the whimpering man, who Sam could see was visibly paling, even in the limited alley lighting. He appeared to compose himself, straightening his suit jacket and buttoning it up again. 'These aren't just the local inspectors that I can easily buy off, did you realise the National Crime Agency is involved?' He sighed and tugged the jacket's sleeves down over his cuffs. 'This pains me, David, it really does,' a hint of sadness sat beneath his words as he looked down at his shoes.

At that moment, the silence that surrounded the

scene was broken by the shrill ringing of a mobile phone. All of the blood drained from Sam's face. Her eyes opened wide with fright; her heart began hammering mercilessly against her rib cage as she realised the extent of her current plight.

Jane was returning her call.

CHAPTER ELEVEN

Brad reached inside his jacket pocket and pulled something out. It was a mobile phone. 'Hello? Oh, hi, Richard… no, I'm not at home… yep… yes, Janice's… yeah, Claire's away and I fancied a little extra-curricular… I know I should, but it wouldn't be so much fun then would it?'

It took Sam a little while to realise that it hadn't been her own phone ringing. When it finally came, her relief was short-lived as she remembered that Jane returning her call in the next couple of minutes was a real possibility, or even Chris calling to check on her once he realised how much time had passed. She knew she had to switch the phone off, and not just the ringer, because even a vibrating phone would probably be heard in the quiet alley.

Brad was still on his call throughout the time that all these thoughts were hammering through Sam's head; '…and you're sure it can't wait, because I'm rather, you know, in the middle of things… no, well I couldn't have just let it ring out in case it was Claire…'

Sam's phone was still in her hand. Unfortunately, it

wasn't as simple as pressing the physical power button as this would cause the screen to light up asking for confirmation and give her away.

Brad's henchman had his hand clasped over David's mouth to silence him during Brad's call, but it wasn't necessary. The wounded man had no fight left in him and his body was beginning to slump against his attacker's hefty frame. Sam slowly inched both hands around the sides of her body then behind her back. One hand still held the phone, but she was so close to the wall that the phone's protective rubber case caught on the brickwork and the device was knocked out of her hand.

Her heart stopped.

This was it; she was going to be found. As the phone fell to the floor, Sam pictured its descent in slow motion, waiting for the thud that would condemn her.

'I don't CARE what that old git thinks!' shouted Brad, just as Sam's phone hit the floor and bounced onto her foot, his voice echoing around the otherwise deserted alley. She quietly let the breath that she had been holding exit her lungs, momentarily pleased that Brad was prone to such outbursts. *Now what?* She'd have to crouch down to retrieve the phone, or she could leave it and risk it ringing, but she had no idea how much longer she was going to be stuck here.

Brad was pacing now as he was speaking into the mouthpiece, completely distracted and offering Sam the opportunity she needed. However, his eagle-eyed henchman was another matter, constantly scanning the ends of the alley for witnesses. A couple of times Sam felt his eyes linger on the darkness when she stood rigid, like he could sense her there.

Then she caught another lucky break as David

decided to take the opportunity to try to make a run for it. It was never going to get him very far, but it was just enough for what Sam needed. She didn't waste any time, immediately crouching down to retrieve the phone, then fumbling to hold down the power button, desperately confirming on the screen that she wished to shut the device down. She slipped the phone into her pocket as she stood again, her back flat against the wall to survey the scene once more.

The henchman had easily got David back under control, and now had the weak man in a headlock. Brad was finishing up his call; 'we'll speak on Monday, please don't bother me about the subject again until then.' He crouched down in front of the wheezing man. 'So,' he said, turning his attention back to David whilst tucking his phone back away into the inside pocket of his suit jacket. 'I'm going to need to know exactly who you've told about my involvement in our last endeavour. I would advise you to tell me the truth as quickly as possible so that this doesn't have to last too long.'

Sam tensed up as she saw the henchman's arm encircle David's torso from behind to wrap his hand around the knife handle. His other hand came around David from the opposite direction and over his shoulder, covering the man's mouth to muffle the screams of agony that were to come. 'So, David,' continued Brad, grinning, 'who'd ya tell?'

Sam scrunched her eyes shut tight. She didn't need to be able to see the scene in front of her to know that Brad's henchman had just twisted the knife viciously where it was nestled in David's gut, his suppressed but clearly agonised screams had done the job just fine. When the worst of his wounded noises had passed, David's mouth was released long enough to let him speak, and Sam unclenched her fists slightly, realising that she had almost dug her nails right through the skin of her palms.

'I swear, Brad… I didn't tell no-one. They didn't care about where the money came from… just grateful,' David said between jagged breaths.

'You swear?' Brad queried tilting his head to the angle of David's, his voice was like a small child's asking someone to pinky promise. Sam only just closed her eyes in time to miss the horror show this time, so sudden was the movement. 'Yes, yes, I'm SURE!' wailed David.

'Good!' said Brad, pleased. He straightened up before continuing, 'I did suspect that to be the case, you've always been so discreet in the past. But I had to be sure, you understand that?' he looked to David as though the answer to this was a cause of genuine concern for him.

'Course, Boss,' David confirmed, visibly relieved that this crazed businessman in front of him appeared to be coming around.

'Of course, if I find out you're lying, I will hunt down everyone you've ever loved—'

'Not lying, I'm not, I swear, Boss!' David turned his head to the side and spat blood onto the tarmac. 'So, hospital now, yeah? I think I'm in pretty bad shape.'

'Well David, I'm afraid we can't take you,' Brad began pacing, 'you see, it's only a matter of time before the police catch up with you, and you've just confirmed that you're the only person besides us that knows of my involvement with you,' he stood still and turned to look at David. 'So, with you gone, I can sleep easier at nights.'

'Gone? What—' David began to protest as his confusion made way for complete understanding, but Brad just spoke over him, 'Phil, do the honours please. Then get him in his car and I'll see you back inside.' With that, Brad adjusted his suit again and knocked on the fire door. It was opened almost immediately by someone inside that Sam couldn't see, and Brad stepped back into the building, the door closing again behind him.

Brad's henchman, Phil, didn't hesitate before carrying out his orders. Sam held her breath, unable to look away despite the sheer terror of what she was seeing. She tried her best to mentally shrink back into the wall and just be one of the bricks, motionless and invisible, as Phil wrestled the knife out of David's belly.

The dying man tried his best to put up a fight, but in truth, there was no fight left in him, with the knife removed it was now flowing freely out of the jagged hole in his abdomen and onto the ground where he kneeled. His head slumped forwards onto his chest, a line of bloody drool hanging from his lip.

Phil grabbed a handful of David's hair with one hand and yanked his head back sharply, slicing through the flesh of his throat with the already bloodied knife. He then tossed his victim callously onto the floor, face first, and stepped over him, heading in the direction of the pedestrian gate at one end of the alley. Sam was thankful that it was not the one that involved him passing close by her shaking body.

As she remained rooted to the spot, Sam could not take her eyes away from David. He had fallen in such a way that he was facing towards her, his eyes locked on hers as the last of his blood and breath left his body.

She knew that even if she hadn't been too terrified to move, and the threat of danger from Phil was not still imminent, there was very little that she could have done to save the man, but it was still a vision that would haunt her till the end of her days. If she had not gone to the toilet mere minutes before this ordeal, she was sure she would have peed herself through the sheer terror of what she had just witnessed.

Sam knew that she had to leave, David was gone; Phil the Henchman was gone, for now, and he, or Brad, or anyone else for that matter, could come along at any minute and spot her pale frame when not distracted with petty issues like torturing people.

She willed her body to slowly peel itself away from the wall and attempted a small side-step in the direction of the pub's fire door. Her legs were trembling still and her whole body felt numb, but she pushed on. The door wasn't far away, but it felt like miles. When Sam reached and opened it she allowed herself one last look back at David, whose body was now bathed in the warm glow of light from inside the building, his lifeless eyes still staring at the spot where Sam had previously stood, she became overwhelmed with guilt. 'I'm sorry,' she whispered in his direction, tears beginning to form in her eyes, before suddenly registering the sound of a car pulling up not too far away, followed by the sound of the gate in the chain link fence being opened. Not waiting another second, Sam yanked the door open fully, temporarily drenching the blood-stained ground in warm light. She charged through the door and pulled it shut hard behind her, making sure that it locked fully so that she couldn't be followed.

Composing herself as best she could before returning to Chris and her friends, whom it felt like she had left a lifetime ago, she turned towards the staff door that led back to the pub's front of house.

Phil left the gate open behind him, he didn't want any obstacles to slow him down when he was dragging a body through an alley. As he approached, he gave a cursory look into the alcove next to the club's fire exit that housed the bottle bins. He had once caught a guy out here smoking a spliff when he was supposed to be on-shift, and a witness like that tonight just wouldn't do.

He was pleased that his boss had suggested putting David's body into the idiot's own car, it was so much easier than worrying about tarpaulins and an evidential level clean-up of his own car boot.

The man's musings were interrupted as the grisly scene he was responsible for in the alley was suddenly flooded with light. Looking up ahead to where the light came from, he saw a young woman with short, pink hair entering the building across the alley from the strip club. She was wearing a numbered sports shirt of some description and Phil was just able to read the name on the back of it before the heavy fire door slammed shut hard behind her; "Thunder Kiss".

CHAPTER TWELVE

'Hey, Sam, you okay?' asked Travis, his voice laced with concern as he saw how visibly shaken his work-mate was. Sam looked at him for a moment, taking a second to register where she was and what Travis was doing there. The crate of bottles he was holding suggested he was on a run to re-stock the fridges, and this knowledge somehow brought her consciousness back.

'Uh… yes… thanks, sorry, Travis.'

'You sure? Cos you don't look so good.'

'Well, I'm not feeling fantastic actually, I think I'd best call it a night.'

'Okay, well I assume you've got someone who can see you home safely?'

'Yes, thanks, Chris is with me, and I've got the girls too, you know how protective they can be,' she forced a smile and proceeded back to where she had left her friends in a different life.

'Hey, babe!' said Chris as she returned to her table. 'We were starting to worry about— hey, are you okay?'

As Sam opened her mouth to tell Chris that she

would explain everything once they were in a taxi on the way to the police station, Brad's words to David came to her, echoing around in her head like the lasting remnants of a bad dream; *"I will hunt down everyone you've ever loved."*

'I'm not feeling too hot,' Sam told him and Honey who was watching her face intently. 'Do you think you could take me home?'

'Of course,' he said, immediately picking up Sam's hoody and offering her his hand.

'Looks like we're moving on anyway,' commented Honey. The team were collectively finishing drinks, picking up previously discarded coats and bags, and moving towards the doors.

'Let's say our goodbyes and I'll get us a taxi.'

When he saw her, she was part of one big collective gaggle of revellers, all piling out of the pub together. It was clear to Phil, observing from where he was parked nearby, that there would be no way he could get to Thunder Kiss right now.

'I'd better get this sorted before Mr. Dixon finds out,' he muttered to himself. He pulled away from the kerb, driving off in David's car, the dead owner's body tucked safely away out of sight in the boot.

'Are you sure you'll be okay?' pestered Chris when they were on Sam's doorstep, 'you don't seem yourself at all.'

'I'll be fine, it's just been a long day, and a few drinks obviously didn't mix well with it. I'll call you tomorrow. Thanks for bringing me home.'

'Anytime gorgeous,' Chris smiled. 'Go on, I'll see you inside,' he kissed her forehead and stepped back to allow her space to unlock her front door. 'I'm at football practice in the morning, but I'll come by later in the day, okay?'

Sam nodded and went inside. She waved from the doorway as Chris returned to the waiting taxi. Safely locked inside and alone, she went straight to her bedroom and broke down.

Her body shook from the ferocity of the sobs, as she let all the tension from the last hour seep out of her muscles. She wasn't thinking about what to do next, that could come in the morning, for now she just needed some release. Complete and utter exhaustion overcame her a few minutes into her outburst, and she fell asleep where she lay, still fully clothed, and with her face stained from the tracks of her tears. On waking late the next morning, it took Sam a minute to remember why she was still clothed and had slept on top of the covers of her bed. Looking down at what she was wearing, she remembered that she had gone to the after-party and at first assumed that it had gone on really late and got really messy. As she sat up, however, she was pleasantly surprised to note that her head was not spinning. It was then that the memory hit her, a vision of David's face contorted in agony as Brad had kicked the knife deeper into his stomach, and Sam raced to the bathroom as bile rose up in her throat. She vomited into the toilet then sat beside it, very still, for a few minutes, her skin drained of all colour.

In the harsh light of day, the events of the night before had not gone away. *It really happened, and I have to do something about it.* Sam knew she had to go to the police.

After taking a long shower and changing her clothes

to more appropriate daywear, Sam decided to risk eating some toast before she headed out. *Hopefully if I just have it with butter it might stay down*, she thought to herself, switching the toaster on at the wall before dropping the bread in. She turned the TV on at another wall socket for some background noise to keep her company.

Sam was only half listening to a news story about a body being found in the boot of an abandoned car when her phone rang, startling her. She rushed to the lounge to get it, stubbing her toe on one of the last few boxes she had yet to unpack from when she moved in. Sam vowed to herself as she winced, not to leave it another six months before she finally got round to clearing them from her home. 'Hello?'

'Hey Sam, just checking-in to see how the hangover is doing!' said the cheery voice of her boss at The Tin Whistle.

'Hangover isn't too bad thanks, I went straight home from the Whistle actually, I, er, wasn't feeling great.'

'Wow, that was early, what the heck were you drinking?'

'Not like that, I mean I was actually feeling unwell in general, not alcohol-related.'

'Oh, right, that might have answered my question then, I was calling to see if you could cover an extra shift later on today, the football's on from four this afternoon and Travis has had to pull out, so we could do with an extra pair of hands.'

A vision of the alley behind the pub flashed into Sam's mind, David's blood pooling on the uneven tarmac. Just the idea of going back so soon made Sam want to vomit back up her two mouthfuls of toast. 'I... I'm really sorry, I still... I'm not feeling quite right.'

'Okay, no problem, thought I'd ask. You get your-self well, we can manage here.'

'Thanks for understanding,' Sam didn't wait for a response from the man before hanging up. She re-turned to her toast, looked at it disdainfully, then deposited it into the food waste bin beneath her sink. Sam thought again about Brad's threat to his dying victim, and immediately her thoughts were of her parents, Jane, Chris, and her friends at Stormy City. How far would Brad's wrath stretch if he ever found her?

I can't really identify him. All I have is a first name and a description from a dimly-lit alley. But the po-lice need to know what I know, it could be more use-ful than it seems to me; maybe the last piece in a puzzle or something.

She caught sight of her red-eyed reflection in a mirror, and mentally chastised herself for automatic-ally acting like a scared victim. *Toughen up, Sam. It's only a trip into town to tell someone a story. You can do it.* She allowed herself a couple of deep, calming breaths with her eyes closed, which served to physic-ally unbalance her a little. *Guess I'll be walking into town then. Thanks head, it hardly seems fair to have a hangover on top of the stress.* With a sigh of resig-nation, she grabbed her bag and stepped out of the house and onto the street.

The calm, sunlight-peppered streets belied Sam's mood as she headed in the direction of her suburb's high street. Sam's own home was in a gentrified area, part of a new estate of almost identical houses. They had been built on the site of an abandoned hospital that had finally been torn down after years to make way for them, much to the delight of the residents in the large Edwardian houses across the street.

After a few minutes the Edwardian buildings gave way to some inner-city style terraced housing, broken up occasionally by corner shops and alleys leading to the backs of the houses.

There was a delivery truck parked outside a shop across the road from a mosque, delivering bottles and cans of drinks. The driver threw an empty plastic crate into the back of a lorry and it hit the insides of the vehicle with a resounding crack. Sam, already on-edge, jumped about a foot into the air at the sound, her fight or flight response sending her heart rate soaring. She wasn't the only one either, two young men who had been standing in the entrance to one of the alleyways between the residences were staring out into the street, alert. They were both looking keenly in opposite directions past each other to different sides of the mosque, and Sam noticed that each of them now had a hand beneath their coats, seemingly secured around something at waist level. *Undercover armed cops*, she thought to herself. *No one has claimed responsibility for the terror attacks yet, but it looks like the police seem to think they know who's behind it.*

The men relaxed a little when they realised the source of the noise wasn't a threat to anyone. *Perhaps they're just here to protect the worshippers at the mosque from other people's prejudices and assumptions*, Sam thought, but she still hadn't convinced herself by the time she'd walked around the corner and out of sight.

Squinting uncomfortably into the sun, Sam reached the police station in her suburb. She took a deep breath, reminding herself that this was her only realistic option; she couldn't just do nothing.

The reception clerk was holding a mug of tea in both hands as Sam approached the front desk. 'Morning, love,' the clerk greeted her, 'couldn't just be a dear and leave that door open for me could you, please? These men in uniform, the first sign of warm weather and the air con is up to max.'

Sam smiled despite herself as she propped the door open.

'Thank you. Right, how can I help you?'

Spotting the woman's neat, manicured nails, Sam consciously stopped picking at her own cuticles before lowering her head and her voice to speak. 'I witnessed a crime. I'm not sure if it's one that might have already been discovered and reported, but it was a serious one… and I was there… and I need to tell someone… that I was there…' her voice trailed off

'Okay,' stalled the clerk, seeing Sam's nerves. 'I'll get someone to come down and take a statement—'

'No!'

The woman jumped, startled.

'I mean… It needs to be a… a Chief Superintendent,' Sam specified, remembering Brad's comment about paying off inspectors. 'Please, it's really important that it's someone high-ranking.'

Sam's panicked response had clearly convinced the clerk that she needed to tread carefully, and she spoke with a soft tone as she handed Sam a clipboard. 'Okay, so our Chief Superintendent is out all day today on personal business, but her Superintendent is due in before too long. If you're okay to wait, have a seat just behind you there, and you can start off by filling in your contact details on this form. It doesn't need any information about what you're reporting yet, you can save that for when you're ready. Okay?' she smiled comfortingly.

Sam nodded her thanks and extended a shaking hand to take the clipboard and pen that she was being offered. The kindly desk clerk placed a supportive hand over the top of Sam's briefly as the items were passed over. Sam sat down where the woman had indicated, and wrote a false name at the top of the form. *I'm not quite ready to trust everyone here just yet.*

After having written down the address of an Indian takeaway whose flyer was on the table next to her as her fictional alter ego, Sam looked idly out of the building's main door. She had accepted that it might be a few minutes' wait for the Superintendent, but she was feeling too tense to settle down into the tub chair she was seated in. Instead, she passed the time by running through the details in her head again, however horrific, to keep them fresh.

She looked out through the passing pedestrians, commuters, and dog-walkers alike as the visions played out in her mind. Cars and bicycles ebbed and flowed past the traffic light at the nearby junction as she pictured David stumbling out into the alley, held up by the bouncer-like guy. Then she saw his face, Brad's - but this one wasn't in her head.

CHAPTER THIRTEEN

Sam's blood seemed to freeze. In the coffee shop across the street, Brad had stood to shake hands with a tall man who appeared to be waiting for his coffee to-go.

The men chatted in a friendly manner, both apparently laughing at each other's jokes, until the tall man's coffee arrived, and he made to walk past Brad to the door.

Sam couldn't see a huge amount of detail from her vantage point, but over Brad's head she did see the tall man's face fall as Brad produced what appeared to be an envelope and presented it to him. The tall man snatched the envelope and peered inside discreetly. He tilted his head up to the ceiling, like he was asking a higher power for forgiveness.

From behind, Sam could tell that Brad was speaking from his hand gestures. He offered his hand forwards to the tall man, who rapidly tucked the envelope into his shoulder bag and walked straight past Brad, ignoring his outstretched hand.

Sam watched, rigid and unable to look away as Brad grabbed his things and followed the man out of the coffee shop. Here, Brad got into the back of a car that was parked at the kerb outside and it immediately pulled away. The tall man checked the traffic with a scowl on his face and then crossed the road towards her. Rather than turn when he reached the pavement, he came straight up the steps and into the police station, adjusting his expression as he crossed the threshold. He smiled at Sam who continued to stare at him, then walked past the barrier by the reception desk. 'Morning, Rose.'

'Good morning, Jake, take the scenic route today did you?' the desk clerk teased.

'Cheeky! I got held up getting coffee, I ran in to Bradford so stopped for a quick chat.'

'Well, there's a young lady here that's come to report a crime but is insisting on speaking directly to the top brass. Do you have some time?'

The man glanced over to where Sam was still rigid, staring. He mumbled something to the clerk about being swamped and terrorist attacks then sighed. 'Give me five minutes to settle in then grab someone to escort her up to my office.'

Overhearing all this, the horrifying truth of the safety of this police station hit Sam. As the desk clerk turned to update Sam on the apparent Superintendent's availability, she abruptly dropped the clipboard containing her false details onto the table next to her, stood, and hurried out of the building, jumping onto the first bus that pulled up at the stop outside.

After a short detour in the wrong direction on the number thirty-nine bus, relief flooded over Sam as her second bus of the day turned the corner onto her street. She approached the steps to her front door then stopped dead. A figure was waiting there, partly obscured by next door's unkempt ornamental trees.

The figure moved back and turned its head slowly in Sam's direction. Relief washed over her for the second time in the last few minutes as she recognised the close-shaved hair. 'Chris. What are you doing here? I thought you had practice this morning?'

Chris jumped down from the step and bounded towards Sam, hugging her tightly.

Sam let herself be absorbed by his strong embrace for a few long moments, savouring the protective feel of his arms that just yesterday would have probably been the cause of an argument.

Chris kissed Sam on the forehead when she finally pulled away from him.

Composing herself, Sam walked past him and unlocked her front door, deliberately keeping her face away from her boyfriend so that he couldn't see the tears of relief that were pooling in the corner of her eyes. 'You haven't answered me yet,' she kept her voice as steady as she could manage. 'How come you're not at practice?'

'I saw the news,' Chris said in an equally unconvincing calm voice. He pulled her inside as soon as the door was open and slammed it quickly shut behind them.

'You saw him, didn't you?' it was more of a statement than a question. Chris looked extremely flustered and unsure of himself; a little annoyed with Sam whilst simultaneously fearing for her well-being.

She was unsure of how to answer, *he clearly knows.* 'Saw what? I don't know what you're talking about. What on earth's gotten into you, shoving me in the door like that!' she fired at him, hoping to delay things long enough for her to work out what he knew before she gave in to his desire to protect her and told him everything.

'You saw David Steele's body. Hell, maybe you even saw him attacked and murdered, last night at the Tin Whistle.' He grabbed the TV's remote control from the arm of the sofa, cursing when the screen wouldn't come on. After he'd flicked the power on at the mains, he switched to a twenty-four-hour news channel to watch the newsreader solemnly updating them on the latest developments in a recent murder.

'A breakthrough has occurred in the David Steele murder case this afternoon, with police investigators discovering what is believed to be the scene of the attack that ended his life.' The picture on Sam's TV switched from the newsreader's serious expression to the scene of an alley that was only just recognisable as that behind the Tin Whistle, for it had been transformed into a full-scale crime scene. Police tape ran across both chain link fences, bright spotlights lit the whole area up, and white-suited Scenes of Crime Officers were everywhere, with a particular concentration around a dark patch of ground where Sam knew David's body had bled out.

Sam slumped down heavily on the sofa as the newsreader explained that police were appealing for any possible witnesses to the crime to come forward. The camera panned around the alley, trying to show as much of the scene as they possibly could from the media confinement behind the police tape. Sam shuddered as the memories presented once more.

She had forgotten that Chris was there until he sat down beside her, his frustration seemed to have evaporated at the sight of the expression of surrender on her face. Gently, he took her trembling hand, 'Talk to me, Samantha,' he pleaded, 'I know you sometimes go out back of the pub for some peace, tell me what happened.'

Sam inhaled slowly. 'Yes,' she said, so quietly it was barely more than a breath. 'I saw everything.'

Sam told Chris about the events she had witnessed, from the torture David had endured to his murder. She told him about Brad, the man that had threatened everyone David held dear if he had revealed their dealings.

'So, you actually saw the guys that killed him? You could pick them out of a line-up?'

'You can lose the enthusiasm, I already tried to report it to the police, that's where I've just come back from.'

' "Tried"?' Chris looked at her, confused. 'Did you change your mind?'

'No. Well, yes. I mean… one of the men was there.'

Chris's mouth dropped open.

'Well, not there in the police station, he was across the road, but with the police Superintendent.' Sam tilted her head up as she recalled what she saw. 'He gave the policeman something.'

Chris recovered. 'He paid him off?'

'No,' said Sam quickly, 'the policeman seemed really angry, I think it was more likely blackmail.'

Chris exhaled loudly. 'You have to tell somebody.'

'Who, Chris? Who can I tell? How do I know he doesn't have the rest of the police force under his control too?'

He thought about this for a moment. 'There must be someone we can report it to, a way to go straight to MI-5 or something,' he suggested, clutching at straws.

'Chris! You seriously think we can just wander in

the front door of Thames House and insist they listen to us? This isn't an episode of Spooks, it doesn't work that way in the real world. I'm sorry, but I'm on my own with this one.'

He looked at Sam, hurt at her dismissal. 'You have me.'

'I'm sorry, I didn't mean—'

'We could call with an anonymous tip; I'd keep you safe.'

'It's too risky, Chris,' Sam spoke softly as she responded to his suggestions. 'There are ways of finding you from a phone call and I don't wanna risk endangering my family and friends. Look, I tried to do the right thing and report what I saw, the guys there didn't see me in the alley with them, so as long as I don't draw attention to myself, I'm safe.' *Realistically*, she thought, *what more can I do?*

'That's crazy, babe… you can't just leave it. I told you, I'll help look after you, you need to report this to someone.' He started pacing, 'Okay, how about we go to the press instead of the authorities?'

Sam considered this a moment. 'But I don't have a shred of evidence, it's just my word, and police corruption is a pretty big accusation.'

'Well, you could leave that part out of it. We go to the press, they have to protect their sources, we could tell them everything. Who was the guy anyway, what did he look like?'

Sam opened her mouth to answer Chris, but no sound came out.

Staring past her boyfriend, eyes fixed at a point behind him, she slowly raised her arm. 'Like that,' she whispered, pointing at the face that currently filled her TV. 'That's him.'

CHAPTER FOURTEEN

'Bradford Dixon?' said Chris incredulously. 'Owner of Dixon Defences?' His voice getting louder and more disbelieving with each word. 'My fucking BOSS?'

'I'm sorry, but it's the truth. Don't get mad at *me*,' snapped Sam.

'You're wrong, it can't have been him.'

Sam's heart was pounding in her ears, threatening to drown out the confident voice from the news that she recognised so clearly from the night before.

'—Yes, I do have reason to be in a good mood. The sun is shining, and the young children in this deprived neighbourhood where I grew up have now got a clean, safe place where they can play.'

The voice of the news anchor played over scenes of Brad pushing kids on bright, shiny swings; 'Dixon Defences were awarded a multi-million-pound defence deal with the government just last week in the wake of the explosions in the city earlier this month. Bradford Dixon wanted to give something back.'

'It's important to share the wealth, and these kids could do with some good coming out of the atrocious attacks that our fair city has had to bear witness to in recent weeks. We, at Dixon Defences, are proud to say that we have the opportunity to play our part in ensuring that this type of thing never happens again.'

The TV went dark and silence followed, shaking Sam out of her trance. She turned to Chris as he threw the remote control down onto her sofa. He blinked at her slowly. 'Seriously?'

Sam nodded back.

'Do you know what he is to this city? He is the guy that built himself up from nothing. The guy who built an empire,' he gestured big, 'but kept it local,' he gestured small, 'because that's the kind of guy he is. Because he cares. He's the guy that gives back. Hell, he's the reason I have my job which I love, because of the skills I learnt on *his* youth training scheme. He's the guy—'

'He's the guy that murdered someone right in front of me less than twenty-four hours ago!' shot back Sam. 'I'm sorry that he is all this to you, that he's on this pedestal and yet still a really shit human being, but it was *him* Chris. *He* did it,' she gestured to Chris and his continued gawp of disbelief, 'and this is the attitude I'll be up against if I try and report it to any-one.'

'Well, yeah! You want to accuse Bradford Dixon, Bradford fucking Dixon, of murder! You're not going to get a welcome package, that's for sure.' He took a deep breath and ran his hand over his stubbly head. 'How could you not know it was him? He's involved in, like, *everything* in the city.'

'I haven't lived here all my life like you, remember. I've only properly been here a few months.'

'But he's *everywhere*! His company sponsors the

sports teams, and the charity events, and the awards ceremonies and, well, everything!'

'Okay, so I'm obviously not that observant, sorry!' Sam shot back angrily.

She slumped down onto the sofa and let out a sigh that did nothing to relieve the tension she felt in every single muscular fibre. 'I think it's best that I just try to forget what I've seen,' she mumbled into her hands. 'It will be safer for everyone.'

Chris stood silently where he was for a full two minutes, trying to process everything. Every now and then he would take a breath as though about to speak, but then seemed to think better of it. Eventually, he sat down beside Sam and took her hand in his.

'I really hate to say this Samantha, but I'm inclined to agree. No-one is going to believe you.'

Chris stayed with Sam for the rest of the afternoon, neither of them saying much. The silence was a comfortable one between them, but that comfort could not dispel the paranoid thoughts that continued to swim around Sam's head.

She tried to occupy her mind by reading a book, as the news channel continued to play in the background, its audio muted. Her concentration was repeatedly broken by Chris glancing across the sofa at her.

Craving the mundane, Sam jumped up. 'I'm going to call Mum and Dad.'

The phone was picked up after two rings. 'Sam!' came her mother's excited voice, 'how are you?'

'I'm fine, Mum,' she forced herself to reply in a jovial tone. 'It's good to hear your voice. How are you and Dad?'

'Just great, Sweetie. Looking forward to our cruise

in a couple of days!'

'Have you packed the kitchen sink yet?' Sam asked knowingly.

'I've packed enough, thank you!'

'She's packed more than enough for some of us,' Sam's father shouted in the background. Her mother must have put her on speakerphone.

'Hi, Dad.'

'Hi, Samantha, all okay there? No more trouble in the big, bad city?'

Sam flinched at the question. 'Yep, it's all fine, no need to worry about me.'

'I'm not worried, I've told Chris to keep an eye on you while we're away,' he joked, 'not that he'd need any telling.'

'How is Christopher?' her mother jumped in.

'He's fine thanks, Mum.' Chris waved an arm lazily from the sofa. 'He says "hi".'

'How's the rollerblading going?'

'Great thanks,' Sam didn't bother correcting her mother, 'I was watching a game yesterday, then helped manage the line-ups for the second half. Hopefully soon I'll be playing one.'

'Well, let us know when you are and we'll get it in the diary, okay?'

'That would be great.'

They chatted for a few more minutes about Chris, her parents' upcoming cruise, and Sam's career prospects. *Calling them was the right thing to do.* The sense of normality it had afforded Sam comforted her, but only for a short while.

After about half an hour of trying again to read her book, Sam broke down.

Chris immediately abandoned the tea he was busy making in the kitchenette and came to her side.

'I feel so lost.' Sam blubbed, nestling into the comfort of his chest. 'I'm so relieved now that someone else knows, but I've no idea of what to do next. How do I move on from this? I feel so guilty about doing nothing about what I've seen.' Sam could feel the strength in her personality withdrawing into a dark corner as she allowed her emotions to consume her.

'Okay, so firstly, there's nothing that you can do, we already agreed on that. You can't bring the guy back; it's unlikely that you could bring his killers to justice without endangering yourself; and he was hardly a saint anyway.' He kissed the top of her head as her shoulders continued to shake up and down beneath his embrace. 'Don't let this cause you to withdraw, Samantha. You've become so much more confident in yourself in the last few months since you've joined Stormy City, and I can see how much happier you are because of it. Don't let this drag you back, we can get past it together.'

She extracted herself from beneath his arms as Chris relaxed his bear hug. She leaned back to better be able to look straight into his eyes, 'you're acknowledging that roller derby has been good for me?' It was delivered somewhere between a joke and a sarcastic dig. Chris picked up on the latter.

'Look, I'm not saying I get it, but I'm not an oblivious asshole, I can see what it's done for you.'

Sam lay her head back down onto his shoulder and he stroked her hair quietly for a few minutes. *He's right, derby has helped me get my confidence and self-esteem up. It could probably do it again.*

'What are you thinking? You still feel lost?'

'I'm thinking I'm going to get back to normal as quickly as I can. Back to work, and back to training.'

'That's my girl. Want me to give you a lift to work

in the morning?'

'No, I'll be fine,' she said decisively, 'Faroz said last week that she wanted to meet up and walk in together anyway, so I'll have company.' *I just hope I'm doing the right thing by sweeping this under the rug.*

CHAPTER FIFTEEN

'Thanks for meeting me, Sam. It just makes it a bit easier at the moment. I've been going in to work with Julie, but she's on holiday this week.' Faroz subconsciously tweaked the position of her hijab as she spoke.

'It's no problem, I'm quite pleased of the company to be honest, it's been an… odd weekend.'

'Everything okay with you and Chris?'

'Yeah, it's not that, it's just… I have a lot going on at the moment.'

'Okay, well if you want to talk…'

'Thanks, but no, I'm fine. How have you been getting on anyway? You're obviously still getting flak from people? It's been weeks now.'

'Yeah, but folks tend to have long memories when half the iconic buildings in their city get destroyed.'

'I didn't think any group had claimed responsibility?'

Faroz laughed. 'Sam, surely you've worked out by now that to the public, it's always the Muslims' fault, even when it's not!'

'Oh yes, I do keep forgetting about that.'

Their jovial mood was broken by a glaring man who spat towards Faroz's feet as they passed.

'What the hell?' exclaimed Sam, turning to look at the man's back as he carried on walking.

'Just leave it, Sam,' Faroz instructed sombrely. I'm used to it, it's just a little less intimidating if I'm with someone else.'

Sam suddenly felt fired up. *Murderers might be beyond my pay grade, but ignorant pricks like this I can definitely handle.*

She felt a tug at her arm as she puffed herself up. 'Please don't, Sam.'

A couple of minutes later someone called something unintelligible aggressively at them from across the street. Sam broke the silence that they had been walking in. 'Is it always like this for you?'

'Pretty much,' Faroz sighed, 'but it has been significantly worse since the recent attacks, and to be honest it's increasing each day that goes by without responsibility being pinned on anyone.'

'Then why still walk to work? Wouldn't it make sense to get the bus or a taxi or something.'

'Because I love this city, Sam. I love the architecture, the smell, the sounds. And I won't be put off by assholes. The heightened aggression is temporary. Give it another month and hopefully we'll be back to it just being "show us your head, Muslim bitch".' She smiled at Sam, whose face was full of disbelief.

'You have to report some of these things, Faroz, it's not right.'

'It's not worth it, not at the moment, the police don't care about the little stuff right now, all they care about is catching the terrorists.'

Their route to the elderly care home where Sam worked took them close to the edge of the area devastated by the collapse of one of the targeted high-rise office blocks. Construction barriers remained in place as the operation to make the ruins safe for proper demolition and re-construction had not yet been completed. Sam glanced at a section of the rubble that could clearly be seen to have once been a kitchenette. She shuddered; *something always freaks me out about seeing inside walls on the outside.*

The women found further reminder that tensions were still running high as they spotted armed guards at the entrance to the bus station. 'I can't believe that everything is still this bad, weeks on,' Sam marvelled.

'Yes, and those guns make me feel less safe, not more! I wish they wouldn't always arm the police as soon as these things happen. Anyway, happier things… what are you up to this week, anything nice?'

'Just derby practice, we're recruiting so there's a taster session this week. You should come and give it a go.' Sam knew full well that her work colleague wouldn't.

'I'm far too old to start something like that.'

'You're twenty-five!'

Faroz smiled at her, 'Yeah, and?'

'Well, we've got a charity skate-a-thon this Saturday in the park, why don't you pop along to that, meet some of the girls, see if we can change your mind?'

The women reached the care home, Faroz making up some excuse about being busy at the weekend too. On entering, Sam's gaze immediately flicked to the TV on in a corner of one of the lounges. The initial media excitement surrounding the crime scene behind The Tin Whistle seemed to have died down, and it had now been a good few hours since the violent murder of David Steele had been given more than a cursory mention on the looped news channel.

'Oi, Samantha!' shouted a bald man from a sofa in the corner. 'It's about bloody time, now get your arse over here so I can whip it at chess.'

Faroz burst out laughing as she hung her jacket up. 'He's keen!'

'He just enjoys the trash talk,' laughed Sam, 'and the fact that I let him win,' she whispered.

She turned her attention to the man on the sofa, 'You get yourself a pair of skates and meet me on-track, Alf, and I'll whip you back.' *I think work is going to be just the distraction I need today.*

'Hi, Honey, where do you want me?'

'Jeez, Sam, you're eager,' Honey checked her watch, 'the newbies aren't due here for another half hour yet!'

Sam waved goodbye to Chris through the window as his car pulled away out of the car park.

'You didn't manage to convince him to join us as a ref yet then?'

'No, he's frustratingly disinterested in getting in-volved, said he had plans with his mates from foot-ball, so he'll come back to pick me up at the end.' Sam absently watched his taillights disappear around the corner.

Honey eyed her suspiciously. 'Everything okay with you two?'

'Yes, sorry, just thinking,' she shrugged it off and smiled at Honey, who appeared to remain uncon-vinced. *Typical Honey and her genuine concern for people's well-being. I'll probably have told her everything by the end of the session.*

'Okay, if you're sure. Hey, did you hear about that murder outside the Tin Whistle? Some guy with a sort of rock star sounding name. It must have been the night we were there, a few of the girls were really freaked out by it, they're thinking of changing to another afterparty venue for future bouts. Sam? You absolutely sure you're okay?'

Sam shook off the mood that had crept over her at Honey's reminder, conscious of how white her face must have gone. 'Yeah, sure. Listen,' she said, changing the subject, 'there was a reason I've come in early, besides just to help out with the arrival of the new girls. I managed to persuade Jane to come along. Now that they're sober, I wanted a chance to talk to the girls about her condition before she gets here and give them a few tips for how best to deal with her silence. I don't want to mother Jane, I want her to get out there and meet everyone, but I really want her to enjoy it and feel like she could fit in here… so, if you can spare a couple of minutes…'

'Sure.' Honey smiled, 'anything for a friend of Thunder Kiss. Give me two seconds.'

Honey went off to a corner of the cafe where Belle was checking over the spare kit that the new skaters would be borrowing. Sam saw her nod her head at Honey's words, before raising her whistle to her lips and blowing it. The shrill noise instantly brought the ten or so other rollergirls that were already present to attention, the high pitch ingrained into their subconscious now, creating a Pavlovian response following months of drills that all end with the sound of Belle's whistle.

Belle was already kitted up, as always, and proceeded to skate over to the sofa area of the cafe, plonk herself into a seat, and waited for the others to follow suit.

CHAPTER SIXTEEN

Sam headed over to join the other women on the cafe sofas. 'Thank you,' she said quietly to Belle, who nodded an acknowledgement her way.

'Okay guys, some of you already know this, so I'll skip over the pleasantries, my friend, Jane, who will be joining us tonight, suffers from an anxiety disorder that sometimes means she cannot physically speak.'

'My wife's a speech therapist,' interjected Nikki, 'and she's never mentioned anything like that. Are you sure it's an actual thing?' she asked sceptically.

River rolled her eyes, 'Oh yeah, cos your wife knows everything about everything, Nicola.'

'NIKKI! I've told you before, River, don't call me Nicola, I don't like it!'

'A lot of professionals don't know about it,' Sam stepped in quickly, recalling Jane's own complete lack of a diagnosis despite visits to several speech-based professionals. She returned to addressing the group as a whole, 'Even when she *is* more comfortable with the people and the situation, she will still often resort to gestures such as nodding and shrugging, just through years of habit, she's not being rude!' a small titter emanated from the group at this comment and Sam's accompanying smile, relaxing the mood a bit.

'So, what can we do to make things easier?' asked Cantget softly.

'Well, for starters, don't ignore her just because she doesn't respond to you, give her pointers on her technique as you would any of the other newbies. Also, remember that she's not deaf, you don't have to speak slowly, or loudly, or try to sign things to her, she understands you perfectly well. Treat her like a person and not a freak, and eventually we'll get her there.'

'No worries, Sam, we'll be sensitive about it,' responded Cantget supportively. 'Guys, can we please all make sure that if we split off into groups, at least one of us here manoeuvres ourselves into whichever group Jane is in, so at least one person there will be prepared for her silence.'

Sam smiled appreciatively at her as Belle stood to signal that their pow-wow was over. 'Okay, let's go get our shit together, the new girls will start arriving soon,' she announced.

'She sounds like hard work,' River commented to another woman as she went back to her kit.

Sam was about to follow her and say something when she heard the squeak of Thora's bearings screaming out to be cleaned, as the rollergirl approached her with a handful of papers. 'Can I put you in charge of waivers? Everyone needs to fill one of these out, so grab them as they come in the door.'

'Sure, no problems,' Sam said, taking the papers ready to catch people as they entered the building's foyer.

'Great, thank-you, I didn't want to end up with someone like River being the first person that anyone new gets to meet!'

'Are you suggesting that some of us have more… abrasive personalities than others?'

'Well, yes!' Thora laughed, 'you're also naturally a lot quieter and more reserved than someone like myself and we don't want to overwhelm them either.'

After three or four of the new skaters had arrived, looking excited and nervous at the same time, Sam had soon forgotten all about her worries of the previous week as she immersed herself in the task of making them feel welcome and guiding them in the right direction. Jane arrived when there were still a good few people yet to turn up, which worked well as Sam couldn't leave her post at the door to escort Jane around, leaving her friend to integrate herself without any hand-holding from Sam.

'It's great that you've come. I promise you won't regret at least giving it a go,' she beamed as Jane moved on to give Thora her payment for the session and fill out a marketing questionnaire for Cantget.

With five minutes to spare until the official start time, all of the expected new skaters had arrived. Honey delivered a short speech to the assembled newbies, during which Sam put her own kit on.

It felt good, pulling her skates back on. She hadn't realised just how much she'd missed the sport and her friends in the few days that had passed since the game. A lot had happened in that time and it felt like a long time ago.

Travis skulked into the room in the middle of Honey's induction talk. He smiled sheepishly at Sam as Belle shot him an unimpressed look. *I guess he's still in her bad books for his no-show at the bout,*

Sam thought, noting the red rings around his eyes.

In the background, Honey was going over safety information and "what to expect from your first foray into the full contact sport of roller derby", finishing by assuring them that they *will* have all fallen over by the end of the session, 'So get that worry out of your heads from the start.' Those closing comments brought the guaranteed nervous titter of laughter that always accompanied that section of her speech.

Now fully kitted up in her skates, knee, elbow and wrist guards, helmet and gum shield, Sam volunteered to lead the newbies through to the main hall.

Once everyone was assembled in the hall, Belle took charge. She introduced herself to the attentive crowd, many of who were either rolling slightly backwards or frozen solid for fear of toppling one way or another once they had established some semblance of balance.

'The first thing you all need to learn, which you will be fed up hearing by the end of the session,' began Belle, 'is to use the correct stance.' She stood firm on her skates, legs apart, knees bent, body angled at the hip and shoulders back, demonstrating a squatting position. 'Keeping your centre of gravity low means that you have less distance to fall to the floor if you are knocked over,' she continued, 'and also keeps you solid and makes it harder to move you.' She relaxed her position and gestured for Sam who was nearest to her to aid her in the demonstration.

Sam knew her role as she had seen this demo done before. Her heart sped up at the realisation of what was expected of her, and the responsibility of getting it right for her audience.

'If you are standing upright and unprepared, then a

hit from an opposing player is going to move you from where you were,' Belle informed everyone. She then stood as she had just described, and Sam took a deep breath, no time to mentally prepare herself.

She took a few strides towards Belle, tensed her muscles, and delivered a hard hip-check to her coach's side, putting everything she had into following the move through with her full bodyweight.

Belle was knocked sideways and stumbled a bit, taking her a second or two to right her balance before she was able to resume a stable standing position. 'So, you can see that if I stand like that, I might not necessarily go down, but I'll lose my position on-track, and waste time trying to regain it, during which time the damage has, in all likelihood, already been done. Now… if I get low and wide, I can get really stable and be in a good position to not only take a hit, but to counter it. For this demo, I'm not going to counter-hit, I'm just going to attempt to withstand Thunder Kiss's hit and defend my position.'

Sam repeated her earlier procedure of positioning herself a little way from Belle to give herself a few strides to wind up into the hit. She knew that this one would need more force and an aggression that Sam knew was lacking in her game.

She closed her eyes for a second and focussed her thoughts on the spot on the floor beneath Belle's feet.

As Sam approached, Belle's whole body, low and wide as she had described, tensed up, solid as a rock.

Sam this time managed to align her own body beautifully so that not only her hip, but the whole legal blocking zone on one side of her, from mid-thigh right the way up to her shoulder, contacted Belle's side in unison.

Despite the resulting perfect display of how to give

a hit, this time Belle didn't budge an inch.

Sam had just enough time to think that this was pretty much what it must feel like to hurl yourself without apprehension at a brick wall, before she registered that she was falling. She had bounced right off Belle, the force of their sudden contact taking her feet out from underneath her and into the air in front as she landed hard on her rear, just about managing to twist at the last moment so that she didn't land on the base of her spine.

Belle had not moved.

A gasp came up from the watching crowd of newbies, until they saw the amused look on the other rollergirls' faces, concluding that this type of fall was clearly a common occurrence and not as bad as it seemed.

Belle smiled down at Sam and offered a hand to pull her back up. 'Lesson learnt?' she asked the room, who all nodded back. 'Your next lesson was in there too,' announced Belle, 'if you do fall on your arse, make sure you favour a cheek, because you don't want to land on your coccyx, believe me!'

Sam took a timid bow to a round of applause, rubbing her favoured cheek. *That's going to be a doozy of a bruise.*

CHAPTER SEVENTEEN

For the rest of the session the newbies were all being taught together with occasional one-on-one help when it came to some of the trickier moves, and these were occasions on which Sam noticed Honey would often pair up with Jane, who, to Sam's delight, had done nothing but grin the whole time.

Sam watched Jane when everyone was practicing using crossover manoeuvres on the track's bends. She was no longer holding her partner's hand for support, as the newbies had been doing to begin with, and the broad smile on her face spoke volumes.

As Sam watched, she saw a slight shift in her friend's facial expression. Jane's legs begin to power into long strides on the track's straights and as she approached the bends her body sunk low to the ground, giving her strides extra length and allowing for some really deep, wide crossovers. She was powering past the other newbies, garnering the attention and quiet respect of the team skaters for a lap or so before she went too wide on one of the bends and her feet slipped out from underneath her.

Sam sprinted over as her friend's body collapsed

onto the floor. She slid onto her knee pads, stopping at Jane's side as she rolled over with a delirious look on her face. 'Awesome,' she whispered.

Sam laughed, and the rest of the team who had been watching took their cue from this, clapping and cheering her fall and recovery before turning back to their own newbies.

'So, now you have your first fall over with— '

'And I didn't die!'

' —and you didn't die,' Sam laughed, 'let's get up and carry on.'

'Hell yes!' Jane got to her feet the way Belle had shown them all earlier; avoiding splaying her fingers on the ground to prevent getting them run over, and started off around the track again. Her style was a little less gung-ho this time, but nevertheless still putting the muscle power into each stride to power her around the track.

'She's going to be great,' came Belle's voice from behind Sam.

'She really is. I'm not sure she's ever had somewhere to belong before. Hopefully here she can thrive.'

The session wrapped up soon afterwards, with most of the newbies eagerly asking when they could come back.

'Are you staying?' Honey asked Sam, 'we're doing jammer-focussed drills.'

'Yep, let me just say goodbye to Jane.'

'I saw her go into the toilets, I think.'

'Perfect,' smiled Sam. She headed into the toilets and found Jane in front of the mirror attempting to rearrange her hair. 'Helmet-hair is an unfortunate side effect of roller derby, and it can't be fixed I'm afraid,' she told her friend seriously.

Jane subconsciously glanced at the cubicle doors before replying, having concluded that they were alone. 'That was brilliant, Sam! I can see why you got so into it, so quickly!'

'Did the girls look after you okay?'

'Oh yeah, they were great. Especially Honey, and Cantget was trying her best! Her derby name is Cantget Yourhandson right?'

'Right,' said Sam.

'So, she doesn't realise the actress's name is actually pronounced Johansson, not Yohansson?'

'Apparently not, and I don't have the heart to tell her, it's been her skate name for about three years now!'

The two friends giggled. 'Right, I'm going to stay for the next session, are you okay leaving by yourself?' asked Sam.

'I'll be fine, see you same time next week if not before?'

'Absolutely,' confirmed Sam. The two friends hugged. 'Take it easy,' she called as she left to return to the hall with the others.

Sam found the following session tough. She knew she showed promise as a jammer, being quite speedy and light on her feet, but there was a lot more to it than that. She currently lacked the aggression that was also required to force your way past opponents, as well as the courage to take the chances that would see her achieve her goals on-track and she knew that she needed to work on these skills.

Honey saw her frustration during one of the drills and came over. The skaters acting as jammers were aiming to create a hole in a solid wall of three bodies of skaters who represented the opposing blockers, by repeatedly hitting the wall at different points until one of the blockers made a mistake and left a gap. Sam just simply wasn't hitting the wall hard enough to cause them any difficulties.

'Watch me, Sam,' instructed Honey, as she took her friend's place in the drill. She slammed her shoulder at the point where two of the blockers bodies met, then shifted over to the other side of one of the women to do the same there, causing enough upset to catch a glimpse of light through which she then threw her body, scattering blockers in her wake.

'It's easy for you, you do it all the time,' Sam mumbled.

'I DO do it all the time, which is why you should take on board what I'm showing you,' responded Honey, 'and I started somewhere too you know,' she added.

Sam dug deep for some determination to switch up her defeatist attitude and found just enough to give it another go. She positioned herself behind the wall of her league mates.

'Good,' said Honey. 'So, make the first hit really count. Mentally prepare yourself, you want to be where they are, you *need* it, like you need air. Bring your body low so that as well as launching your shoulder forward into the target area, you're directing some force upwards as you pop into the hit, you'll find that when blockers are all tensed up and ready, they're not expecting force from that direction.'

Sam gave it a go and it clearly did make a difference to what she'd been doing before. She moved immediately on to the other side of the middle blocker in the wall and repeated the action, and it was only two hits after that before the wall broke enough for Sam to follow through the shoulder hit and squeeze the rest of her body into the gap she had created.

'Excellent,' reviewed Honey before skating off to help the next group.

Travis caught up with Sam during a water break, 'You doing okay?' he asked.

'Yes thanks, just frustrated with myself for holding back,' Sam replied.

Belle's whistle interrupted them and called everyone to attention. 'Right, lads, we're going to do a bit of apex work and then we'll split into teams and scrim for the last twenty minutes,' she announced to excitement from the gathered skaters.

'You mean we're gonna stop doing drills and play some actual roller derby? About time!' mocked Honey as she swigged some more water.'

Belle maturely stuck up a french-manicured middle finger in Honey's direction, the hint of a smile at the corner of her mouth.

Honey blew a kiss back and Sam nearly spat her water out she was laughing so hard at them.

'You two crack me up!'

CHAPTER EIGHTEEN

Belle positioned two of the more experienced skaters on-track protecting the inside line. 'Okay, as a jammer, if you can draw these blockers away to the outside, great, you can now pass on their inside. However, if the one protecting the inside stays there, blocking your path, you still have the option of an apex jump... Honey, would you mind? You're best at this,' Belle asked.

Honey smiled, stepping onto the track a long way behind the two-man wall to give herself a long run-up. She was able to execute a jump that took her partly over Thora's foot, and partly over the out-of-bounds area on the other side of the track tape. When she landed, both feet were back on the track within the boundary, and she was now in front of what had started as an impenetrable wall. It was an impressive move to see executed as expertly as Honey was capable of, and the awed silence in the hall expressed that everyone else was thinking the same thing as Sam right then.

Nikki and Sam formed a group with Honey who lined herself up on the inside for Sam to practice a simple approach and jump.

Sam was finding that she didn't have the courage to properly jump over Honey's foot, so was instead slowing down as she got close then gingerly stepping over.

'Sam, if you try and do that in an actual game, the blocker where I am will hip check you the fuck off of this track. You need to be fast and be gone before she can think about what to do about it.'

'I know!' said Sam, exasperated, 'but my feet just won't do what my head is telling them to, or maybe it's just not telling them, I don't know, either way, it's obviously not happening today. I'm sorry!'

'Stop saying you're sorry for Christ's sake! You should be bashing us out of the way and shouting "fuck you" over your shoulder as you coat us in a cloud of dust from this badly-swept floor.'

'Try it with a decoy move to the outside added in,' suggested Belle who had just skated up next to their little group, 'the extra stuff to think about might distract you from the fear.'

Sam did as she was instructed and fared a little better with a very timid jump. She clipped Honey's ankle during the move and Honey stumbled backwards. 'Shit, Honey, I'm so sorry,' Sam exclaimed sincerely.

'Sam!' snapped Belle. 'Like Honey said, will you please just stop saying sorry!'

Honey turned to face her. 'Step up, attack that shit and disappear on out of here,' she slapped a fist into the palm of her other hand as she spoke.

Softening up, Belle continued encouragingly, 'We all need something we need to work on. It's about time we found out what yours is,' she added with a wink in Sam's direction as she skated over to advise the next group.

The trio swapped roles, and Nikki had a little more luck than Sam. Being less experienced, she wasn't expected to achieve a perfect jump, but she did give it her all, making some little hops over Sam's offered foot.

Four short, shrill blasts from Belle's whistle signalled the end of the drill and everyone moved towards the centre of the hall. 'Okay,' addressed Belle, 'let's scrimmage!' She surveyed the women in front of her, most of who were wearing black tops of various descriptions. 'Tell me some of you brought white tops with you!' she said, exasperated. A few people went over to their kit bags and quickly changed into white tops. Sam was already wearing white but grabbed a spare white top from her bag which she threw over to Honey to put on.

'Cheers!' Honey smiled at her appreciatively.

'Looks like we'll have two Thunder Kisses on the white team tonight then,' stated Belle as she eyed up the back of the top that Honey had just pulled on.

'Hopefully some of Honey's jammer magic will rub off on it for me for next time!' grinned Sam, as she applied some black hockey tape to the back of Honey's shirt, changing the player number on it from sixty-five to sixty-six. Travis gave her a grateful nod.

They separated into two teams according to shirt colour, each one with a league member who was currently not skating due to injury acting as their bench coach.

Sam jammed first, allowing herself to be swept up into the moment, to be too caught up in what she was doing to concern herself with thoughts of murderers and police blackmail.

At the end of their session, Belle called everyone in to the middle of the hall to get drinks and do cool down stretches together. 'Did we all enjoy that then?' she asked, the question being met with nods and grins from the red faces all around.

Honey took her helmet off, shaking her long pink hair to try and get some shape back into it.

'Okay,' said Belle, 'we're all big girls and boys here and we know which of our muscles each of us needs to concentrate on individually, so just do your own things, but make sure you *do* do them!' she warned. 'Right, while you do that,' she continued, 'a little reminder about our sponsored skate-a-thon at the weekend instead of our usual practice. We'll be meeting in the corner of the park nearest the tennis courts. I want everyone to wear their Stormy City t-shirts to promote the league, and best behaviour please, you're representing Stormy City in a public, family-orientated environment, so keep a lid on the language.'

Everyone turned to look at Thora. 'Oh yeah, fuck-ing typical, all look at me!' she laughed.

'Okay, finish up your stretches everyone. I'll see you all on Saturday at the park.'

Travis had already taken his protective gear off, having said very little to anyone all session. At Belle's dismissal he scooped all his kit into a bag and left without another word.

'He must have somewhere to be in a hurry,' Chris appeared from behind Sam as she finished off her cool down, kissing the top of her sweaty head. 'Are we going on Saturday?' he asked her.

'I sure am, do you not remember sponsoring me?' she teased him. 'But it's up to you if you want to join me.'

Chris's presence reminded Sam that the last two carefree hours had only been a temporary respite. With roller derby no longer a distraction, she began to feel quite vulnerable again. 'Right, let me get this kit put away and then you can escort me home,' Sam addressed him.

Honey caught up with the couple as they were about to leave the foyer. 'You did well tonight, Sam. You just have to work on—'

'Overcoming my fear, yes I know,' Sam smiled at her friend as she pulled on her Black Veil Brides hoody, ready for the change in temperature that would greet her outside.

'I'll wash your top before I return it, you *really* don't want it back tonight dripping in my derby sweat!' Honey laughed. Her expression then turned sincere, 'Are you okay now?' she asked quietly.

'I am thanks, Honey. I'll see you for the skate-a-thon on Saturday.'

'Excellent. Oh, and remember to avoid the football ground, they're starting some work there this week-end.'

'More work? Didn't they just finish a new stand or something last month?'

'I dunno, you know I'm not into football. I think Dixon got a load more money recently so has stuck it into a few projects, so this is probably phase two of his takeover of the city or something,' Honey laughed. 'His name seems to be everywhere these days.'

Sam stopped in her tracks. 'D-Dixon?'

'Yes, Samantha,' Chris said calmly, 'Bradford Dixon of Dixon Defences, his brand sponsors the city's football and rugby clubs.'

'Really Sam, you need to start learning some

things about this fair town that you now call home.'
Honey bade them goodbye as they all exited the building together. She was immediately side-tracked from going to her car as she was beckoned over by a couple of women who were chatting together over cigarettes out of the wind under shelter of a bike store.

'You okay, Samantha?' Chris studied his girl-friend's face intently.

'I just hadn't really realised before just how in-grained Bradford Dixon is into the essence of this town.'

Chris said nothing but put a reassuring arm around her shoulders and guided her towards where he had parked.

As Sam's eyes automatically scanned the car park for approaching vehicles, she spotted an occupied van parked away from the harsh glare of the nearby streetlight. Squinting through the windscreen, she could make out two figures sitting in the front. Her heart began to race as she wondered whether leaving the house and returning to her normal routine so soon after what she had witnessed had been the most sens-ible thing to do.

Chris had been attempting to distract her by telling her about his evening as they had made their way across the tarmac to his car. 'Then I said to Giggsy, "well, if you're always going to—" '

'Chris,' Sam interrupted quietly, squeezing his arm gently. 'Look over there at that van. Do you think —?'

'I think you're paranoid Samantha. Not just cos of what you've seen recently. There's something in the air, everyone is on edge because of the attacks and that's adding to your own paranoia.'

Sam was preparing a retort when a car came around the bend of the road. Sam stopped walking, watching the moving shadows creeping across the tarmac as the light from the car's headlights drew nearer. For just a second as the car passed by, Sam held her breath and a brilliant glow was cast over the parked van and both its occupants, during which Sam could clearly make out their faces.

CHAPTER NINETEEN

The faces of the van's occupants were lit up long enough for Sam to be sure that she did not recognise either one of them, and also to see that neither of them was focussed on her. They were both staring hard in the direction of Honey and the other skaters. *Likely just a couple of young guys who have finished playing squash at the centre and are checking out the hot rollergirls in short shorts and tight leggings before they head home. Who can blame them?*

Pleased that it was nothing to worry about, Sam tuned back in to the story that Chris had resumed recounting, as they reached his car and drove off home.

'Thanks for taking me tonight,' Sam told her boyfriend as they arrived at her house. 'I needed it, both to get back to normal and to have you close. I'm feeling much better about everything now.'

'Good. Just be careful for now still, okay?'

'I will,' Sam smiled at him. He leaned over from the driver's seat and Sam kissed him goodbye. 'Thanks again,' she said as she exited the car and headed up the stone stairs to her front door.

Chris watched her, as always, until the front door was closed behind her. Sam heard him drive away as she dumped her kit bag on the floor, unzipping it to start the process of airing out her sweaty pads and wrinkling her nose as the aroma reached her.

Crossing to the kitchenette, she turned on the oven and then thought better of it, choosing to order pizza instead.

She decided to give Honey a call whilst placing her order on the pizza company's website, her friend should be home by now. Sam wanted to thank her derby wife for the support she had shown Jane during the Newbie session that evening. She tried Honey's mobile number which just rang through to voicemail. Sam hung up without leaving a message, it was something she wanted to say personally so it would have to wait for another time.

Sam checked the status of her pizza order and saw that she'd have just enough time for a shower to get the rollergirl stink off before it arrived. Sure enough, she was dressed and just pulling a brush through her wet hair when the doorbell rang.

Phil took another mouthful of the fairly simple but delicious lasagne that he had been served and glanced at his silent phone for the umpteenth time. He could hear Mr. Dixon at the next table with a business associate, discussing the meteoric rise of Dixon Defences' stock value in recent weeks.

A managerial-looking man in a suit came over and offered Phil a complimentary drink. 'Good to see you again, Sir. Cormano's Italian appreciates your re-peated custom, is there anything that I can get for you this evening?'

'Not tonight thanks, Tony. I'm on the job, I'm

afraid,' Phil said. 'I should probably have my wits about me in case the boss calls,' he nodded his head in Mr. Dixon's direction.

'Oh, I hadn't realised that Mr. Dixon was in this evening,' he leaned in to Phil conspiratorially, 'these new kids we have at front of house, they tell me nothing! Know nothing! I'll let them know to add your bill to the Dixon Defences' account. Do excuse me.' The man moved straight to Mr. Dixon's table where his welcome was met with a clap on the back from Mr. Dixon who introduced the man to his business associate.

'I have a soft spot for this man,' Phil heard Mr. Dixon explain, 'he was the first one to sign up for a unit in this leisure complex when we began redeveloping the site.'

Phil's phone began to judder gently across the table. Putting his fork down, he grabbed the vibrating phone, not bothering to check the caller ID. 'Why has this taken so long?' he asked gruffly.

'Philip?'

'Uncle Alf,' Phil relaxed his shoulders at the sound of the voice on the end of the line. 'Sorry, I was expecting someone else. What's up?'

'It's these damn cushions, Philip. There's always too many on the chair and I can't sit on it properly to watch my shows. You know how I like to watch my shows in my chair.'

'I know, Uncle Alf. Why don't you get some sleep now, and I'll pop round in the morning and help you move the cushions, okay?'

'And my slippers, Philip, I like them fluffy, and these ones are too flat.'

'Okay, I'll—'

'You know what your dad would say, don't you?'

Phil winced at the mention of his father.

'He'd say that fluffy slippers aren't manly, but really, what kind of a man was he anyway? No man should ever hit a woman like that, let alone their only child. I remember this one time when I came round —'

'Uncle Alf,' Phil cut the old man off, subconsciously checking around him to see if anyone had heard his Uncle's words; he certainly didn't need to hear any more. 'If you're okay for this evening, that would be great, as I have to go, I'm waiting for an important call, but I promise you I will pop by tomorrow.'

Alf mumbled something incoherent and then hung up. Phil suspected that he'd fallen back to sleep mid-sentence, it wouldn't be the first time.

He picked up his fork again and returned to the lasagne to try and distract him from memories of his violent childhood, but he had lost his appetite. He'd come to terms with his past a long time ago, choosing to be the bully instead of the victim, but speaking to Uncle Alf always seemed to bring some old feelings to the surface.

Picking at the cheese on the top of his garlic bread, he was reminded that he owed so much more than a fancy meal and steady pay check to Mr. Dixon, the businessman that had literally fed and clothed him when they had met shortly after Phil left home for the last time.

Shortly afterwards, Phil gave up on his food. He was wiping his mouth with the napkin that had been protecting his high-end suit when his phone vibrated again.

He checked the caller ID this time.

'There'd better not be a problem,' he stated flatly,

speaking quietly so that the other diners could not hear him.

'No, well, er…'

'Do you have the girl or not?'

'We do, we've got her, but she's not talking.'

CHAPTER TWENTY

'What do you mean she's "not talking"?'

'Well, we've roughed her up, quite a bit actually, and she's still not telling us anything, insists she has no clue what we're talking about.'

'Clearly you're not doing it right,' Phil sighed. *I'll have to get involved myself after all.* He glanced across at the table where Mr. Dixon was sitting, speaking animatedly about something. The plates from their main course had been cleared away and dessert menus were on the table. Phil calculated time for coffees and cognacs afterwards, then he'd be free to go and see what the problem was.

'Give me an hour, then I'll come to you,' with that he hung up.

Accepting a dessert menu from the waiter, he scanned it, preoccupied. *It's odd, that the girl won't talk.* He guessed that rollergirls were likely to be on the tough side, but didn't expect one to be quite so resilient, they weren't exactly trained in the art of withstanding interrogation.

He still didn't have a theory when he pulled his car up on a quiet country lane alongside an expansive wall. He got out, sent a quick text to declare his arrival, then waited next to an intricately carved wooden door built into the wall. A minute or so later there was a clunky noise of metal on metal, and the door was opened from the inside.

Phil entered and closed the door behind him, blocking out the road and prying eyes with it.

The area beyond the wall was completely unlit and pitch black, even the shadows seemed to have shadows.

'Ethan?' Phil's whisper seemed to come eerily back at him from the leaves of the trees all around.

'Here,' came the reply from just to one side of him in the dark, where Phil then saw a small beam of torchlight. Wordlessly, the pair walked together for a few seconds in the dark until they came upon some eroded stone steps that led up to the doors of a small chapel. Despite its modest size, the entryway was an imposing sight in the dark, the torchlight playing shadows all over the extravagantly sculptured stonework as they entered.

'She's in here,' Ethan said, thrusting his head in the direction of a room he currently held the door open to. Phil, saying nothing, stepped past the youth into what used to be a cloakroom.

Some pieces of ornately carved furniture remained, including a couple of bookcases full of tattered bibles. The top of one of these was laid out with a number of tools and surgical-style instruments with varying amounts of blood on them. Against the other, another youth was leaning with his arms folded, looking bored.

In the middle of the room was another piece of leftover furniture, a wooden chair which was currently occupied by an athletic-looking young woman with pink hair. Her ankles were bound awkwardly to the bulging carvings of the chair's solid feet, and her wrists were secured onto the chair's arms. Blood dripped onto the floor from the fingertips of one hand which was dangling lifelessly over the end of the chair arm. Phil could tell from the swelling on the fingers of the other hand that at least three of them were broken.

The woman's head was hanging low on her chest, her breathing ragged, she was just on the verge of consciousness. The pink hair that cascaded around her shoulders was matted with blood from a wound on one side of her head. On her bottom half she wore shorts and long, starry socks, leaving her thighs fully exposed to whatever sharp instrument Ethan and his accomplice had used to make a large number of very small, shallow cuts. One of the cuts was much deeper and followed the line of what looked like an old scar on the side of her thigh.

Phil pulled a leather glove from his pocket and put it on. Grabbing the woman's hair, he roughly pulled her body forward away from the chair so that the name on the back of her Stormy City Rollergirls team shirt was visible. *Well it does say "Thunder Kiss".* She groaned quietly as he let her body fall limply back into place again.

'It's not the right girl,' he stated matter-of-factly.

'It has to be!' cried Ethan defiantly, 'you said "Thunder Kiss, with pink hair". That—' he continued, gesturing to their captive, '—*is* Thunder Kiss, and she has pink hair.'

'I said it's NOT her!' Phil shouted, beginning to lose his cool. 'Christ! I thought that description would be enough, how many people do you usually see with pink fucking hair?' he said, more to himself than the others.

'How are you so sure, I thought you only saw her from the back?'

'It's not the right pink, and it's too long,' Phil said uncomfortably, *Christ, I sound like a fucking fashion designer.*

'Jesus! How many fucking shades of pink hair are there?' asked Ethan, frustrated.

'Well apparently a few,' Phil responded, calmer now and considering their next step. 'She might still be able to tell us where the girl we need is. We still *have* to find her.'

Just then, the woman made a strange noise and all three men turned their attention to her. The sound was quiet and difficult to recognise at first, but they soon realised that she was laughing.

As she slowly struggled to lift her head up to face her tormentors, Phil could see the reason for the muffled noises. Her nose was broken, the drying blood from her nostrils covered her mouth and chin. One eye was also swollen shut from what must have been an impressive right hook from one of the young men. Yet despite all of this, she was laughing, and it was getting louder, defiance apparent in the sound and in her one visible eye.

Phil had never known anything like it in someone they had just picked off the street, some of the more hardened criminals, yes, but not a young woman snatched up from after her sports practice. *Maybe she's had a really rough upbringing and it's given her a serious mental toughness or something. I could relate to that.*

'Who the hell *are* you?' he mused quietly, shaking his head in confusion.

'I'm Honey Trap,' the woman responded, her

bloodied lips parting into a sneering grin, 'pleased to fucking meet you.'

She followed these words by spitting a mouthful of blood and saliva onto the front of Phil's tailored trousers, before returning to amusing herself with quiet giggles.

Phil punched her hard in the side of the face, irate and not caring which of her existing wounds his fist connected with. The giggling stopped, and Honey Trap slumped over sideways in the chair. Phil removed his glove and turned to Ethan, flexing his fingers. 'There'll be other ways of finding the girl we need,' he said.

Ethan's accomplice spoke for the first time, 'The guy that we pressured, the bartender, he told us the team's practice schedule. Their next one is at the same venue on Tuesday. We can get her then, but you're clearly going to need to come to help ID the right one.'

'Monday will be too late,' stated Phil, 'this needs to be taken care of quickly and it's already taken too long.'

'We did overhear those others saying something about meeting up Saturday,' Ethan chipped in. 'Check the website and see if there's anything on there.'

His friend got out a smartphone and navigated to the Stormy City website. He smiled, 'Yep, it's all here on the main page, they have a charity sponsored skate-a-thon planned for Saturday in the park in town. It'll be public, but we have time to work something out before then.'

'Excellent,' smiled Phil, 'then we definitely don't have any more use for this one,' without bothering to look at her, he gestured towards the unconscious Honey Trap. 'Bring her out into the main room, I'll finish her off. Then get rid of the body,' he instructed, 'but not in the river like the last one, find a skip somewhere or something, it doesn't need to be discreet.'

'Sure thing, boss,' replied Ethan.

'Message me when it's done.'

CHAPTER TWENTY-ONE

Sammy was absent-mindedly picking at the corner of a dressing on the inside of her elbow as Jane approached. 'Hi,' said Jane quietly, towering over her seated friend and casting a shadow across her table. Disapprovingly, she realised the significance of the dressing. 'You donated blood?'

'I did. I like to do my part.'

Jane's face remained stern.

'You know I hate to miss an appointment; it makes me feel guilty.'

'Sammy, you're doing endurance this afternoon, you're mad,' she squinted up at the sun, 'and in this heat too, it's supposed to be scorching later on.'

'I'll be fine. I'll hydrate, and I can't stay the whole time anyway as I have to leave early to get to work.'

'Which work?' Jane sat down at the cafe table beside her friend.

'The pub.'

'I honestly don't know why you work two jobs; you don't need to.'

'You sound like Chris now, he was asking the other day why I don't make more of my degree,'

Sammy took the lid off her ciabatta roll and wrinkled her nose at the contents staring back at her.

'Have you thought that maybe he's right?' Jane peeled the offending gherkin slices off the top of Sammy's melted cheese and popped them into her own mouth. 'Why don't you?' As soon as she'd said it, Jane could see that Sammy was about to snap at her. She likely didn't need this from both of the most important people in her life. She swallowed quickly, 'Just consider it, I mean.'

Sammy appeared to think carefully whilst she replaced the top on her roll. 'I think it's a loyalty thing now. I do enjoy working at the pub, I like the people, and it's fun, but I guess I mainly work when there's events on and they need extra staff, so I feel I would be letting my manager down if I stopped going, and a skilled full-time job wouldn't sensibly allow time for me to still help out there.'

'And the care home?' Jane asked softly.

'Same thing I suppose. They badly needed staff when I was volunteering during my years at uni, and I guess after the first couple of jobs I applied for didn't work out, and they offered me a full time place, it's kind of hard to leave them and the residents in the lurch.'

Jane stared at her attentively, imploring Sammy to look further into herself.

'If I'm really honest with myself, I'm also reluctant to make the move. I don't feel confident enough to apply elsewhere, and I also don't have the heart to stand in front of either manager and hand in my resignation. I'm okay with things as they are for now, maybe someday I'll feel different.

'How's things going with your job anyway?' Sammy finally took a large bite of her roll, preventing her from further speech whilst she chomped away on the chewy bread.

Uncomfortable with the sudden shift in focus onto herself, Jane took a moment before she replied.

'I went for another interview last week.'

'That's great! How did you get on?'

'The usual. I missed out to a graduate. It's like my skills from actually working count for nothing compared to people who've been sitting in a lecture theatre for the last three years. No offence.'

Sammy shook her head dismissively, *"none taken"*.

'It's probably not even their skillset that I'm substandard to, it's their forwardness, confidence. I can bang out reliable code till the cows come home, but I can't sell myself the way they can. I'd love to go for a position where I'd manage a team, but even if I could cope with that, I can't easily convince an interviewer that I could.'

'So are you not even trying for those jobs then? You're sticking with applying for coder positions?'

'Computers don't need you to talk to them and employers expect coders to be socially awkward. It makes life a lot easier.'

'Easier doesn't mean better though, Jane, you should push for what you want; try harder, don't just give up!'

'Says the girl who insists she's not good enough for the team roster yet,' Jane shot back, a little taken aback by Sammy's candour.

'Well I'm not,' Sammy mumbled. 'Seems I'm still not aggressive enough.'

'So... fix it. If it's as simple as just telling your brain to try harder, just do it.'

'Okay, I get it, I'm sorry, Jane.'

'No worries, even *you* sometimes need a reminder

that my anxiety isn't a conscious decision.'

'That I do.' Sammy sipped her drink. 'So, anyway… Roller derby.'

Jane smiled, 'Yes, roller derby. I loved it, Sammy!'

'Yes, we get that a lot from first-timers, it's addictive.'

'It feels like a place I could really belong, the people are great, so open and helpful and really inspiring.'

'Okay,' Sammy laughed, 'don't overdo it!'

'Sorry, I know, it's just… they just get on with it, you know? Cantget said she suffers with social anxiety, can you believe that? Yet you said she coaches sessions sometimes? And Thora… she spends half the session on her ass on the floor, but she just jumps back up and gives whatever it was another go until she nails it. You're a phenomenal bunch.'

'They are.'

'No, Sammy. *You* are. You need to recognise that you should include yourself in that.'

Sammy reached over and hugged her. 'Want me to grab you a drink? I recommend this berry smoothie thing I have; it's got some exotic-sounding name.'

'I'll go, thanks.'

Jane got up and went into the cafe where two elderly ladies in aprons were behind the counter, talking.

'Did you hear about that family that got caught up in the attacks?'

'The one where only the father survived?'

'Yeah, that one. Well he's only gone and died now too from his injuries; they were right near one of the buildings when the bomb went off.'

'Awful business,' she shook her head in disbelief then took her apron off. 'I'm just popping to the toilet.'

Jane was perusing the chalkboard menus, covered in different drinks, all with at least five different ingredients.

The elderly server turned and saw Jane. 'Oh, sorry love, I didn't realise you were there. What can I get for you?' She stared at Jane expectantly over the top of her spectacles.

Jane looked at her and smiled.

'Lots of choice isn't there?' the woman began to drum her fingers on the countertop as she waited for Jane to make a decision.

She hadn't finished reading the descriptions, but Jane could sense the familiar feeling of butterflies in her stomach coming on, so quickly concluded that Sammy's smoothie did sound pretty good. 'B-berry jamboree, please,' she said quietly.

'Sorry, dear, you'll have to speak up, my hearing isn't what it used to be.'

Jane's throat began to constrict. She couldn't bring herself to speak any louder so she leaned as far across the counter as she could and repeated herself.

The woman nodded and Jane unclenched her fists a little as she went behind a divider to prepare the drink. She returned with a cup and saucer and a small jug. 'There you go love, the bag's in and your milk is separate so you can make it as strong as you like,' she said, smiling at Jane as she rang the total up on the till.

Jane forced a smile at the woman as she paid then took her "very strong tea" outside.

'Didn't fancy the Berry Jamboree then?' Sammy asked casually.

'No, seemed a bit too much like hard work.'

'Okay, but I think you're missing out.'

'Probably.' Jane looked around her, keen to change

the subject. 'It's nice, people getting on with things, there's definitely been a shift in attitudes. I finally see an air of defiance around the city now.'

Sammy glanced in the general direction that Jane was looking in. 'I don't see that at all. This park used to be much more carefree. There's something different about the way people play with their kids, not letting them so far away and stuff.'

'You think? I prefer to look on the bright side,' she said, noticing the couple playing frisbee, young siblings arguing over a powerful-looking Nerf gun, and a couple of dads chatting as they pushed their toddlers on the nearby swings.

Suddenly, a puff of air passed Jane's cheek and the cafe window behind her shattered.

CHAPTER TWENTY-TWO

Sammy jumped in fright as Jane ducked.

The heads of all the parents in the play area whipped around to check on their kids; a couple who were walking with an infant in a baby carrier both ducked and jumped off the footpath, the father's hand instantly moving protectively to the head of his precious cargo; a number of other people who had been lounging on picnic mats had leapt up, ready to sprint if needed.

Jane turned to see that the cafe window was actually still intact. The source of the sound of shattering glass became apparent when one of the ladies that had been serving in the cafe wandered outside holding a dustpan and brush whilst cursing under her breath. As she stooped to sweep up the broken bottle from below the table behind them, Jane noticed the foam dart from a Nerf gun lying on the now-empty table.

Jane puffed out her cheeks then exhaled dramatically. 'Looks like you win that one, Sammy. People are still pretty on-edge, you and me included.'

'That was a minuscule flinch,' she retorted, looking a little like she'd been caught out revealing a big secret. 'If Chris were here, he'd have thrown me under the table out of the way though,' Sammy laughed uncomfortably.

Jane shot her a quizzical look. There was clearly something on Sammy's mind.

'He's been a little over-protective of late.'

'Surely that's a good thing, that he's supportive and he cares.'

'Well, it's a pain when it extends to roller derby, he's worried I'll hurt myself and I know he would prefer for me to stop playing.'

'He'll come around. He'll soon recognise all the good that it's done for you. He's only looking out for you, he really cares for you, you know. I see it in the way he looks at you, little sideways glances and the such.'

Sammy narrowed her eyes suspiciously, 'You're really advocating for him today, what's up? I thought you weren't that keen on him.'

'Just because I don't speak to him doesn't mean I don't like him! Don't confuse those things.'

'I won't.' She paused a beat. 'Before you arrived earlier, I was thinking about when we were younger, and how you used to speak fine at home to your parents, but not a single word came out to anyone all day at school.'

'Yeah, I think you saw me as a challenge, most of the other kids and even some of the teachers gave up on me pretty quickly.'

'Remember the first time we spoke?' a grin began to creep across Sammy's face.

'Haha, in the girls' toilets at school you mean?' Jane smiled back. 'Yeah, classy huh?'

'Was it planned? I can't quite remember.'

'No, I think we were just in there doing our hair or something and I knew we were alone so the words just sort of came out,' Jane smiled to herself, remembering how her condition had improved a little after she had opened up to Sammy. 'It was after that that I started to purposely drag other friends in there to talk to them too! I guess I must have been at ease in the toilets for some reason!'

'Thank goodness you've branched out a little since then!'

'Well, I do try my best not to allow my SM to get in the way of life,' Jane dropped her gaze to her drink, 'most of the time,' she said, painfully aware that everyday tasks were still a constant source of stress for her.

They finished off their drinks then went to join the roller derby league near the tennis courts.

'Chose a great day for it, Belle!' said a woman who was stretched out on a picnic blanket, the sunlight reflecting brightly off the plaster cast on her left leg.

'Yep. Weather's fantastic and the park is rammed... which might make avoiding people on pathways a bit more of a challenge, but it will do wonders for fundraising and promoting the league,' Belle beamed.

'You're going to get a tan line at the top of that plaster cast,' River warned the woman on the picnic mat.

'It's not always about looks for all of us, River,' she replied, not bothering to open her eyes as she soaked up the sun's rays, 'I'm just getting my vitamin D.'

River scoffed and found a patch of grass away from the others on which to sit down and put her skates on.

Sam looked past the injured skater to a table that had been set up with Stormy City merchandise. Skaters' partners and families that had come along to help out were carefully positioning fliers at the front. She spotted Chris there too, stacking up bottles of water under the table and out of the way of the sun's immediate grasp. He stood up straight and beamed as he caught sight of Sam, 'Hey, gorgeous.'

'Hey yourself,' Sam ran up to him for a hug.

'Jane,' Chris acknowledged her with a curt nod from over Sam's shoulder as they parted from their embrace. Jane responded with an awkward smile and a small wave of her hand.

Sam opened her kit bag, 'I'd best get my skates on.'

'I've offered to be official waterboy, so I'll hand bottles out to skaters as they pass. Jane, they said they could use some help at the merch table if you're up for it.'

Jane smiled and nodded in response, then went to join the activity at the table, positioning price labels near the relevant items.

Looking up at Chris from where she sat on the ground, Sam noticed that he had just the slightest smile on his face as he watched the families around them, pushing young children in buggies, and shouting at the slightly older ones to watch where they were kicking their footballs. He was a world away in his head and wondering exactly what he was thinking about made Sam feel a little insecure. Once her paranoia about everything else had cooled down, she promised herself she'd speak to someone about her feelings where Chris was concerned. Maybe Honey.

'Hey,' she said suddenly, looking around. 'Where's

Honey? She's not usually late to this kind of thing.'

'I was thinking that myself,' Thora plonked herself down on the grass next to Sam. 'I'm sure she'll be here before too long; I don't see what she could possibly be doing that would keep her away from a public space where she can spread the word about Roller Derby to the masses. That would just be a wasted opportunity to Honey.' She lowered her voice, 'Travis is a no-show again too, apparently he did text Belle this time at least, said he wasn't feeling great.'

'He's missed a few events recently.'

'Yeah, I think he might be using again and maybe suffering little withdrawals between paychecks.'

'That's exactly what I said to Samantha the other day,' said Chris.

'Well, not quite so eloquently,' Sam mumbled.

Fifteen minutes or so later, Belle called the skaters to attention to say a few words to them and the members of the public who had gathered. 'So, half of the money raised by this sponsored skate today will go towards buying new loan kit items for Stormy City, so that more people can come along to our taster sessions and discover our amazing sport. The other half is destined for the Sophie Lancaster Foundation, who work extensively to put an end to prejudice against subcultures.'

There was still no sign of Honey, but Sam was sure she would have good reason for not being there.

'Skaters,' Belle continued, 'have fun and be safe; everyone, please give generously, there are donation buckets at the end of our merchandise table over there.'

The group of spectators had increased in size, drawn by the sight of the small crowd and the cluster of skaters in uniform, and the merchandise table seemed to already be doing steady business. Sam could see Jane smiling as she helped work out change and restock the keyring tub.

She set her phone up to begin tracking the distance as she skated it and soon the modest crowd was cheering the skaters as they set off doing their laps around the park.

Ninety minutes and forty bottles of water later, the skaters stopped for a short break and a chance to refuel on the stacks of jelly sweets that had been stashed under the merchandise table. Sam was delighted to see Jane conversing with a couple of the people that she was running the table with. It didn't look like long, animated sentences yet, but from a distance she could see Jane's mouth moving a little in response to dialogue from the others.

'Yep, she's talking to them,' Chris sat next to Sam, offering her some of his ice cream. 'Still not saying a word to me though.'

'I know it's frustrating, Chris—'

'Damn right it's frustrating, I really want to like my girlfriend's best friend, but how can I be expected to have any kind of relationship with someone that won't speak to me?'

'Can't.'

'What?'

' "Can't" speak to you, not "won't".'

Chris sighed. 'Look, I know you're going to say don't take it personally, but it's pretty hard not to.'

Sam put her hand reassuringly on his forearm. 'Jane finds it harder with you than with others, because it's important to her too,' she said calmly. 'It's that pressure that she's putting on herself, because she wants it so badly, that is making it extra difficult for her. It's a vicious circle, but the fact that she's struggling shows you mean a lot to her.'

Chris sighed and finished what remained of his ice cream in one go. 'Well, when you put it like that…'

'And she sides with you a lot too.'

'Really? Like with what?'

Belle approached then, interrupting the couple.

CHAPTER TWENTY-THREE

'How do you feel about a few short exhibition jams?' asked Belle, beads of sweat glistening on her black skin, 'I know it's on tarmac, but we could take it easy, just give the public a rough idea of what the sport's about?'

'I'd certainly be up for it,' said Sam, 'we should make use of the attention we seem to have attracted, aside from the fundraising, it's what we're here for'

Belle thoughtfully nodded her agreement. 'Thora,' she sighed at her teammate, 'will you put that cigarette out, you're supposed to be an athlete.'

'Na-ah, "affleet",' she made quote marks in the air with her fingers, 'with effs. You don't get a blocking booty like this by skipping out on the cheeseburgers.' Sam grinned as Belle moved away shaking her head and reminding a giggling Cantget as she passed that e-cigarettes weren't any better.

Belle blew her whistle.

'Okay, Stormy. Those happy to play a few demo jams, please head into the tennis court over there. All you folks wondering exactly what roller derby is all about, why don't you come over and join us, and I'll talk you through what's happening.'

A dozen or so members of the public whose curiosity had been piqued gathered outside the chainlink fence with Belle, whilst the Stormy skaters lined up on an imaginary track on the tennis court, Sam taking up position as a jammer. 'Remember guys, fifty percent, and positional blocking only, contact to a minimum,' Belle then turned to the assembled crowd, 'we normally have a bit more protective gear on us than this, so we're taking it easy.' Sam saw Thora give a thumbs up to one of the younger spectators who was staring at them in awe.

'Five seconds!' called Belle, and the group immediately tensed, waiting for the familiar sound of her whistle.

The team ran through two jams, slowly and carefully, allowing Belle time to explain the key gameplay points. Chris stood watching them, arms folded across his chest. Sam spotted a raised eyebrow from him on a couple of occasions after she had spun on her toe-stops past blockers who had accidentally given her too much space by the tennis court line that was serving as their inside track boundary. *Maybe he's starting to appreciate the skill that's involved.*

Belle called for a couple of members of the team to come out of the courts, and to Sam's surprise, she saw Jane come in wearing Cantget's skates and pads. 'Er… what are you up to?' Sam asked her.

Jane smiled and shrugged, taking up a position on the jam line next to Sam, as another of the new skaters joined the blockers.

'Right, these guys haven't actually played before, but they're both extremely competent skaters. Remember we are just walking this one through, let's show these folks how gentle we can be with our

Baby Stormclouds.'

Ah, that's what Belle's getting at. Sam thought back to how intimidated she was in the early days by the idea of being body-checked by someone whilst on skates. *I guess it makes sense to help attract new people to the sport.*

'Five seconds!'

On Belle's whistle, Sam and Jane both moved forwards into the pack of skaters clustered in front of them. Moving laterally across the track's width, Sam was struggling to get past the blockers in front of her as a result of not wanting to push on them too hard. Jane looked to be having an easier time of it herself, as the blockers around her were being extremely cautious with regard to not knocking into her too hard, and so it was Jane that Belle ended up pointing out to the surrounding crowd as having established the lead jammer status.

Sam escaped her blockers soon after and began to race Jane around the imaginary track. She caught her friend up as they were both closing in on the pack. Jane began flapping her left hand wildly in front of her, and her blockers took the hint and made a space for her near the inside line. Sam headed for the middle of the clustered skaters, slowing down to ensure that she didn't hit anyone too hard, as per Belle's instructions, but she saw that Jane wasn't slowing her speed at all.

Sam winced, waiting for the inevitable clash of limbs, but at the last moment, Jane lifted one foot, and then the other, jumping over the outstretched leg of an opposition blocker before landing on her knee pads in front of them and rolling over.

There was a moment of silence as everyone waited to see if Jane was okay. Sam hurried over to her friend, who gave a thumbs up from the floor as she reached her, and the skaters all cheered.

'Well, Jane, ideally you need to do that so that you don't go over the line, and you would land on both feet rather than barrelling across the track,' Belle informed her seriously. She then broke into a huge grin, 'But that was freaking AWESOME! I can't believe you had the guts to give that a go after coming to one practice! You're gonna be something special.'

Sam was pleased to see the excitement on her friend's face as she took the praise, but she couldn't help but feel a little inadequate that Jane had just executed a move that Sam struggled to force herself to even attempt.

'Nice moves,' said Chris as Sam made her way over to where he was now sitting by her kit bag.

'Now's the time for a toilet break if you need one,' Belle reminded everyone.

'Oh, good plan, I'll be right back,' Sam quickly swapped her skates for trainers. 'I've got to leave early to fit in a shower before I go for my shift at the pub later,' Sam checked her watch, 'it's probably not going to be worth me putting my skates back on after that.'

'I'm going to stick around here for a bit, it's a nice day to be outdoors, and I think I heard someone say that they need more water, so I'll go pick some up soon.'

'Okay, just watch my stuff for a minute, then I'll say my goodbyes to everyone.' She jumped up and kissed Chris on the forehead before setting off in the direction of the toilet block next to the car park.

Cantget passed Sam on the path, 'Here, you'll want this,' she threw a roll of toilet paper to Sam.

'Cheers! Good preparation,' Sam wrinkled her nose as she approached the park's public toilets. *Cleaned at least once a day, huh?*

Phil was feeling cramped from sitting squashed up in the passenger seat of Ethan's tiny car for the last couple of hours. He had better places to be but he knew he needed to identify the woman personally this time. *There's been too many slip-ups in this operation already.*

Next to him, Ethan laughed as he watched an elderly man struggling with the car park's new cashless pay machine.

'Hey,' snapped Phil, 'don't mock the elderly, they've done more for our generations than you will ever comprehend.'

'Whatever you say,' Ethan said, sounding bored. 'How much longer—'

'That's her,' Phil sat up suddenly and indicated the girl with short, pink hair who was just entering the ladies' toilets across from where Ethan and himself were parked.

'The one wrinkling her nose up, carrying the toilet roll?' Ethan asked.

'That's the one.'

'You going to make yourself scarce then? We don't want her spotting you.'

'Yep, I'll go when she's gone back into the park. You go in to keep a closer eye on her, and I'll see you later at church.'

Ethan nodded, stroking at his goatee beard and turned his attention towards the toilet block to watch for the girl emerging, which she did after a couple of minutes.

Phil's phone began ringing as he exited the car a

minute later. He checked the caller ID and answered immediately as he walked.

'Hi Philip, I'm sorry to bother you, but your Uncle Alf is asking for you. He seems to be expecting you, something about cushions and fluffy slippers?'

Shit. Phil stopped walking and pushed his palm against his forehead. *I forgot all about it in the midst of this mess.* 'Thanks, can you let him know that I've been held up, but I'll be over as soon as I can,' *whenever that will be.*

Sam tossed the toilet roll into Cantget's kit bag as she passed it. By that time, the skaters were re-grouping, ready to set off again on Belle's signal. Sam gave the assembly a quick wave and was met with return gestures of waves, blown kisses, and some shouts of "see you soon, sweetie!"

Heading next to the merchandise table, she thanked the volunteers there, the family members and injured skaters, for giving up their time to help out.

'I'll see you soon,' Jane said quietly in Sam's ear as they hugged goodbye.

'Yes, you will, and you're doing great by the way.'

'Sounds like you are too, I heard that you'll likely be rostered for the team next season.'

Sam pulled away quickly to look at Jane. 'Really?'

Jane giggled, 'Yep.'

'They said that in front of you?'

'You know how people forget themselves around me, they hardly notice I'm there.'

'Wow, okay. Thanks for that,' Sam gave Jane another quick squeeze. 'See you soon!'

'Oh, I get a hug too, do I?' said Chris as she returned.

'You get the biggest one, obviously.'

They kissed and Sam suddenly realised how much she hated that she had to leave him now. 'Will you drop by the pub later? Else come over when my shift's done?'

'I'm meeting a friend later on for a drink, but I'm sure he won't mind if we divert the venue.'

Sam squeezed his hand in thanks.

'Right, I'd best go get that water.'

Sam collected her kit together and bade him good-bye, heading back up the path once more towards the toilets and car park. Being such a sunny day, the path, like the rest of the park, was busy and she had to dodge a number of toddlers on scooters coming the other way.

As the car park came into view, she saw a man crossing it up ahead of her. He was dressed in light trousers, a fitted t-shirt and a baseball cap that was pulled down low over his face, instantly making him look suspicious, even on a day this sunny. *I wonder if he's been trying to break in to parked cars. I hope mine isn't one of them.* She drew closer and the man turned briefly as he entered one of the cars, his face momentarily visible to Sam as he did so. The sight stopped her dead in her tracks. She could never forget that face, it was Bradford Dixon's henchman, and the man that had ended someone's life before her very eyes.

Sam was abruptly brought back to the present by the feel of something sharp pressed against her side.

CHAPTER TWENTY-FOUR

Instinctively, Sam looked down and saw something silver glistening brightly in the sunlight that fell through the trees next to her. The black handle of a knife was being held by a youth with short, dark, spiky hair and a trendy goatee. The youth's eyes were dark and uncompromising as he spoke, 'Move. Now.'

Sam remained fixed to the spot, too scared to do anything. She felt the knife pressing harder against her clothing.

'You *will* feel this blade if you don't come with me right now.'

Oh dear god, he's not trying to mug me, he's going to drag me into the trees and rape me.

The young man spoke again, 'Even if you're not concerned about your own well-being, you should know that we have your friend, Honey Trap; picked her up thinking she was you,' he allowed himself a small chuckle before leaning in and whispering into her ear. 'Of course, we don't really need her anymore, so we're quite happy to kill her if you don't co-operate.' Then he threw his head back and laughed as a family passed them on the path, like he thought what he'd told her was a really good joke.

Sam was still stationary, so Goatee slowly and deliberately repeated his instruction, 'Move.' Putting one shaky foot very carefully in front of the other, Sam began to move forwards towards the car park. He had his free arm around her waist, holding her close to him and keeping the pressure of the knife against her body as they walked.

'Hey Sam!' the cheery voice didn't seem right under the circumstances and cut through Sam's confused consciousness, jolting her back to the park's public footpath.

'Er, hi, Nikki,' she responded without much enthusiasm.

'I'm not too late, am I? I came as fast as I could, but the wife only just got home with the car, hope I haven't missed much.'

Sam couldn't seem to work out what the correct response would normally be, her brain wasn't functioning properly under the stress and terror that she was feeling.

Nikki's distracted demeanour faded as she saw the man at Sam's side and a quizzical look crossed her face. 'Who's your friend?'

Sam felt the knife blade shift a little harder against her and got the message loud and clear, *I need to get my game face on.* She avoided Nikki's last question completely, 'It's all still going on, you haven't missed much. I just needed to leave early to get rollergirl stink off me before I go out later.'

'Oh, that's right, you're working at the Whistle aren't you? I remember you mentioning it now.'

Sam wasn't really listening, her mind was working overtime trying to think of some way to alert Nikki to her predicament, to get her to get help without endangering either of them. 'Well, you haven't missed much yet, I think Jane was about to make a speech to everyone, so if you hurry you can probably catch that.' Sam turned away and began to walk again, hoping that her attacker would follow suit and not notice the inevitable look of confusion that would appear on Nikki's face at any moment. 'Catch you later, Nicola,' she called over her shoulder, deliberately dragging out her friend's full name. Sam just hoped it would be enough.

'Yeah, uh, see ya,' replied Nikki, who set off jogging in the direction of the park.

'Well played,' muttered Goatee, 'I thought for a moment that you were going to seize up again there. It's lucky that you didn't.'

'Yeah, lucky for who?' Sam said through gritted teeth.

As they stepped out of the trees and into the open space of the car park, Sam's heart began to beat loudly in her ears. She was running out of time to do something to get away, but still wasn't sure what. Sam had no way of knowing if he was telling the truth or not about Honey, but he knew her skate name, and she certainly wasn't here, on a day when being kidnapped was probably the only thing that could have kept her away.

To Sam's relief, she suddenly heard the familiar squeaking sound of bearings that were badly in need of a clean. 'Hey, Sam, Nicola told us she saw you leaving,' said Thora, emphasising the name their friend despised.

'You didn't say goodbye, so we thought we'd try and catch you,' chipped in Belle as the pair eyed the man next to her suspiciously.

'Who's this yummy specimen?' Thora gestured

casually to the youth. 'You know it's not a great idea to meet up with your bit on the side at the same park as your actual boyfriend.'

'I'm a friend of Honey Trap's,' he smiled. Sam suspected he was using Honey's name as a reminder to her to dissolve the situation, but she still planned to stand her ground for now. She had no guarantee that they even had Honey, let alone that they would let her go free once they had Sam in her place. The man at her side had already made it clear that they would be happy to kill Honey as they no longer needed her, and so Sam's best shot at helping her friend was to let someone else know that she was in trouble.

'Yes, that's right, he's friends with Katie Honey,' she told her teammates, praying that he didn't know Honey's first name was actually Sarah, seeing as he kept referring to her friend by her skate name.

'Any idea where she is?' Thora asked him. 'No one's seen her today and usually she wouldn't miss a public outing like this.'

'Er, no. I don't. Sorry. Come on Sam, we'd best go.' With that, he began leading Sam over towards a little red car that was parked a few feet away from them. Not knowing what else to do, Sam let him guide her and stood obediently next to the youth who was still gripping her waist as he withdrew the hand holding the knife so that he could unlock the car.

Without warning, Goatee's body slammed up against the side of the car, the sudden impact relieving him of his balance and causing his body to crumple to the floor. The manoeuvre pulled his arm from Sam's waist, spinning her around as he instinctively tried to hold on to stop himself from falling.

As Sam turned, the reason for Goatee's sudden

spasm came into view. Belle was busy backing away from the scene of the body check that she had just delivered to the young man, her face ashen as she stared at the ground in front of her. Thora was a few feet away, her hands on her hips defiantly until her closed-mouth grin dropped as she also caught sight of the knife that lay on the floor next to Goatee's car keys.

'Run, Sam!' Belle screamed at her, as Goatee was regaining his senses and reaching for the knife. Sam did not need to be told twice. She began to run towards her own car which was parked a couple of rows over. Digging around in the pocket of the hoody that was tied around her waist, Sam muttered with gratitude as her hands closed around her car keys and she had the doors unlocked before she had reached the vehicle, ready to dive into it.

Goatee was close behind her, but Sam managed to get into the driver's seat and lock the car before he could reach her. Clearly desperate, he slammed his body up against her window, elbow leading, trying to shatter the glass. The first attempt unsuccessful, Sam would not be allowing him another try. She started her engine and pulled away, tyres screeching. As she flew over one of the car park's many speed bumps, she caught sight of Thora and Belle, both skating hard back towards the path between the trees, Belle with her phone to her ear.

Sam made it out onto the main road and through the nearest set of traffic lights just before they changed to red. As she flew through the lights, she could see Goatee was only just getting into his car. She turned up a side street as soon as she could so that she would be out of sight of the main road by the time Goatee was travelling along it.

At the next traffic light, she fumbled around for her phone before remembering it was still in her kit bag, left on the ground in the car park. There was no way to call anyone till she got home. She drove as fast as she dared.

Ethan couldn't believe his bad luck. Phil being seen by the woman - Sam, as her friends had called her - wasn't such a disaster, as Ethan was there ready for her and the distraction actually allowed for an easier approach on his part. The other matter, being body-slammed against his car by a girl on roller skates, well, that part he would probably leave out of his story.

Clearly that bitch said something to tip off her friends. His little car reached a queue for the traffic lights that were currently red, and he knew that he had lost her.

There was no way that he could go back to Phil empty-handed. He could always run, but they'd likely find him and then it would be worse. No, he had to be smart, tell Phil what had happened, but only when he had a new plan. *Think, what else do I know about this woman and her movements besides the roller derby practice schedule?* The barman, Travis, might know more, and it would help that Ethan now knew her name.

The memory hit him as he thought about Travis and the pub. *That girl on the path mentioned Sam working a shift at a pub; the Whistle.* Ethan smiled to himself as he realised that it was, in fact, the pub Travis worked at too.

Okay, so she's not likely to make it in for tonight's shift now, but Travis will know more about her. Ethan smiled to himself, he knew just how to make sure that Travis would cooperate.

CHAPTER TWENTY-FIVE

Travis's lanky form was splayed out on the sofa in his low-rent flat, watching TV. The flat was located above a Chinese takeaway and always smelt like prawn crackers. He had grown accustomed to it, and it helped in a small way towards masking the general man smell of the place that came from seldom washing dishes and only taking infrequent trips to the local launderette once he'd worn all of his clothes at least twice each.

A knock at the door roused Travis from the zombie-like state he had managed to attain as he watched some afternoon quiz show. Ethan, Travis's drug dealer, was standing in the doorway and pushed his way past Travis and inside without waiting for an invitation.

'Ethan, that money, I—'

Ethan waved a hand dismissively in the air. 'I'm not here to collect the money, although you do realise that you are on extremely thin ice with that? You're now a week overdue,' he paused and gave Travis a sideways glance, that didn't reassure him at all.

'I do, Ethan, I'll get it for you. I've worked loads

extra at the pub, although I did have to miss a shift to meet with you the other day when you wanted info on the roller derby team, and another when they closed us down because of the crime scene out back. I tried, but I couldn't get the boss to give me an advance. I just need a little more time, if there's any way that we could defer till payday, I'll definitely have it for you then.'

Ethan let out an exaggerated sigh as he observed Travis' desperation. 'This keeps happening Travis. It's not good for business, and at some point soon you know I'm going to be ordered to make an example out of you. The boss can't look like a pushover, and word gets around. I won't be able to protect you much longer.'

'Please, Ethan. Just a few more days!'

'When's payday?'

'Last day of the month.'

'I tell you what, you give me some information, and I'll get the boss to extend your deadline until then.'

'Really? Of course, sure, anything, Ethan.'

'Fantastic. I need to know where Sam, the roller-girl, lives,' Ethan delivered casually.

There was a moment of confusion before Travis narrowed his eyes suspiciously.

'She does work with you, doesn't she?' Ethan pushed.

'She does, but why do you want to know where she lives?'

'Never mind, all you need to know is that giving me the information means you not needing to worry about meeting your payment this month until you can afford it.'

'Do you supply her too? You're not going to hurt

her, are you?'

Ethan smiled, 'Why, Travis, do you have a thing for that sweet little girl?'

Travis did have a soft spot for Sam, but he knew her interests lay elsewhere, and he was noble when it came to such values, so had never pushed the point. He looked downwards and mumbled his reply, 'That's none of your business.'

'Of course it's my fucking business! If it's stopping you from letting me know where to find her, then it's exactly my business! Now you tell me or you've got three days to pay up what you owe.'

Travis's head snapped up at this, he knew he wouldn't be able to meet the payment that soon, but he didn't want to endanger Sam, which he was fairly sure is what he would be doing by giving Ethan what he was asking for.

'I'll throw this in to help you make up your mind,' Ethan offered, holding up a small transparent bag with white powder in it.

Travis's response to the sight was almost physical. Because of his financial difficulties, his last fix had been some time ago, and the craving was something that he could not ignore as he teetered on the verge of withdrawal.

'No charge,' Ethan clarified, swinging the tiny bag from side to side between his fingers.

Travis hesitated only a couple of seconds.

'Fine,' he snatched the bag from Ethan's hand before the offer could be retracted. Turning his back on the smiling man, he rummaged around amongst the rubbish and unpaid bills that lay on the coffee table. Finally finding his phone, he began scrolling through some photos. 'I don't know where she lives, but I do know where you can find out.' With a hard stare he turned the phone around and showed Ethan a photograph. 'This didn't come from me,' he stated firmly, fully acknowledging the depths of this selfish act of betrayal.

He sent the photo and Sam's full name to Ethan who nodded as his phone sounded its arrival then left. Travis sat alone, trying his hardest to hold back the tears that threatened to break the surface.

Phil's phone vibrated in his pocket. *This had better be Ethan with some good news, or at the very least, a solid plan to make up for his failure.* He fumbled around till his hands closed on the device. 'Samantha Beaven, huh?' He smiled as the image that Ethan had sent him filled the screen. It showed the girl, Thunder Kiss, posing with a friend in front of a yellow rose bush. She had on a polo shirt with something embroidered on the chest, a uniform of some sort. Phil used his fingers on the phone's screen to zoom in on the area then threw his head back and laughed with glee.

After locking the front door behind her, Sam went to the kitchen, switched on the kettle at the mains and set it boiling, out of habit more than anything else. But then a nice camomile tea might be just what she needed to calm her nerves and gain some perspective.

As it heated up, she took the stairs two at a time to her bedroom and dragged a weekender bag out of the cupboard. She immediately began pulling clothes and underwear from the wardrobe and drawers and stuffing them into the bag.

What she had experienced earlier was not, she knew, a random attempt at mugging or kidnapping.

Goatee had mentioned that they had picked Honey up thinking that she was Sam, but they still didn't have Sam, meaning they weren't finished yet.

The adrenaline was wearing off, and Sam sat down on her bed, suddenly feeling quite faint. She was now wishing that she hadn't donated blood that morning, but who knew she'd be running for her life later that day?

The house phone rang, and Sam jumped at the sudden interruption in the otherwise silent building. She checked the caller ID before answering. 'Chris!'

'Samantha, are you alright?' her boyfriend's voice was thick with concern, 'I called your mobile, but you didn't answer, I was so worried!'

'I'm okay, I left my phone in my kit bag at the park. Chris, I'm leaving town. I'm going to the police, but not here, somewhere else, far away, where his influence isn't so strong.'

'I'm coming with you. I'm just getting in the car now with your kit bag and I'm coming straight over, okay?'

'Thank you.'

'I'm so sorry it's taken me so long; I didn't hear about what had happened until I got back to the park with the water.'

'Chris, it's okay. Just… get here soon, alright?'

'Samantha, don't worry, if they knew where you lived they'd have come for you at home in the first place, not somewhere public like the park.'

'That's not why I want you here quickly, I— I just want you here.'

'Right. I'll be there as soon as I can.'

Phil bounded up the front steps of Oakwood Residences, a carrier bag with a brand-new pair of fluffy slippers swinging from one hand. 'Afternoon, Bhavna,' he greeted the receptionist with a charming smile, 'how's he doing?' he signed in to the visitors' register as he spoke.

'Lovely to see you, Philip. He's up and down today I'm afraid, but he's expecting you. He's in his room,' she nodded her head down the corridor that stretched out behind her desk on the right.

Phil lifted his hand to tip an imaginary hat as he walked away.

Reaching his Uncle's room, he took a moment to compose himself. Something about the old man always turned Phil into a little boy in his head when he was around him. He strode in.

'Philip! About bloody time!'

'Uncle Alf, I came as soon as I could, there's no need for that tone.'

Alf dropped his scowl a little. 'Did you get them?'

Phil produced the slippers from the bag. 'Fluffy enough for you?'

The old man's eyes lit up when he saw them.

'You are a good boy; don't you listen to what your father tells you.'

'Dad's dead, remember, Uncle Alf? Years ago now,' Phil delivered the line softly, as he did every time.

'What? Oh, yes, my mistake. I forget things you know, it's my age.'

'No worry, old man,' Phil said and patted the back of his Uncle's hand. He stared out of the window at the yellow rose bush in the home's garden, 'Uncle Alf, there's someone I'm trying to find, and I think you might know where. It's a young lady, with bright pink hair,' he showed the old man the photo on his phone that Ethan had sent him earlier.

'Yes, of course I know her, that's Samantha,' he leaned in towards Phil conspiratorially, 'she's my favourite.'

'Why's that then?' Phil asked him, not really caring.

'She lets me win at chess,' he sat up proudly, 'and she thinks I don't know what she's playing at.'

Sounds familiar. 'So, she treats you well then?'

'Absolutely, she's a lovely girl.'

Now the big question, 'Do you know where she lives?'

CHAPTER TWENTY-SIX

Phil sauntered back up the corridor after staying with Uncle Alf for a few minutes. He had sorted out the cushions for the old man, and although he had expected it, he was frustrated that Uncle Alf had no idea where the girl lived. He stopped as he reached Bhavna at the reception desk and flashed her a smile. 'Uncle Alf has just been talking to me about one of his carers, a young lady called Samantha?'

'Oh yes, he is rather fond of her, always asking for her on her days off,' Bhavna laughed.

'Yes, he seems very taken by her. I wanted to send her some flowers as a thank-you for being so good to him. Would it be possible to get her address for their delivery?'

Bhavna's smile turned into a pursed-lipped version of her earlier grin, her eyes darting briefly to a shelf next to her shoulder then back to Phil. 'I'm afraid I can't give out employees' personal information, no matter how well-meaning the reason. You could always get something sent here for her though.'

Well, it was worth a shot, 'Thanks, I'll do that then. See you soon.'

Bhavna waved as Phil turned towards the door, 'Take care.'

He had taken two slow steps, trying to work out his next move, when shouts could be heard from behind the reception area, down the opposing corridor to Uncle Alf's.

'BHAVNA! Phone and first aid!'

Thinking quickly, Phil stopped walking and patted his pockets like he was checking for something.

Credit to Bhavna, she was fast with that first aid kit, and was already off down the corridor towards the commotion before Phil needed to work out what to do next as an excuse to stick around. He leapt back across the reception area, behind the desk and immediately strode to the shelf on the wall where Bhavna had inadvertently glanced when talking about employees' personal information.

He thumbed through the folder, scanning the staff photos as quickly as possible looking for the girl that he had seen in the park earlier. He could hear shouts from the elderly residents but couldn't quite make out what they were saying, it was enough to let him know that Bhavna was still needed down the corridor, calming people.

Samantha Beaven's face jumped out at him and he quickly snapped a photo of her personnel file. He hastily replaced the folder on the shelf and rounded the reception desk in time to hear Bhavna's footsteps returning to her post. Phil threw himself around the corner in the direction of Uncle Alf's room as she emerged into the reception space. Taking a couple of steps back, Phil forced a deep breath and then strode out as though he had been walking for a good few seconds.

'Left my phone, of all things,' he informed her,

waving it where she could see it in his hand. 'Take care, Bhavna, see you soon.'

Bhavna was busy with other things and barely looked up as he exited the front door.

Sam threw the last of her toiletries into her washbag and took the luggage downstairs to wait for Chris. After pacing the lounge three times, she powered the TV on at the mains and then aggressively prodded the remote control at it to switch it on. The background noise was a welcome distraction to the earlier silence in the building, and Sam felt a little of the tension of the last hour or so dissipating.

She began to feel angry, how dare these people threaten her in broad daylight? A little spark of her strength of character was beginning to return as she ran over the earlier events in her head; if the others could save her from a knife-wielding youth, then she could damn well save herself from this whole situation. She began to pace again, her mind working overtime to come up with some solution.

The news was on TV, showing a standard shot of a crime scene, with police tape blocking off the end of an alley and forensics officers crowded around a large rubbish skip. A voiceover was explaining the scene '—the body has been identified as that of a local school teacher. There is currently no obvious motive behind her murder.'

Sam wasn't really taking in the story, she was still on-edge, waiting for Chris, her thoughts jumbled, as she stared unseeing at the screen in front of her. The scene switched to a newsroom, where the anchor began speaking more about what was known about the victim's life. 'Sarah Honey was also known to some in the area by her skate name, "Honey Trap", which she used when playing with her roller derby team, Stormy City Rollergirls.'

Sam's hands flew to her mouth. She felt sick.

A large image of a smiling Honey, framed by her long, pink hair, filled her TV screen as the newsreader continued; 'This woman is understood to be the same girl that was victim to a kidnapping four years ago when she was held by a former school friend at his family's holiday home in the Peak District. The incidents are believed to be unrelated.

'On that occasion she successfully evaded her assailant and managed to alert the authorities, unfortunately, this time the twenty-four-year-old singleton hasn't been so lucky.' He paused solemnly for effect. 'Jessica Raines, our reporter on the scene, has more. Jessica…'

Jessica was positioned at the end of the alley, just in front of the police crime scene tape.

It's my fault. Because I didn't go quietly. I got her killed. Oh my god. Sam collapsed into her sofa and began sobbing, her entire body shaking violently as she did so.

Jessica began her report; 'The police were alerted to the presence of the murdered woman's body in the early hours of this morning by early kitchen crews at the nearby restaurants. Full results of the initial forensics from the scene haven't been released as yet, but we do know that the time of death was around thirty-six hours ago, and that there is some evidence that the victim was abused, possibly even to the point of torture, prior to her death.'

Torture? Honey died in pain because of me. Because of what I saw. Sam began sobbing, weighed down with guilt.

Wait, thirty-six hours? So, she was already dead

when I was attacked at the park. The relief softened Sam's guilt slightly, but she remained frozen on the sofa, unsure. Honey was dead, these people would stop at nothing.

 A knock at the door made Sam jump. She ran to answer it, eager to have Chris just hold her for a minute whilst she mourned the passing of one of her best friends.

'Chris!' she cried as she fumbled to pull the door open, 'they've killed Honey!'

A man's torso filled her doorway, 'Not Chris. And that bitch brought it on herself.'

Sam looking up into the smiling face of Bradford's bodyguard.

CHAPTER TWENTY-SEVEN

Sam's scream caught in her throat as Phil barged his way into her house, his bulk forcing her back into the lounge. He was followed by someone she didn't recognise, he appeared wiry, and not as smartly dressed as Phil, in a tracksuit and trainers.

She turned to run, though not sure where to. She just needed to get some space from these men for long enough to grab a knife or something.

Before she had a chance to go far, hands grabbed her roughly by the shoulders and dragged her over to throw her down onto one of the sofas. The casually dressed guy held her there while Phil spoke. 'You're a tough one to track down, Miss Beaven.' He was strolling slowly around the small open plan area as he spoke, looking around at Sam's decor. 'Or should I call you Thunder Kiss?' He stopped abruptly and turned to look at her, 'You know you really fucked things up when you gave your friend your shirt to wear, and not just for me, she didn't do too good out of it either.'

Sam said nothing as tears began to form in the corners of her eyes again at the mention of Honey and her fate. Her captor roughly pulled her upright so that she was seated on the sofa, then positioned himself behind her with his hands firmly on her shoulders, holding her in-place.

'We haven't been formally introduced, I'm Phil by the way.' The bodyguard looked around the room again, 'Cute place you have here,' he furrowed his brow, 'what's with all the purple?'

'I like purple,' Sam muttered matter-of-factly.

Phil stood still, sizing her up for a moment, then he shrugged and spoke again, resuming his pacing. 'Do you know why we want to speak to you?' *he makes it sound so civil.*

'You want to know who I've told,' Sam answered quietly, not looking up.

'Give the girl a gold star. Right, but we can't do it here, we'll move on as soon as your boyfriend gets here.'

Sam's gaze shot upwards to stare, horrified, at Phil.

'I know you're expecting him, you thought Gregory and I were him when you came to the door.' He stopped pacing to stare straight at her, leaning in, 'We know you're bound to have told him about what you saw, kid. Then it's just a matter of knowing how many others he's told.'

On cue, there was an urgent knocking at the door. Sam took a deep breathe in, ready to scream a warning to Chris, but Gregory had already put his hand over her mouth. Phil smiled at her, then turned to go and answer the door. Sam could only watch, horrified.

A well-built man in light trousers and a tight-fitting t-shirt opened the door to Samantha's house. In one fluid movement he had grabbed Chris by his clothing and pulled him inside, closing the door swiftly behind them with the other hand. Chris turned to face his assailant, now standing between himself and the front door. *This must be the bodyguard.*

He tensed up, ready to launch himself at the man. 'Er, I wouldn't if I were you, Christopher,' the suit stated, gesturing with his eyes over to where Samantha sat on the sofa. Samantha was so busy watching Chris with concern etched into her face, that it seemed that she hadn't noticed the knife that the man in the cheap tracksuit behind her had in his free hand. He was holding it loosely, but close enough to her neck that Chris would not be able to get to him in time if he decided to use it.

The bodyguard patted him on the back. 'Let's try and get this all sorted out civilly shall we? We don't want any more bodies to deal with if we can help it.' The TV was still on behind Samantha, and the local news was now playing in its slot after the national stories. Chris saw Honey's picture on the screen and the frightened look on his girlfriend's face and concluded that compliance was going to be their best bet, at least for now.

'Okay,' responded Chris. 'Let's be civil.'

'Excellent,' the bodyguard rubbed his hands together. 'Let's all go for a little ride then shall we.'

'Where to?'

'Well, anywhere is better than here of course, in case we're interrupted. I do know a delightful little place ideal for our purposes though. But first, mobile phones please.'

Chris was reluctant to hand his over, but Tracksuit still had his knife readied on Samantha, so he had no option but to oblige. The bodyguard took it to the kitchen where Samantha's charger was visible on the bench top and plugged it in. 'That's lucky, perfect fit,' he said, pleased. 'Now it just looks like you forgot to take it with you on your sudden trip away to de-stress.' He turned to Samantha and held his hand out.

'I left mine at the park,' she told him.

He looked at her suspiciously.

'Really! I swear!' she implored. 'It was in my kit bag which I dropped when I ran away.'

Chris thought better of reminding her that he had her bag.

The bodyguard nodded to Tracksuit, who felt the pockets of Samantha's sleeveless hoody. A cursory glance at her skin-tight sports capris told him that there was no phone there either. He shook his head.

'Right then, shall we go?' the bodyguard encouraged jovially. 'As we've got no option but to go out the front, this needs to look peaceful, and above all, convincing. Christopher, Gregory here shall accompany you in your car and I will take Miss Kiss, as now that I finally have her, she will not be leaving my sight again for the foreseeable future.'

'NO!' shouted Chris, making a start towards Samantha as she stood up from the sofa.

'There is absolutely no way that you two will be travelling together, so get over it right now,' the bodyguard informed him firmly. He looked at a set of keys on the kitchen bench and picked them up, examining the main fob which was a purple roller skate. 'I'm guessing these are yours then,' he said to Samantha, holding the keyring up for her to see.

Samantha didn't respond, she just looked away.

'Gregory, pass me Miss Kiss's bag that she has so kindly packed for us, let's keep up the charade of these two leaving town together.'

Tracksuit leaned over and collected the bag as instructed, with the other hand firmly clamped around Samantha's elbow, steering her around the furniture. The bodyguard gestured for Chris to leave the building ahead of him. Chris shot one last look towards Samantha, managing only a slight twitch of one side of his mouth, and not the reassuring smile he had intended.

Once outside, Chris warily led Gregory to his black VW Passat that was parked a few yards along the street. He got in first, with Gregory's arm already in the car and pointing a gun at the driver's side as he slid stoically into the passenger seat. Chris saw the bodyguard a few cars down, throwing Samantha's overnight bag into the boot of a nondescript blue saloon as she entered the car on the driver's side, now wearing a hoody with the hood pulled up and her head hanging low, like she was staring at the ground.

'Don't worry about them, just drive straight, and I'll tell you when to turn,' Gregory instructed, a slight foreign accent to his speech. He settled in and rested his gun hand in the crook of his opposite elbow, allowing him to keep the barrel trained on his driver. 'As long as you don't try to play the hero, everyone will get to where we're going safely. I can't make any promises for once we arrive, of course,' he chuckled to himself.

It was all Chris could do to hold back from lashing out at the man.

'I'm going to tell you a story about Phil there,' Gregory gestured to the blue car as they drove past where it was parked, and Samantha pulled out behind them. 'He used to live on the streets. Left home as soon as he could to get away from the abuse and the beatings.' Gregory kept his eyes on Chris as he spoke, whether as a precaution or just to intimidate was unclear. 'So, one day, he sees the boss getting mugged as he gets into his car. The guy is threatening the boss with a knife and the driver can't intervene without risking the boss getting cut.

'So, Phil steps up, stealthy, behind the mugger. He yanks him back by the collar, spins him round onto the floor, and beats him to a pulp - cos it's all he knows, right? They had to pull him off the guy, and then the driver finishes him off with a boot heel to the head while his face is on the kerb. Phil's just standing there. He's not bothered, right, probably seen worse. So, the boss offers him a job, there and then. Takes it seriously too, doesn't let anything endanger the big man. You feel me?'

Gregory delivered the last piece of information with a reassuring tone. It made Chris feel anything but.

Sam saw Chris's car in front indicate and turn off the main road and down a single-track country road. Stiff from spending a good hour on the road, she indicated also. She followed him down the tarmac, a high wall close up against one side of the cars as they drove. The wall continued round a sharp bend, and it became apparent that it surrounded a large property, maybe a stately home or manor house.

Ahead of them, Chris's car slowed to a stop by an ornate wooden door set into the old stone wall. 'Pull over here,' Phil instructed. Sam did as she was told and turned the engine off. Her passenger suddenly reached beneath his seat and pulled some sort of leather restraint from underneath it. Her heart momentarily jumped into her throat as she saw the shiny buckle and tough material held tightly in the hands of her captor. On closer inspection, she saw that it was a coiled-up dog lead, and her sigh of relief was so loud it caused Phil to give her a quizzical look.

'If you see anyone, we're just out looking for our runaway dog, okay? Try anything, try to signal them in any way, then you *and* they are dead. Understand?'

Sam nodded vigorously, *I really don't want to be witness to any more violence if I can help it, and certainly not the reason for more deaths.*

'Good. Get out.'

As Sam obliged, Gregory and Chris got out of their car too. As they all reached the wooden door it swung inwards, and Sam had another heart-stopping shock as a youth with a goatee appeared.

Goatee leered at her as she entered the door and passed next to him, with Phil keeping a close formation to bring up the rear of the little group. 'Hey, Sam, good to see you again,' he closed the door and locked it behind them. 'I'm just sorry it was so brief earlier.'

Sam saw Chris tense up at these words, the realisation apparently hitting him that this was the man from the park. She watched as his eyes briefly scanned the youth and dropped to the knife in Goatee's hand. *He won't be able to reach the knife before Goatee reaches me.* Chris seemed to have worked that out too, his muscles unclenched. The two men exchanged knowing looks of menace instead, the silent altercation eventually interrupted by Phil's voice; 'Gregory, take Christopher here to the shed then make him comfortable… and keep an eye on him.'

Gregory nodded then strode over to Chris. As he

walked, he produced a roll of duct tape from a pocket which he proceeded to use to bind Chris's hands behind his back. With his knife to the back of Chris's neck, Gregory manoeuvred the man around a tall hedge and out of sight of the others.

'Ethan,' Phil addressed Goatee, 'take care of the cars please. Miss Kiss and I have some talking to do.'

'With pleasure,' Ethan unlocked the door then threw the key to Phil who then went to lock the door behind him.

This is my chance.

Phil had his back to Sam and she was out of his reach.

She began to run.

CHAPTER TWENTY-EIGHT

'We'll hurt him first,' Phil called out casually. 'Before we kill him I mean. He'll pay the price if you go now, and it will be costly.'

Sam slowed her flight. She turned her head to see Phil nonchalantly pocketing the key in his jacket, he hadn't even looked up at her yet, one hundred percent confidence in his words' ability to stop Sam in her tracks.

Because she knew he meant it.

She stopped running and turned her body to face Phil, her feelings of defeat manifesting as defiance. 'You know I'd tell you everything you want to know without all this, don't you?'

'I believe I do,' Phil put his hands in his pockets, still standing casually next to the door.

'Then why? Why all the effort? The risk, the violence, the loss of life?' exasperation came pouring out with Sam's words.

'Miss Beaven, you've seen first-hand what happens to people who fail my employer or pose any kind of risk to his operations. He knows nothing of your involvement at the moment, and I'd like to get this all tidied up to keep it that way, it's sort of a "you or me" deal. So, I need to be sure that you're not going to miss out any important details. In my experience, there's only one way to ever be really sure.' He lifted his head to look at her. 'I also enjoy it just a little bit.'

Resigned to the fact that now was not the time, Sam began to trudge back through the long grass towards her tormentor. *He's a psychopath. He enjoys other people's pain, and I'm stuck here with him, alone.* She had no choice but to comply for now, for Chris's sake. She knew she had to think quickly, to come up with another way to get them both out of this increasingly dire situation. It was clear that speed or strength would not help them in this case, Sam needed to be smart, to outthink her captors. Honey had managed it, years ago when she was younger. *I can't just give in. Honey didn't, and I owe it to her memory to try to be as strong as she would have been.*

Even if all she could do was buy them some time and hope that help came, Sam promised herself that she wouldn't just give up.

An idea began to form in her head, but she would have to appear strong and resolute for it to work.

She reached Phil who smiled at her, then without warning, pulled his hand from his coat pocket and hit Sam hard across the cheek with the back of his hand. The shock of the blow caught her off-guard, causing her to stumble and fall to the floor. 'Don't try anything like that again. Now get up and walk that way,' Phil pointed in the direction that Chris and Ethan had gone.

Sam got shakily to her feet. She'd been body-checked pretty hard by Belle before, but there was an emotion driving this hit that seemed to physically vibrate through her jaw. She forced herself to just shake it off and recover quickly, ignoring the throbbing around her cheekbone, and set off walking alongside the tall hedge.

As they came around the hedge, a small chapel came into view. Manicured grounds stretched away from them and in the distance a grand stately home loomed against the sky. The chapel had, for some reason, been built away from the house, tucked into this little area by the boundary wall.

The thick wooden door to the chapel was ajar. Sam looked questioningly at Phil and he gestured for her to proceed into the building. Her eyes were met with a murky light, the sun trying to fight through the build-up of moss and algae on the chapel's small stained-glass windows. A short aisle led out ahead of her, just five rows of pews on either side of it.

The floor was a mix of wooden floorboards dotted with large stone slabs, both gave their footsteps an eerie echo. Instinctively, Sam knew that this was where Honey had died.

In the shiver that slowly crept up her spine to the back of her neck, making her shoulders tense, and in the air that hung thick around them, somehow she could just feel the presence of death. The building had likely borne witness to an impressive share of secrets, but it certainly wasn't telling.

'You can sense it can't you?' Phil's voice cut through her thoughts. 'The pain, the mortality. It hangs in the air.'

Sam shivered involuntarily. The place smelt cold and damp, reeking of years of disuse, and neglect, and death. The building's high-vaulted ceiling suddenly began to feel very oppressive to Sam and she had to search for the strength to overcome the panic that was starting to bubble up inside her.

'I think it's the smell,' Phil continued, 'it's sometimes hard to detect unless you know it's there. We have a cleaner who has expertise in this particular area, of course, but sometimes it's still hard to get it all, you know. The blood soaks deep into the wood, I reckon it's that that gives this place its air of mortality. You smell it, and you know you shouldn't be here.' Phil was steering Sam towards a small area to one side of the chapel on the opposite side to the lectern. 'Of course, in your case you don't get a say in the matter.'

A single wooden bench sat there, fixed firmly to an extravagant railing, probably where a few choir singers would have been located when the chapel was last used for more respectable purposes. Phil shoved her roughly down onto the choir bench and tied her wrists together with a set of thick plastic restraints, bounding her to the ostentatious railing. When he was finished, he turned and walked back up the aisle towards the chapel's entrance, removing his phone from his pocket as he moved.

Sam watched him go, silent. When he was past the doors and out of sight, she tested the strength of her bonds. Neither her ties nor the railings were showing any signs of give. The oppression of the surroundings slowly crept up on Sam as daylight faded further, and she imagined the scent of the blood rather than actually smelling it, but it still seemed to suffocate her; *Honey's blood*.

Sam drifted away inside her head, the little courage she had shrinking back into a corner.

Phil returned shortly after he had left, apparently finishing up a telephone call. '—see if you can get hold of Alvarez, and make sure the job gets done 'cos this guy's a loose end, he's the final link between us and those rollergirls... No, I'm assured he won't have told anyone and won't have planned ahead.'

Sam wasn't paying much attention to what Phil was saying, still feeling dragged down with thoughts of Honey's final hours being spent in this place, but one word did penetrate her wandering thoughts, "plan".

Sam focussed her efforts now on how best to manipulate the situation to be in her favour. She had already thought of a plan outside, but the sudden backhand across the face from Phil had distracted her at the time.

Sam looked up at the thug standing in front of her, cocky and menacing. Taking in his appearance, Sam realised that she had to match him in sheer arrogance if he was to believe her. She had to truly believe her own words and appear outwardly to have an unwavering confidence in her convictions.

She pictured Honey again, drawing on memories of her strength and her take-no-shit attitude, and Sam's own promise to her departed friend that she would live up to what Honey always told her she could be.

'Well?' Phil asked her, his hands clasped loosely in front of him.

Sam quietly took a deep breath, preparing her voice to answer steadily. 'Well what?'

'Come on, I already told you what we're here for. Who else have you spoken to about what you heard?'

Showtime. 'What I heard?'

'This isn't a fucking game, little girl,' Phil spat, losing his cool, 'the murder, the conversation, the people you saw, any and all of it.'

'Oh, that pesky business. No one,' mustering some courage, she locked eyes with him, 'yet. But carry on like this and it'll be in the national papers by Monday.'

Believe it. Make it real. Convince him.

'Possibly Tuesday, depending on when they find my body. I'm assuming you plan to kill me anyway, once you've heard enough?'

Phil wasn't fazed, not yet, but he was looking a little confused. After a period of silence between the two of them he spoke, 'What exactly are you playing at?'

'I'm not playing at anything. You just underestimated me, that's all. The "loose end" that you plan to get your mate on the phone to tie up might not be sharp enough to plan ahead, but I am.'

Phil was trying to remain impassive, but there was the slightest twitch of his face muscles, and Sam could tell that if she hadn't convinced him fully that she had some sort of insurance policy, he now wasn't sure that she didn't. It would be enough, for now.

His face suddenly changed, the muscles stabilised; he was back in charge again, and seemed dangerously pleased about it. 'That "loose end", is your bartender friend, who, incidentally, sold you out,' he grinned. 'Now who's underestimating who?'

CHAPTER TWENTY-NINE

Travis was slumped on his sofa again, coming down from an extremely small high that he had afforded himself before work. He'd placed a small quantity of the white powder that Ethan had left him with directly onto his tongue and his cravings had somewhat subsided long enough for him to turn up at the Tin Whistle and complete his shift. The manager's words echoed in his mind still, "It's not like our Sam to just not show up, not call ahead with a damn good reason. I hope nothing bad has happened to her."

The TV in front of him was on, although Travis's glassy eyes weren't really focussed on the screen, his thoughts were elsewhere, thinking of Sam. He couldn't stop thinking about what might happen to her and how he would be partly to blame. Sarah Honey's face smiled up at him from his TV screen and he ran his hands slowly through his hair, trying to banish thoughts of what her final hours must have been like as he pulled his fingers through the strands.

He knew that her death was his fault. Ethan had called to arrange a meet with some guy he worked for, a well-built bloke in a suit. Travis had had to pull out of his shift at the pub when the football was on, usually their busiest time, and his boss wasn't too chuffed. He had done it anyway, as Ethan's employers were not the type of people that you let down, even at the risk of your job.

The guy had wanted info on the Roller Derby league. It sounded like he'd seen one of the shirts and that was all he knew, but he wanted to know more. More about who they were, where they practised and when. Travis had told him the league's name and found their practice schedule for him on their website. It had seemed a little odd to him at the time, but he had supplied the information without question.

The backlit scene in front of him changed to show the alley where Honey's body had been found for what felt like the fifteenth time in the last hour. Travis pulled at his hair again then began sobbing, clawing at his eyes in a subconscious attempt to make the images in his head go away.

He raised from the sofa suddenly and went over to the kitchenette. Glancing over the menu for the Chinese takeaway below him, he opted for one of his favourite dishes, beef chow mein, and telephoned down to place his order. Travis barely heard the owner's usual banter and the fact that there would be a long wait for his food tonight as the place was really busy; he had caught sight of the bag of white powder on the worktop. When he hung up his call, Travis snatched up the bag then rummaged around on the shelf beneath the coffee table. Scattering aside unpaid bills and a couple of lads' magazines he found the thing that he was looking for. Hastily he opened the lid of the retro-styled Superman tin and took out his drug paraphernalia.

Turning the bag over and over in the fingers of one

hand, Travis watched the substance inside moving around as if it were looking for an escape route. He could be stronger than this, he'd been without the drug for a short while now anyway, he could just tip it down the sink and move on with his life, with bettering himself.

In the background, the newsreader continued to talk about Sarah Honey's life and the children she had taught, the lives she had touched.

It was too much for Travis.

He arranged the entire contents of the bag into lines on a small mirror on the coffee table. Snorting them desperately, the voice on the TV seemed to echo in Travis's head repeatedly; 'She will be sorely missed; this is truly a tragedy; such a young life cut short.'

He sat back deep into his sofa cushions and exhaled noisily. After a few minutes it became apparent to Travis that the drug was not making him feel any better about himself or any less guilty about Honey's death, or whatever was going to happen to Sam. In fact, nothing was ever likely to make him feel good about himself again.

Jumping up from the sofa, he wandered back to the kitchenette. He pulled an almost full litre bottle of vodka from a cupboard before returning to his slouched position on the sofa to drink himself to death.

Sam couldn't tell what time it was, but there was a sense of settling-in around her in the way that some birds seemed to be making their roost on the beams that held up the vaulted ceiling, entering in through a broken stained glass window high up on one wall.

As the darkness crept in, Sam's eyes began to feel

heavy. It had been a long day, and she was exhausted, but even sitting by herself in the silence she could not actually sleep, the adrenaline still hanging around in her system. It wasn't over yet. She knew her only hope was to keep up the facade of having insurance, of someone telling her story for her after she was gone. If she could do that for as long as it took for someone to come looking for them, then herself and Chris just might stand a chance at getting out of this alive, and hopefully in one piece.

She stretched her jaw, one side still throbbing gently from Phil's earlier hit. There was the sudden sound of movement outside the chapel followed by Phil returning having changed into a dark suit. He approached Sam then took a seat in a pew near her. 'No-one will find you here, Miss Kiss.'

Sam blinked quickly before the tear of despair that was threatening to form could start to take shape.

Phil looked at the disrepair around him, 'I knew the guy that used to look after the grounds. The owner lives abroad, couldn't give a shit about the house and its heritage, so he's never even visited. Left the key with my friend too.' He leaned in towards her, gesturing to the walls around them, 'So there's nothing to tie any of us to this place on paper. That's why it's so perfect. That and the graveyard of course, there's nowhere better to bury a body than an actual graveyard.'

'Why didn't you bury David Steele here? Why did you let his body be found if it risked leaving evidence behind?'

'David was a message to our other associates, so they know that it's best not to fuck things up.'

'And Honey?' the name caught in Sam's throat as she thought about her friend's final indignity of being left in a dumpster.

'Honey… was a message to you.' Phil let his words float in the air a moment, the faintest of echoes bouncing off the cold stone that surrounded them. 'Okay, you have my full attention now. What's the deal with your insurance policy?'

Sam took a second to compose herself. Pushing her uneasiness to the back of her mind, she replied as confidently as she could. 'It's pretty standard really. If anything happens to me, then a good friend, who is not part of the Stormy City Roller Derby league, so you won't find them, will release everything I know to the media. Everything. You will without a doubt go down for David Steele's murder, Bradford I guess as an accessory, or conspiracy to commit, I'm not sure of the exact legal term. You can imagine the fallout, I'm sure.' She studied Phil's face to see if he was giving any signs of being convinced and then remembered the one detail that she had almost over-looked. 'The same goes for Chris, if anything hap-pens to him, full disclosure to the press and other media outlets.' *That was close*. Sam had no doubt that Phil would have exploited any loophole, had she not been specific enough.

'I see. You expect me to believe that you had the foresight to make these plans and yet haven't repor-ted anything to the police?'

'When I found out who Bradford was, I figured he probably had the police on his payroll,' she explained honestly. 'I didn't think it would end well for me,' she managed an ironic smile.

'Smart girl. Now, what about if you just tell us what we want to know, which is what you heard that night, and who else you've told about it. Then we promise to let you both go afterwards. That way everybody's happy.'

'Really? You think I'm that dumb? I don't exactly trust you, so I won't be telling you anything until Chris and I are home safely.'

Phil looked pensive. 'Well, if this is the case then myself and my employers may need some time to work out how best to proceed with our plans for you both. I'll just go and check in on your boyfriend first, make sure he's… comfortable.' Phil's phone rang and he removed it from his pocket and checked the caller ID, 'You'll have to excuse me, Miss Kiss, I need to take this.'

CHAPTER THIRTY

Phil opened the creaky chapel door. It was almost pitch black inside the decaying building, the moon offering just enough light to make out large shapes and distorted shadows. If he had to admit it, the place gave him the creeps, but he considered that an effective feature as it was likely that his "interviewees" felt the same way.

His eyes slowly began to adjust to the dark and he saw that Samantha was awake. He was feeling tired of this whole manhunt and just wanted the job over so that they could move on to the next phase of their plan, preferably without Brad ever having to know anything about this hiccup.

Mustering up some arrogance, he swaggered up the chapel's aisle towards his captive, his shoes clacking on the stones as he walked. *I'll open with the news about the bartender, rattle her straight away.*

'You're awake, good,' he drew himself up to tower over the small figure on the bench.

The young woman lifted her chin up to look directly at him, defiance etched into her features.

Bitch. I know more than one way to shake up a silly little girl like you. 'The last person to give me that look was beaten, killed, and dropped in a dumpster.'

Phil could see that she was trying to remain subversive and ignore him, but her mask had faltered. 'Honey Tra—'

'You don't get to say her name.' Samantha said through clenched teeth.

I've hit a nerve. 'Okay then. Your buddy, she wouldn't want any more bloodshed, she'd consider the price paid already. So why don't you tell me what I want to know.'

'You don't know anything about her, or me.' She turned her head away.

Another tough cookie. Great. Phil grabbed her chin and pulled her head to face him as he spoke directly into her face. 'I have news on your bartender friend. He felt so bad over giving you and your friend up that he decided to save us some effort; he overdosed tonight. Yet another one to add to your body count, Miss Kiss. When are you going to start talking and make all this stop?'

'ME? I'm not the one going around killing people!'

'You may as well be. Because we will carry on until you cooperate,' he leaned in closer, 'and we will start with those that you love most.'

The facade fell, Samantha's features betrayed the terror that he knew she'd been trying to hide. Phil suddenly realised what he'd said, and that her insurance didn't even matter. He'd found her Achilles' heel.

'You didn't plan for that did you? Just for yourself, not the welfare of your nearest and dearest,' Phil smiled, triumphant, 'and I suppose also only for if you actually turn up dead, not for if you're believed to have left town with your boyfriend.'

He saw the whites of Samantha's eyes bright through the gloom, darting around as she tried to think of something to say. 'I— I need to check in regularly, else the information will be released.' Her voice was desperate, and Phil knew that she saw he wasn't buying it anymore.

'Funny how you neglected to mention that earlier. It makes me think that's not quite true, Samantha. In fact, maybe this whole insurance policy of yours is a work of fiction.'

She looked horrified. *Bingo*.

'That's the truth of the matter isn't it? No one knows where you are, anyone that thinks they know will think you've gone away with your boyfriend. If anything happens to you or him here, no one will ever know, so nothing will get released. Well, this changes things somewhat.' Phil straightened up to leave. 'I'll be back in a few hours, after I've paid Christopher another visit.' He marched out of the door before Samantha had managed to utter a cohesive sentence to his back.

He closed the door to the building behind him, shutting her away into the dark to be alone with her grim thoughts about what her immediate future might hold. Phil had decided to wait for Bradford to be contactable again before he made any move on either of his captives. He was pretty sure now that Samantha had been bluffing about the entire insurance policy, but the blowback if he was wrong would affect Bradford more than it would himself. A decision based on that risk had to be made by someone above him. He was going to have to come clean after all.

That bitch. I'm going to enjoy ripping her heart out.

Travis became aware of his physical body long before his memories returned. Semi-conscious, he knew that he was not well. Beeping noises reached him from somewhere nearby, and a strong smell of bleach irritated his sensitive nostrils. As he became more aware, an intense pain in his throat and chest took him off-guard and he instinctively tried to cough to alleviate the tickle. The act was excruciating, and he suppressed any further attempts.

The beeping had quickened in these last few seconds, and the sound must have attracted someone's attention, as he now realised that he was no longer alone in the room.

'Calm yourself there, son,' a woman's kindly voice spoke to him as a hand came to rest gently on his shoulder. 'You're in the hospital. We had to intubate you when you came in as you couldn't breathe by yourself. It's an uncomfortable thing to have done so we've had you sedated for a few hours and unfortunately you will be in rather a lot of pain for a while.'

Travis opened his mouth to reply and a straw was placed into it. 'Don't try to speak yet, you'll be very dry. Have some water and then rest some more, you've been through a trauma tonight. We'll keep an eye on you, us and the Lord, don't you worry.' The woman patted his hand and then left the room, her footsteps clopping away down a corridor into the distance.

Travis had not yet opened his eyes and didn't feel the need to now either as the drowsiness returned and began pulling him back down with its heavy fingers.

Back in a semi-conscious state, memories started to drift back to him. Taking the cocaine, drinking the vodka, passing out. *What an idiot*, Travis thought to himself, *you know better than to drink when on coke, what the hell were you thinking?* Honey's smiling face from the news reports flashed into his mind, and everything came rushing back to him in an instant.

He had wanted to die.

Honey had been killed and tortured, and he'd helped enable it. Sam was probably dead now too and he'd done nothing to stop it. He was better off dead.

Something that the nurse had said suddenly floated into the foreground of his muddled thoughts, *"We'll keep an eye on you, us and the Lord..."* Travis wasn't particularly religious, like many people he would declare himself a Christian, but didn't really do anything to back the statement up. He did, however, strongly believe in a higher power, be it a Christian God or something else, and a failed suicide attempt felt like a message. *Maybe I have a defined purpose in life, that's why I didn't die tonight.*

His thoughts became less rational as he began to drift off back to sleep. Sam's face peered up at him from a hole in the ground, frightened and resigned to her fate. It hit him then and he almost awoke properly, *she's still alive!* He was still alive too so that he could right his wrongs by finding her and protecting her. Yes, he would rest now so that soon he would walk out of hospital a changed man, tasked to help the unfortunate that had lost their way like he had. He would start with fixing this situation with Sam, regardless of what she thought of him once he came clean about his part in it all. Honesty would be another trait of this new person that he was to become.

He felt at peace with the world as he drifted fully off to sleep, the remnants of the sedative still having an effect.

By the time the man quietly entered Travis's room he was in an extremely deep sleep. His heavily sedated mind was only vaguely aware of a physical pressure from above as the man held a pillow down over his face. A pain in Travis's already damaged windpipe was the last thing he felt as his muscles lost a futile battle to bring oxygen to his starving lungs.

CHAPTER THIRTY-ONE

With every clack of Jane's cowboy boots on the pavement she tried to convince herself that she was just being paranoid. She had tried calling Sammy on a number of occasions the evening before, none with any success. *She probably just went to bed early after her ordeal*, Jane tried to tell herself, *you're just being silly*. She knew that Chris had rushed over to Sammy's house to check that his girlfriend was okay, so she had at least been in safe hands, but it didn't hurt to check.

During the two-minute walk from the bus stop next to the fish and chip shop to Sammy's house, Jane's thoughts turned increasingly less optimistic. She was dwelling on the fact that she still could not raise Sammy on the phone this morning. *Something just doesn't feel right.*

She turned right up Sammy's street and surveyed the cars double-parked along its length as she made her way towards her friend's abode. She passed Sammy's car before reaching the house, and a curs-ory glance over it didn't reveal anything unexpected. No valuables had been hastily left on show, and nothing was in there that wasn't usually left there. All looked fine here, yet Jane remained unsettled.

As she had expected, there was no response to her hard knock on the door, or to the stones she threw up at the bedroom window, just in case. Tentatively, anxious of what she might see, Jane peered through the venetian blinds of Sammy's kitchen window and into the space beyond. There wasn't much to look at, everything seemed to be in its place, except the phone on the countertop in the kitchen, plugged into a charger. Although hardly indicative of strange goings on, it was unlikely that Sammy would go out without it.

Jane slid her own phone from her pocket, and hit redial yet again, watching the charging phone through the window. The screen on it didn't light up with a photo of Jane's face, nor dance a vibrating jig across the countertop as she listened to the monotonous ringing coming from the earpiece of her own phone. Jane pocketed her phone and continued to peer through the window, aimlessly hoping for a clue as to her friend's whereabouts.

Suddenly, the screen on the charging phone lit up with a notification, the backlight revealing a selfie photograph of a smiling Sammy with Chris's muscular arm around her, holding her close. *It's Chris's phone!* Jane stepped back onto the pavement, looking in both directions up the street for Chris's car. She didn't see it anywhere. She relaxed a little, *perhaps they've gone somewhere together, it would be understandable if Sammy wanted to get away for the night, although I do wish she'd told me.*

Turning to leave, a realisation stopped Jane midstride. She went back to the window to check and confirmed that she'd been right. The kettle was switched on at the mains. Squinting further into the lounge, she stared at Sammy's main TV and could just make out a tiny red glow emanating from the dark frame around the screen, the mains for the TV had been left on too.

Jane called the police as soon as she arrived home. She was trembling as she dialled the local number, practicing her opening line over and over in her head. The operator directed her call; *so far, so good*.

'Missing persons,' said a hoarse-voiced man after a few rings.

Following the script she had written herself, Jane explained the situation and her suspicions.

'When did you say your friend was last seen?' the man asked Jane, a little too quickly to have been taking proper notes on anything that she had just told him.

'She was seen by some friends yesterday afternoon during the attempted abduction. I know her boyfriend went to her house to check on her soon after, but I don't know what happened when he got there. He's rather protective, so may have gone looking for her by himself,' Jane fought back the panic, 'or something has happened to both of them.'

There was silence on the other end of the phone for a beat, during which Jane could just hear office noises in the background, almost like the policeman wasn't paying any attention and hadn't actually realised that Jane had finished speaking.

'Hello?'

'Well, er…'

'Jane.'

'Yes, Jane. We have a twenty-four-hour policy in this area, so there's nothing that we can do for you at the moment. If you call back late tomorrow, then we'll be able to take the first steps in registering your friend as missing. That's assuming that she hasn't come home from a romantic trip away with her boyfriend by then, of course.'

Jane was taken aback by his flippant tone.

'I— I told you, she hasn't planned this.'

'Look, I know you're concerned, but I've been dealing with this sort of thing for years, I've seen it all. Have you any idea how many people try to report someone missing after just a few hours, and we never hear from them again? The alleged missing usually just come home themselves.'

'But— the abduction, the knife—'

'I wouldn't worry about that, I'm sure the two incidents are completely unrelated—'

'So, two incidents, yes?' Jane interrupted quietly.

The policeman sighed, which triggered a nasty sounding coughing fit that lasted for about half a minute. 'Excuse me,' the man said when he had recovered. 'There is no doubt in my mind that the alleged abduction you are referring to at the park was actually a misinterpreted common mugging. Regrettable? Yes; but far less sinister than what you have convinced yourself of.'

Jane took a breath, steeling herself to respond haughtily, but the policeman was still talking, and cut her off.

'You said yourself you weren't there, so ask yourself, how accurately might your friends have recalled, or possibly embellished the details of what they saw?'

Jane had no response, she couldn't defend Belle and Thora on their behalf, she hadn't been there in the car park with them.

'Twenty-four hours, ma'am, and I hope, like so

many others, that you don't need to call back after that time.'

'Jane,' she muttered as the line went dead, 'not "ma'am".'

'Talk to me,' Phil answered his phone abruptly, stopping its shrill ringing from rebounding off the surrounding trees.

The caller attempted to clear his throat, but the voice that came out remained hoarse. 'Someone has just been in touch to report your girl missing.'

'How much did they know?' Phil asked business-like.

'Nothing really, all just suspicion. It was the best friend, she didn't buy the cover, said apparently there were signs at the house that didn't add up to a week-end away with the boyfriend. She was pretty adamant, but didn't have anything concrete, just gut.'

'You've buried it I assume?'

'For now, but she'll be back, she seemed like the tenacious type.'

'Well you can just fix it then too, that's what we pay you for.'

'I'll certainly do what I can.' The caller coughed, a deep, phlegmy cough which seemed to take him a few seconds to recover from.

'You know you really need to cut back on the smokes, Serge.'

'So the doctors keep telling me. I'll let you know if we hear anything else.'

'Appreciate it,' Phil disconnected the call and con-sidered what this would mean for their timetable. *It would probably be wise to try and step things up.* He leaned up against a nearby tree and lit a cigarette, contemplating the different things that he would do to

Samantha once given the go-ahead from Bradford.

188

CHAPTER THIRTY-TWO

'I know you're worried, dear, and I realise it's a horrifying thing to happen to someone you know, but you did say that Samantha escaped her abductor, didn't you?' Jane's mum was making them both mugs of Earl Grey tea.

'Yes, but it's not like her to just disappear and not answer my calls when she'd know I'd be worried.'

'Jane,' her dad touched her arm gently, 'you can't seriously be basing your worries on some plug sockets. I know that Sam is energy-conscious, but she had just experienced a trauma, her routine is bound to have been a little out-of-sorts.'

'It's more than just routine to Sammy,' Jane answered, exasperated. 'It's more even than habit, it's built into her in the same way that you always do that,' she gestured to him trying to place his mug down on the table completely flat so that all edges of its base contacted the surface simultaneously, starting again if he found he had put one edge down too soon. 'She does it when she's over here too, whenever she is anywhere, not just at her own home, remember that time you ended up taking the DVD player to bits because you thought it was broken? Turned out it just needed a PIN entered or something because she'd put it off at the mains when she visited?'

Her mum stifled a giggle.

'Yeah, ok, well how was I to know,' her dad muttered defensively.

'That's not the point, Dad. I just know something's not right.' *What more can I do by myself though? I can't get hold of Chris; all I can do is leave it to the police.*

Feeling utterly helpless, Jane turned her phone over and over in her hands, like if it was moved around for long enough it would reveal the answer.

Her parents began to talk about what films were going to be on TV that evening, and Jane tuned out. *Please ring*, she stared at the device in her palm, willing it to obey, to hear Sammy's voice on the end of the line. Then it dawned on her. She *could* hear her voice. She had kept the voicemail from a couple of weeks ago. It had made her feel so welcome and wanted that she had decided to save it to listen to at times when she could do with a reminder that people weren't all bad.

Jane stood and took her tea into the front room with her, setting it on the coffee table. Settling onto the sofa, she touched some icons on the phone screen and called her voicemail service, pressing the required buttons to replay a saved message. She smiled at the sound of her friend's reassuring tones:

'Hi, Jane, I'm guessing you're in the bath or something. You're not missing much here, just human pyramids and leg-wrestling, all the usual things that classy ladies do on a night out.

'I just wanted to say a great big thank-you for coming to watch the bout with me. I'm so excited that you're considering giving roller derby a go; I've talked to the girls about your SM and they're all really understanding and looking forward to meeting you. We've saved you a place on the next newbie intake, which is on Wednesday. That gives you a few days to change your mind, so don't automatically dismiss it now, mull it over… but I really hope that you decide to come for definite. Love you.'

Jane's smile faltered as she heard something at the end of the recording. The robotic voice instructed her to press the number three to listen again, she didn't hesitate. Concentrating hard, she listened to the message again. This time she didn't really hear the words, she was focussing on any sounds in the background, of which there were none of note, until her friend's parting words.

Just as Sammy finished speaking, there was a noise that could be that of doors swinging open against a wall, and the faint sound of a man's voice saying something, no… pleading. Jane thought that she could also make out some sort of moan just before the call cut off, like the sound someone makes when they are punched in the stomach. *What does this mean?*

Jane stood to pace the lounge and spent the next few minutes attempting to work out what the noises could be, and if it even mattered. It was hardly likely to give any answers relating to Sammy's current disappearance. It felt good at least to be pro-active and to keep her mind busy.

She was still considering the possibilities when she heard the familiar sound of post hitting the doormat. Her dad came into the lounge clutching some letters and began opening them, leaving all the envelopes on the table. Jane absent-mindedly collected them all together and went to place them on the stack of paper recycling that had piled up in their utility room. A local newspaper poking out a few inches down the pile caught her eye. "No progress in alleyway murder investigation," the headline halfway down the page stated.

Dates and facts that Jane began to recall in her mind started to form into a cohesive and viable story. A local criminal, known to the police, had been murdered the night that the league was out in town, and it had happened in the alleyway behind the very pub that they had started their evening at. Jane knew that Sammy often went outside into the alley for some quiet to call her during her breaks when working shifts at the pub. *What if she had gone out there that night?*

Her attempted abduction in the park no longer seemed so random. *Perhaps Honey Trap had somehow got involved too, and they killed her to silence her.*

Something that Jane was now sure of, was that her friend had witnessed the murder of David Steele first-hand - and that it had been recorded on her voicemail.

Phil's phone rang as he stood outside the chapel doors savouring his cigarette. 'Fuck's sake, what now?' He checked the caller ID and froze momentarily. *Oh well, I've gotta let the boss know sometime.* 'Hello, Mr. Dix—'

'I've been trying to get hold of you for twenty minutes now.'

'Sorry, reception's a bit sketchy around here—'

'What's this I'm hearing about you using my resources without my knowledge?'

'It was best handled without your knowledge, Mr. Dixon. Plausible deniability and all that.'

'You don't say! Digging around in Missing Persons, hell, I'm told you even called Alvarez in!'

Phil took a settling breath before delivering his explanation. 'There was a witness.'

Silence.

'But I know where—'

'Sort it out. This could finish us.'

'That's exactly what I'm doing Mr. Dixon, you can trust me with this,' but there was no longer anyone listening.

As Jane entered the police station, she took a deep breath, trying in vain to calm herself. She had decided to visit personally rather than just phone up this time, for one thing, this was now a lot more than just one missing person, but also Jane found face to face conversations to be easier than phone calls due to her Selective Mutism. Her anxiety level wouldn't have fit on her therapist's usual one to ten scale, elevated over concern for her friend, but she couldn't just do nothing.

She waited impatiently for a clerk to come to the front desk, unable to force herself to call for them too loudly. She knocked on the desk a couple of times, and eventually someone spotted her and came over. 'Sorry, I didn't realise anyone was there, you should have given me a shout.'

The butterflies hit Jane. Her speech was, as always, the first thing to go. Her voice came out as barely more than a whisper, and not loud enough for the environment.

'Friend is missing. Think she saw a murder. Voicemail.'

The clerk squinted at her. 'Please can you speak up,' she said loudly, 'I can't understand you.'

Jane became aware of the people waiting in chairs around her starting to pay attention, dropping their reading material slightly to peer instinctively over the top at her. Her eyes wide, she managed to force herself to raise her voice a little, but the vocabulary suffered as a result, 'Friend... phone... sounds... listen!'

'Madam,' the clerk said, shaking her head, 'I don't know what you're trying to say, please calm down.'

Jane sighed, exasperated and frustrated with herself, tears beginning to prickle the corners of her eyes.

'I can see you're worried, is it a life or death thing?'

She nodded. *I've already wasted enough time; it might only be a death or death thing at this stage.*

The pressure had become too great.

Jane now found herself completely unable to utter sounds, coherent or otherwise, and tears flowed freely down her face as she looked desperately around the room for some way to demonstrate what she was trying to say. Feeling like she had already failed her oldest friend, she suddenly spotted a newspaper on the waiting area table. She snatched it up and pointed to the headline of the second story on the front page, about a murder.

'You have information about the Burrows' murder?'

Jane shook her head and pointed hard to the word "murder" on the page.

The clerk at this point could only shrug, looking confusedly at her.

She continued to gesticulate but had lost any real

aim as she became increasingly exasperated with herself and how useless she had become at this time of crisis. *I simply* have *to get this message across!*

195

CHAPTER THIRTY-THREE

By now, the pressure that Jane was putting on herself was only making things a lot worse. She managed to force a few more odd words out, but they were completely incoherent.

She regressed back to that scared little schoolgirl she used to be, feeling the same way she had felt back then when the pressure to get her message across had left her with no option but to walk to the front of the class and write on the whiteboard.

The whiteboard. That's it. Jane leaned across the reception desk and grabbed a pen and notepad. She hurriedly scrawled some words down on the pad and shoved it into the hands of the desk clerk. 'Missing friend in real trouble. Audio evidence on phone. Help ASAP,' she read out.

Jane sighed deeply, the tension lessening in her clenched muscles.

'Inspector!' the desk clerk called over her shoulder, her eyes remaining locked on Jane as though not trusting her enough to leave her unmonitored.

A chubby female police officer on the other side of an internal window lifted her head briefly at the clerk's call, before making her way through to the reception area and to the desk clerk's, and Jane's, rescue.

'This one's yours,' the clerk indicated Jane and handed the chubby woman the notepad, before moving to wave the next person forward.

The policewoman glared at the clerk.

'Well we're still swamped in dealing with the aftermath of a terrorist incident here,' the clerk lowered her voice, 'and you know I can't deal with…' she looked Jane up and down, 'these types.'

'Then why *you* are on this desk is beyond me,' the Inspector retorted loudly and ushered Jane away with her down a corridor. 'Honestly,' she said under her breath, 'some people! Come in here, love,' she steered Jane into some sort of interview room. 'We'll get you some water. I'm Detective Inspector Tanaka, but please feel free to call me Ami.'

Jane sat on one of the soft-cushioned chairs, guessing that this was more of a witness interview room than a suspect one, as it was not at all like what Jane imagined an interview room to look like. Ami roused Jane from her thoughts by handing her a plastic cup of water from a cooler in the corner.

Jane was distracted as she sipped the drink, looking around the room at the children's toys when the policewoman next spoke, 'So I see that you have a friend in trouble, are you able to tell me any more?'

Jane shook her head, *not yet*.

'Okay, well maybe you'll feel ready a bit later.'

She nodded.

'I'm off to the cinema tonight, going with one of my girlfriends to see that new rom com, the one set at a ski resort, have you seen it yet?'

Jane pulled a face as she shook her head this time.

'Not your thing, I guess.'

Jane laughed silently.

Ami continued to ramble on about nothing of importance, and Jane knew she was only doing it to make her more at ease. *Fine with me, it's taking the pressure off, so it's working.* She was reminded once more of school, and the words of her teacher, "just your quiet voice to begin with, Jane, don't feel you have to speak up."

'—with that particular story, I preferred the book. Have you read it?'

'Yes,' breathed Jane gently.

'And did you enjoy it?'

A little louder this time, but still barely a whisper, 'I did.'

'Was it your favourite of the trilogy?' Jane could tell that Ami was deliberately asking her yes or no style questions that gave her the freedom to not use words at all if she wished, or to embellish. This was working for her.

'Preferred the second,' still just a whisper, but Jane could see that Ami wasn't straining so hard to hear her voice now.

The policewoman got up and closed the door to the room, shutting out the hubbub of the outside corridors with it.

'Yes, I liked that one also. It had more of that guy in it from District 4, what was his name?'

'Finnick.'

'Finnick! Yes, that's the one, I loved his character. Who was your favourite?'

'Haymitch, Woody Harrelson's character.'

'From District 12?'

'Yes, I liked how Katniss came to care for him.'

'You seem to be the type that would empathise

with someone caring for a friend,' Ami smiled gently, 'and how is your friend?'

'My friend, Sammy… Samantha… she's missing.' Jane was at her normal volume now, having relaxed into the conversation Ami had persevered with. She sighed with relief, 'I'm sorry, I suffer with an anxiety disorder, it affects my ability to speak.'

'I can see that, my lovely. No worries, we all have our quirks. Okay, has she been reported missing already? Or did you want to do that now?'

'I tried to. A man told me to wait twenty-four hours.'

'Well, I guess in his assessment he determined that to be a suitable time.'

'But someone tried to abduct her yesterday, surely that should be of above-average cause for concern?'

'It certainly would be for me. What makes you think that she's missing rather than just out-of-contact?'

'I'll explain later, because there's more, and it's more worrying.' Jane went on to describe the voicemail message that Sammy had left her on the night of David Steele's murder, and explained her suspicions that her friend had witnessed the whole performance. 'So, it could all be connected, and being a witness is likely the cause of everything that came after.'

'May I hear the voicemail?'

Jane played the message for the inspector who listened intently.

'I can hear what caught your attention. We can get our technical people to clean the audio up a bit and see what we can pull from it. Have you saved the message?'

'Yes, of course.'

'Okay, come with me, and we'll take this to the

tech guys now, then I'll take your full statement. Hey,' she had noticed Jane's worried expression, 'your friend's gonna be okay.'

Jane attempted a small smile in return.

By lunchtime, the police had confirmed with the manager of the Tin Whistle that Sammy had missed her shift the previous day and had also been expected to help at the lunchtime shift. 'But she's already late, and it's not like her to not call ahead and let me know,' he had told the detective that called. 'There was even a time she could barely speak, tonsillitis or something, and she still called to let me know, the rest of them wouldn't of bothered, but Sam's a good kid.'

DI Tanaka returned to the witness interview room where Jane had been all morning, Jane suspected that the woman had realised its cosy appearance had helped to keep her stress levels in check. She had a thin file of papers under her arm. 'These make up the report of your friend's attempted abduction yesterday,' she explained. 'For some reason, it wasn't followed up as it should have been. Someone should have visited Samantha at home to take her statement and offer her contact with Victim Support for the trauma. It was even *more* relevant in this case because it wasn't the actual victim that was reporting the crime,' she pointed at Belle's name on the paperwork, 'so it goes without saying that we would need to speak to her directly at some point to check she was okay. I tried to pin down the lead DS on the case to see why it hadn't progressed at all, but he just brushed me off. He was probably on his way for a cigarette break, it's the only time that guy ever rushes. Still, we can work on our failed procedures another day, for now let's concentrate on finding your friend.'

Jane looked at the meagre selection of papers in Sammy's attempted abduction file. 'So where does that leave us, or more importantly, Sammy?' The face of the youth that Belle and Thora had described to a sketch artist stared up at her. She didn't recognise him at all.

'In light of all the collated information,' Ami saw the confused look on Jane's face and elaborated, 'we have the out-of-character no-shows at work, the attempted abduction,' she ticked them off on her fingers, 'and now the voicemail audio evidence coupled with Samantha's presence at the Tin Whistle on the night that a murder took place. Altogether, it's enough to warrant further investigation, so a trace has been put on her phone, and also a request to bring in has been put out on Chris's car.'

'What about David Steele's killers? Can you do a trace to see which phones were present in the alley that night and track the owners down? Then Sammy would be safe.'

'It doesn't work like that. To trace a phone you have to know which phone number you're tracking, and it needs to be done in real-time. So basically, we can see where a mobile phone is at any given time, but not a GPS history of where it's been. Historically, we can only see which cell towers it has connected to, not an accurate GPS location, so there's no way of working out from that who else was with David and Samantha in the alley that night.'

There was a knock at the door and a young-looking admin assistant pushed it open. 'Boss, we have your ID on that park abduction attempt.'

CHAPTER THIRTY-FOUR

Ami looked up at the young woman who had just entered the room. 'Hit me with it.'

The admin assistant read from a post-it note stuck onto her palm. 'Ethan Madson, twenty-four years old, seems that drug-pushing is his usual thing.'

Ami looked to Jane for a reaction to Ethan's name and this new information.

Jane shrugged.

'Okay, well I guess we'd best find him and bring him in. Do we have a last known address?'

'We do, shall I despatch a team?'

'As soon as you can spare them please. Thanks Susan,' Ami politely dismissed the woman and turned to use a nearby computer terminal.

Jane avoided Ami's gaze as tears of frustration began to form in the corners of each eye.

Some software loaded up, words appearing on the screen slowly, one at a time; "SAFE", "SECURE", then the word "CONNECTED:" big and bold across the width of the screen for a few seconds. Ami entered the name "Ethan Madson" in a search box at the top. 'This software's great, our station's been trialling it for the last few months. It'll pull together all the information we have on this guy and we can run his picture through its CCTV facial recognition feature, and then all the surveillance footage it can find on him will be linked to his name too.'

Jane didn't bother to sound impressed; she couldn't care less.

'I'll run a CCTV search on Samatha too, although I expect that if she has been taken, the perpetrators will have been more careful than that. Do you have a clear photo of her?'

Revealing her phone, Jane smiled sadly as she showed Ami the photo of her and Sammy together that graced the screen as her wallpaper. Cheek-to-cheek they were both grinning madly in the photo.

'Happier times, eh?' Ami took the phone from her and set up a search using CONNECTED.

After a few minutes, Ami spoke up thoughtfully, 'Why do you think Samantha didn't report it? If she did see what we think she might have done, I mean.'

Jane shrugged, 'It hadn't even occurred to me.'

'It could be worth checking her movements the day after, to get a feel for if we're on the right track with this idea of her as a potential witness to a murder.' Ami clicked a few buttons and they waited.

'That's odd,' she said, clicking on different areas of the screen.

'What is it?' Jane leaned forward, slightly alarmed by the officer's tone.

'There's a few hits on our girl on video surveillance, most notably these ones,' she pointed to two specific windows on the screen, both showing Sammy with her prominent pink bob, and both timestamped. 'Here,' she pointed to a still image showing Sammy's face as she entered what Jane assumed to be a building's main doors. 'She's entering this police station,' continued Ami, 'but in this one, timestamped just three minutes later, she's literally tripped up the steps onto a bus outside the station like she's seen a ghost.' Ami clicked to play the video, recorded on the bus's surveillance camera. As she had described, Sammy appeared, tripping up the step to get on the bus, where Ami then paused playback. What horrified Jane was the look of absolute terror that was frozen onto her friend's pale, desperate face.

Phil answered on the third ring.

'She's back then?' he asked, already knowing the answer.

'Yep, and worse than that, I didn't catch her, she's with a DI… talking homicide,' came the hoarse reply.

'Shit,' Phil kicked a nearby rock which swayed serenely in response. 'Hang on, homicide?'

'That's the really big problem. The friend, Jane, is somehow in possession of evidence to do with the Steele murder that apparently links your girl to the crime scene, and no-one is telling me exactly what it is. There's not gonna be anything I can do to stall things anymore, there's too much heat around this. They're running a trace on her phone right now, so you need to get rid of it if you haven't already.'

'She didn't have it on her, so it won't lead to us,' Phil examined his shoe for damage from where it had contacted the rock. 'So, the question is what are you going to do about it?'

'If it were a regular Joe that had been killed there wouldn't be nearly so much drama about a missing girl, but the way CID sees it, a man suspected of involvement in a terrorist attack was murdered, and now a witness to that murder is missing under suspicious circumstances. The feeling here is that she knows something more than just who killed Steele.'

Phil clicked off without any parting words. *So, maybe she was telling the truth about insurance after all, this mysterious evidence could be it*. He walked casually away from the rear of the chapel building, to where a lonely concrete shed sat, wondering what evidence she had on them.

It was a sizeable building, more like a garage than a shed. Gregory was outside enjoying a cigarette as Phil approached. Through the windows he could see a weary but determined-looking Christopher sitting on the floor with his legs out in front of him, tied to a post and watched by Ethan.

Gregory pushed himself off the tree he had been leaning against as he spotted Phil approaching. 'All okay at the chapel, boss?'

Phil walked past him to the doorway of the shed and looked in at his captive. 'It's complicated, but we've still got a few cards to play.'

Christopher was staring at the ground, but words came out of him in a growl as he lifted his eyes to meet Phil's, 'If you dare fucking hurt her—'

'Then you'll what? You need to be aware of your position, my friend. If we decide to hurt her, there'll be bugger-all that you can do about it. She is mine, and I will take care of her how I see fit. Right now, she cannot think for herself, I own her.'

An enraged Christopher began hurling abuse at Phil. Smiling to himself, he exited the building to call Mr. Dixon. Leaving Chris's furious ranting behind him, he sobered up a little, contemplating how his boss might react to the possibility of the girl having some actual evidence on them or their operation.

The phone rang out, so Phil had no choice but to leave him a voicemail, asking for him to call back as soon as humanly possible.

The shrill ringing of a mobile phone temporarily broke the disappointed silence in the police witness interview room. Ami answered it curtly, 'DI Tanaka. …You have?… That's fantastic news… Well, as soon as possible really, there's no reason to hold back… No, I understand… Okay, keep me posted.' Ami clicked off, looking wary. 'There's still no answer on Sam's phone, but the tech team have just got a location on it. We're gathering together a few tactical guys to go and check it out.'

Jane was so pleased that she leapt up and hugged the woman.

A small noise came from through a doorway that lay deeper into the small chapel and Sam winced as thoughts of mice and rats in crypts came to her. She had tried all through a sleepless night not to think about such things, and concentrate instead on her plight, as she knew that things weren't exactly looking good for her. She had heard Phil outside on the phone to someone about Bradford earlier in the morning. He had advised that he remain abroad for a couple of days to secure an airtight and passport-backed-up alibi for what was likely to go down in the chapel. She knew he was unsure about whether to believe her claim of insurance or not, and that that fact was the only reason that she, and hopefully Chris, were still all in one piece.

A scratching sound echoed across the cold, empty space around Sam and she shuddered.

She would have to work hard at convincing him when he next came in, fully commit to the false fact if he asked her about it again.

Sam heard the first noise from the doorway again and could no longer distract herself from the thoughts of what it might be. She had no idea what the room could possibly be used for, she hadn't been far enough into the building to see the rest of the layout. As she contemplated this fact, a young woman about Sam's own age, stumbled through the doorway.

CHAPTER THIRTY-FIVE

Sam was stunned. It had never occurred to her during her stay at this place that there might be others here. The woman was dressed in denim shorts and a bohemian white lacy top. She clung to the doorway, her grubby legs shaking as she hauled herself through into the chapel's main room. Her eyes which were partly obscured by long hair hanging in clumps down her face, were darting frantically around the gloom inside the chapel. She seemed to study each pew for a fraction of a second, scanning for dangers. Even in the gloom, it was easy to see the thick white plastic restraints that encircled each wrist.

Sam swallowed, then found her voice. 'Hey. Can you help me get out?'

The young woman's head snapped in Sam's direction, taking a moment to focus fully on her small presence in the darkened corner. 'Who are you?' she demanded in a tiny voice that betrayed the terror behind the boldly delivered words.

'I'm being held here too.'

The woman looked unsure, her focus switching between Sam's direction and that of the front door.

'You know they'll be waiting out there, don't you? You'll need my help to get past them.'

Her brow furrowed in concentration. A few seconds elapsed then she ran back through the doorway. When she returned a few seconds later, Sam saw what looked like a long nail in her hand. She went around the back of the seat that Sam was tied to and began work on her restraints, digging the nail into the tough plastic and sawing at it.

'Thank-you,' Sam said sincerely, 'I'm Sam. I had pretty much resigned myself to the fact that I'd never see the outside of this place again.'

'I know how you feel. Lacey, pleased to meet you.'

The restraints snapped apart and Sam let out a small squeal of pain as the blood rushed back to her wrists.

'Are you okay to walk?' Lacey asked, turning to support Sam as she stood up. 'We have to go now.'

'My legs are fine, the rest of me will catch up soon enough,' *it has to*.

The two women moved briskly up the aisle, with Sam quietly rotating her shoulders to try and get full feeling back into them. 'Do you have a plan? Do you know where we are?'

'I didn't see much when they brought me in, just that there's a giant wall between us and the outside world, and then we're in the middle of the countryside somewhere. To be honest I planned to worry about the middle-of-nowhere part once I'd got past the giant wall part.'

'Good plan.'

Lacey peeked out through a crack in the chapel's main doors.

'How long have you been here?' Sam asked her.

'A few days maybe, I'm not sure, it all rolls into

one. What are you here for? Ransom too?'

'Ransom? No.' Now that Sam thought about it, that would explain why the other woman didn't appear to have been harmed in any way, despite the length of her stay at Château de Phil.

Lacey's tone changed to one of suspicion as she turned away from the door to assess Sam. 'Then how come you're still in one piece?'

Sam met Lacey's stare, less concerned about what she was implying and more about getting out of there now that she was no longer tied to a railing. 'They want me to tell them what they want to hear, because they don't believe the truth; either way when they're done, they're going to kill me. I've managed to buy myself some time by telling them about an insurance policy.' She checked outside herself, turning her back to Lacey to try and convey trust to the paranoid woman.

'An insurance policy, huh? So, what, you go missing and the police get an anonymous tip-off or something?'

'Something like that, yeah.' Sam was distracted, she'd spotted Phil outside on his phone near the tree line.

'So is it like evidence or something that you have?'

Phil had just hung up on his call and pocketed his phone. Finger to her lips, Sam shrank back from the doors and waited.

Soon after, an impatient Lacey checked outside. 'He's going away. This is it.'

Sam hung back as Lacey pushed through the doors. A few seconds later, after realising that she had left the building alone, Lacey popped her head back inside. 'Come on!' she hissed.

Deep breaths, Sam.

Lacey checked outside briefly once more before coming back in and giving Sam a good shove out the door.

Sam took a second to enjoy the sensation of being in the shade of the trees, shafts of sunlight coming and going around her as their branches swayed. Lacey barged past her, 'We're exposed here, Sam. Keep moving.'

'Moving where? Which way?'

'The gate in the wall.'

'It'll be locked.'

Lacey shrugged, 'We have to try it.'

Sam knew that Lacey was right, but it put them at risk of meeting someone on their way into the grounds. *If only I had a weapon.* Sam looked around her and selected a fist-sized stone from the ground. It fit neatly into her palm and its cold weight was comforting to a scared young woman running on pure adrenaline. She jogged off to keep up with Lacey.

They reached the wall in less than a minute, checking behind and all around them for anyone following as they moved. Lacey checked the gate, 'Locked,' she confirmed.

'Let's check around for a spare key,' suggested Sam.

'You look, I'll watch out for anyone coming after us.'

Sam put her rock down and felt in cracks and crevices in-between the stones of the wall within a few feet of the gate before moving on to look underneath weeds and gravelly rocks at the base of the wall.

'Did you know they were coming for you?' Lacey's voice drifted quietly over the sounds of Sam rustling twigs and leaves.

'What do you mean?'

'When they took you, were you expecting it?'

'Not really, well, not until their first attempt I guess,' Sam winced as she stung her hand on a nettle. 'I got away that time, and then they came for me at home a few hours later.'

'So, if you didn't know, how come you had time to arrange insurance?'

She's really hung-up on this insurance thing.

'Or did you just say you had a plan, and that was enough?'

Sam turned to look at Lacey who was still facing away from her and the wall, keeping lookout for anyone approaching. *When I tell her to drop it, I want her to see my face, so she knows I mean it.* About to get the other woman's attention, Sam noticed something. As the speckled sunlight passed over Lacey, something glinted in the back pocket of her shorts. Taking a couple of steps towards her, Sam saw that the glinting was a knife. If Lacey had been in possession of a knife this whole time, why would she have needed to saw at Sam's restraints with a rusty nail? *Unless she didn't want me to know that she had the knife.*

There's no other explanation.

'You're with them, aren't you?'

CHAPTER THIRTY-SIX

'I have no idea what you're talking about,' Lacey turned to face Sam squarely. The look on her face was defensive, but she had an air of aggression about her. The blind fear Sam had seen when she first stumbled into view had drained from her eyes and had been replaced by irritation. 'I told you, they took me two days ago for a ransom and I've been held here since then. Now can we please get on with our escape?'

'It all rolls into one,' Sam mumbled.

'What?'

'That's what you said before, when I asked how long you'd been here; "I'm not sure, it all rolls into one". But just now you seemed pretty clear that it had been two days.'

'Look, sweetie, I'm traumatised here, I'm sorry if that causes me to muddle up completely insignificant facts.'

'It's about the insurance isn't it?'

Lacey looked at Sam incredulously, 'You are seriously losing focus here. I was making conversation. I don't give a crap about your insurance, or your boyfriend, none of it helps me out.' Lacey began to stride past Sam, 'Let's get moving.'

Sam reached out and grabbed Lacey's upper arm as she passed. Looking her in the eye, she spoke quietly and deliberately. 'I never said anything about a boyfriend.'

Lacey's eyes narrowed and her pupils grew large as her body's fight or flight reflex started to take over. Before Sam had any time to react, the imposter reached behind with her free arm and pulled the knife from the back of her shorts. She flicked the blade out as she brought her hand back around towards the front of her body, slicing it across Sam's flesh in the same elegant motion.

Sam shrieked in pain and released Lacey's arm. Both women leapt backwards away from each other, the cut in Sam's arm pumping out a steady stream of blood that trickled its way down her arm before dripping onto the foliage at her feet. For a fraction of a second, the severity of the standoff eluded Sam as she stood transfixed, watching her blood flowing across her skin.

Looking up, the image of Lacey standing mere feet away from her, knife still in hand, brought Sam back to the present. As she watched, she saw the muscles in the wrist of Lacey's knife-wielding arm tense up, and something in the woman's facial expression shifted from the prior amusement to complete focus.

Sam had seen that look before. Roller derby attracted all types, and for more than one of the women in Sam's league, it was not her only offbeat hobby. Jynx, a tall lady in her forties, had taken up knife-throwing about a year before she began derby, and was quite adept at it by the time Sam met her. Stormy City had come up with the idea of getting Jynx to do a half-time show during one of their bouts, where she threw knives at a board holding photos of the opposing team's players as a bit of good-hearted fun to play up to the rivalry between the two actually very friendly leagues. Sam had watched in awe as Jynx threw each of those blades with complete precision, despite being thrown with what appeared to be a rather relaxed arm, aside from the wrist.

Before each throw, a keen observer would notice Jynx's manner shift from the person that lapped up each cheer, to one that brought her full focus to hitting her target, and tightened up her wrist to prevent the knife from spinning more than required for the short range she was throwing at.

It was that same observation that now warned Sam what was coming before the knife left Lacey's hand. She leapt to one side and hit the ground with a roll as a "choonk" sound told her that Lacey's knife was now deeply embedded into the gate behind her. Scrambling further away from her opponent, she scrabbled to get to her feet, her hand closed over the rock that she had brought with her from the front of the chapel, and she gripped it tightly.

The now unarmed Lacey was upon her before she could fully get to her feet and as Sam tried to get up, Lacey punched her, missing her face and instead punching the ground as Sam wriggled below her. Lacey straddled Sam then fell to her knees, lowering herself to sit on Sam's rib cage and keeping her contained.

Sam managed to roll onto her back just before Lacey's weight would have made it too difficult a task. She swung her arm heavily up and round, catching Lacey on her left temple with the rock. Lacey's hold over Sam loosened, and the force of the blow knocked her body sideways, toppling over onto the ground next to Sam.

There was quiet around the pair now, the sound of Sam's panting the only noise besides the sedate rustling of the trees and the odd bird call.

Lacey was unconscious.

Sam didn't give herself long to recover from the tussle and got shakily to her feet, the rock still gripped in her hand, the whiteness of her knuckles even more apparent compared to the glistening red splodge of the other woman's blood on the underside surface of the rock.

Still breathing heavily, Sam stood over Lacey's limp body. Holding the rock in both hands, she instinctively raised it high above her head, then hesitated. *What the hell am I doing? I can't kill this woman, I'm not one of them.* Disgusted with herself and her temporary lapse in humanity, she lowered her arms and tossed the rock aside. She wiped her hands on her clothes, as if that would somehow cleanse her of the murderous thoughts she had just entertained.

A rustling coming from the hedge reminded Sam that she should push on forwards, especially now she knew she'd been played. She hustled towards the gate to retrieve Lacey's knife from where it was nestled in the wood. As she turned to check that Lacey was still out cold, a rough-skinned hand grabbed her knife arm by the wrist and Sam was brought face to face with a bald-headed, tattooed giant.

CHAPTER THIRTY-SEVEN

Sam struggled against the man's grip. *I can't let him get the knife, it's all I have!*

'Hey, calm down! I'm not going to hurt you; I want to help.'

I have already fallen for that once today. I'm certainly not fool enough to do it again.

'You're not a good choice for the part of the innocent dog-walker,' she hissed.

'So my mother often tells me.' He smiled and let go of Sam, stepping back out of range of her knife hand. He gestured to Lacey's still form, 'I heard you two arguing and then all hell broke loose. Who are you, what's going on, and how can I help?'

Sam's resolve faltered a little. She was beginning to think that maybe this guy was genuine. *No. I can't risk it.* 'I— I'm sorry,' she turned and ran, away from the chapel through the trees, sticking close to the wall for coverage where the shadows were thickest.

She made it about twenty metres before feeling a sudden sting in the small of her back. Immediately, every muscle in her body contracted, completely immobilising Sam who could do nothing to stop herself from plunging face first onto the leafy floor. Lying awkwardly on her side in agony she could hear nothing other than a loud crackling noise, but saw a male figure from the corner of her eye holding down the button on the taser before she passed out.

When Sam awoke, her muscles ached from the effects of the taser and from the awkward position that she was in. She was cooped up in a small, dark space, her limbs slowly cramping, and there was nowhere to stretch them out to. She tried her hardest to push at the solid surfaces that surrounded her, but limited movement of her arms made it difficult, and nothing was so much as budging. Sam had no option but to wait until someone came for her. *When they do, I'll be ready*, she promised herself, and began plotting her moves.

Ami handed Jane a set of headphones, 'The team will be approaching the area where Samantha's phone is any minute now. Pop these on and you'll be able to hear what's happening.'

Jane put down the oversized Winnie the Pooh mug that Ami had served her tea in earlier and took the headphones. She was feeling calmer now and they had moved to an incident room to better monitor the field team's progress.

Ami's phone dinged. 'Oh, that's them now. Switching on comms.' She pressed some buttons and signalled for Jane to put her headphones on.

'Inspector Tanaka, do you read me?'

'Roger, Jones,' Ami spoke into a microphone that was attached to her headphones. 'Are you in position?'

'We are ten-six. We'll be moving forward on foot.'

'Okay. I'm monitoring your progress here. I have the subject's friend present and we're recording audio and movements.' She pressed a big red button on one of the machines stacked up next to her. She covered the microphone with her hand to speak to Jane, 'Jones is that blue dot on the screen to your left. Sam's phone is the green triangle.'

Jane looked at the monitor that Ami had indicated. Under the words "CONNECTED: Tracker", it displayed a road map, mostly green as it was zoomed in to an area in the countryside. As she watched she could see the blue dot moving along a white road, slowly, slowly nearing the green triangle of hope.

The huge mug of tea had left Jane with a desperate urge to go to the toilet, but she couldn't possibly leave the room now. Instead, she sat tensely in her seat, clenching all her muscles and giving herself a generally fraught appearance. A few minutes later, when Jane was contemplating a quick dash to the ladies', Jones' voice came through their headphones. 'We have a visual on a stationary vehicle ahead.'

'Make and model?' Ami picked up a pen, ready to scrawl on the notepad in front of her.

'Looks like a Volkswagen Passat, black. Will confirm when we're closer.'

That sounds like Chris's car.

'That's a positive on the vehicle info,' said Jones then he read out the licence plate.

Jane didn't know Chris's plate number, but she saw Ami comparing it to her case notes and nodding to herself. 'That's the boyfriend's car for sure. Any sign of him or the subject?'

'We're approaching now.'

Jane was suddenly extremely aware of the sound

of her breathing in her ears, filling the audio gap that was made by the silence coming from her head-phones. Ami's hand was poised hovering over the notepad as she strained to hear any background noise.

'No obvious signs of life,' Jones whispered, his poor choice of expression rattling Jane and the colour drained from her cheeks. Ami placed a hand on the younger woman's arm to comfort her as Jones' voice came back through the comms system, sounding intrigued now. 'The vehicle is unlocked.'

The women continued to listen intently as Jones and his partner conducted a cursory investigation of the car's interior. 'Nothing out of the ordinary here or anything that suggests any kind of struggle.'

'What's that?' they heard Jones' partner in the background.

'Skipper, there's a sound coming from the boot, we're getting into position to open it now,' explained Jones.

Jane pictured the scene.

Jones creeping around to the boot of the car, draw-ing his weapon.

His partner with a hand poised over the boot re-lease catch.

A silent countdown passing between the two of them before the boot lid is opened and the two men prepare themselves as best they can for whatever they might find inside.

She held her breath.

CHAPTER THIRTY-EIGHT

The building that Chris was being held in was cold and musty. It lay seemingly purposely in the shade of the trees, that hid it from view of the main house, unable to ruin the beautiful views out across the grounds. The side effect was that the natural moistures from nearby piles of decaying leaves, dewy grass, mossy trees and rainwater all contributed to a generally high humidity level that couldn't be shifted by the sun, it's usually penetrative rays struggling to cut their way through the leafy canopy above. Being an outbuilding, it also wasn't fully sealed or insulated. Strong wooden doors kept the garden vehicles inside safe from potential thieves and vandals, but were not built to keep out the natural elements, and a constant draught crept its icy fingers over Chris's legs. The concrete floor beneath him was slowly numbing his aching backside, which was going to somewhat hamper any plans he might make toward a quick escape attempt.

A small bird was sitting in the rafters, chirping away to itself, oblivious to how inappropriate a soundtrack the sweet sounds of nature were to

Chris's current mood. The thug that had held a knife to his girlfriend's throat the day before, Gregory, was casually draped against a beam in the opposite half of the shed, twirling the knife around in his hand. His control of the polished object was impressive, but Chris was, by now, too worked up to be intimidated.

He had spent a lot of time in silence in the last few hours and had run over every scenario in his head a thousand times. Now he just needed to wait for the right opportunity.

It came in the form of a woman. 'Hey there, handsome.'

At her appearance, Gregory stood up a little straighter, stowing his knife into a sheath hanging from his belt. 'Hey, Lacey. How did you do?' He spotted a dressing on her temple and cupped her chin with one hand, tilting her face to better inspect the injury. 'What happened? If I get my hands on that little—'

'Don't worry, Ethan took the bitch down and she's tucked tightly away now.' Lacey gave Chris a sideways smirk of satisfaction as she delivered this information.

Chris flushed angrily but held back. The timing wasn't right. He satisfied himself instead with working away at the twine that they had used to tie him to a post.

Gregory finished examining Lacey's bandage. 'You should ask for hazard pay for that.'

'On top of those shares we've been given there's no need. Did you see the stock price this morning?'

Chris tuned their voices out. Notably, he hadn't been brought any food at all. It was pretty clear that they intended to kill both himself and Sam once they had got what they wanted, whatever that was.

Gregory and Lacey chatted casually for the next hour or so by Chris's reckoning. No-one came in to check on them, and Chris didn't make any big movements to draw attention to himself. Slowly, the couple became more and more relaxed in both their stance and attentions. *I wonder if they still remember I'm here,* thought Chris, watching as Gregory leant over Lacey to kiss the top of her head.

'How is your head feeling now, baby?'

'Not too bad, the codeine has gotten rid of the throbbing at least.'

'Any impaired vision? Are you seeing two of me?' Gregory asked playfully.

'Two? Now there's a thought,' Lacey replied coyly, oblivious to Chris's intense stare as he analysed the pair, waiting. He had been slowly working on his restraints for the past hour and had eventually been rewarded. The twine that tied his wrists together was still there by no more than a few fibres, enough to hold it together for appearances, but any sudden force would break it.

Gregory grabbed Lacey's ass cheek, allowing the tips of his fingers to slide in underneath the denim of her shorts and very lightly touch her through her underwear. 'I'm serious. I want to make sure you're okay.'

Lacey licked her lips and pouted slightly, making them appear fuller. She leaned upwards and ran them teasingly across Gregory's closed mouth.

Chris tensed.

Gregory parted his lips to receive and return Lacey's affection. 'Do I need to prove to you that my vision is perfect? That everything is functioning like the well-oiled machine it should be?' she teased close to his ear. Whilst he was distracted, she pulled

Gregory's knife from its sheath. Lacey then pulled back away from the embrace and simultaneously raised the hand containing the knife up to her shoulder.

With the grace and precision of a prima ballerina, she forcefully flicked the knife out of her hand. It flew through the air like a missile, all sounds around falling away as two of the three people in the room focussed fully on its trajectory.

The birdsong stopped the instant that the knife's tip penetrated the sparrow's throat. The bird's delicate body descended from the rafters, helped by the gravitational pull of the knife's chunky hilt.

Chris didn't watch it the whole way. He only saw that his captors were now disarmed.

The timing was right.

By the time the bird hit the floor he had yanked his wrists apart, breaking the bonds that had kept him attached to the post. He wasted no time in jumping up and running out of the doors.

Footsteps clattered their approach on a stone floor, and Sam recoiled as light suddenly flooded the confined area that she sat hunched in.

'Out,' instructed Phil flatly.

Sam obliged, shuffling herself towards the bright opening.

'Hurry up, this isn't a game of hide and seek,' he watched her keep shuffling until she was clear of the cubby and able to stand. She turned to see where she had been held as Phil closed the wooden wall panel back up.

'Cool, huh? This place is linked to the guys who were involved in the gunpowder plot. There's a passage linking here with the main house. We've blocked it though, it's a useful tool for these types of situations.'

He pulled her roughly back over to the little bench that had become her reluctant home and re-tied her hands through the railing once more. 'I'd best go and check in on Chris, he'll be worried sick about you after hearing that your little escape attempt failed, tisk, tisk.' He leaned in close to her from behind and whispered in her ear, 'Or maybe I'll just let him sweat a little more.'

Sam's response came out hoarse, dry from the hours spent in the airless cubby, 'You're an asshole.'

His fist struck her on the side of her face, and she cried out in pain.

'You'd better watch your mouth if you ever want to see Christopher in one fucking piece again.'

As Chris's feet pounded the ground beneath him, he knew that Gregory and Lacey wouldn't take long to recover from the surprise of him escaping. It was just a matter of whether they were armed or not when they came after him.

His heart was banging too loudly in his ears for him to hear footsteps behind him, but he didn't dare look round until he'd covered more ground.

He came around the edge of a wooded area and was greeted with a solemn face set into a stone wall. It took him a moment to process that the face was part of a stained-glass window. *Gregory mentioned a chapel. This must be where they're keeping Samantha.* A noise in the undergrowth emanated from the direction that he had come from, and Chris instantly moved around towards the back of the building, deeper into the shade of the trees, hoping that any pursuer would expect him to either run in the front door or make a beeline for the boundary wall to find the gate they had originally entered through.

Once he'd passed behind the chapel and was making his way along the other side, Chris heard faint voices. He chanced a look through the lower corner of one of the windows and saw Gregory speaking to Phil. Straining to hear through the glass, he managed to catch a couple of snippets of their conversation;

'Lacey… separated to search… more manpower… job done quickly.'

So Lacey is out here somewhere. I'd best not stay put for too long.

'Take Ethan… leverage… get it done.' Phil then turned and spoke quietly to a small figure Chris hadn't spotted straight away, sitting with her back to him. *Samantha! Don't worry, I'm coming for you, baby.*

CHAPTER THIRTY-NINE

Moving around the outside of the building, Chris spotted a small window at ground level. The glass had been removed, properly it seemed, as there were no remaining shards that he could catch on his skin, although it was an extremely small gap for him to try to squeeze through. He looked inside, squinting against the thick darkness in front of him. He could just about make out the fact that the window, however low it was outside of the building, appeared to be quite high up the wall of the room inside. *It must be the family crypt underneath the building.* It would get him inside unnoticed at least, and one step closer to Samantha.

Chris hoped beyond hope that there would be a way out of the grave he was entering, as he lowered himself into the hole legs first, squeezing his ample shoulders through the tiny gap before dropping to the ground.

The only light in the room came from the window that he had entered through, and that wasn't much thanks to the trees around the chapel that mostly shaded the building from the sun. A musty smell hit him instantly, and the thoughts of what particles might be making up the scent made him gag. *One step closer to Samantha*, he reminded himself. Looking around and feeling the walls for clues to where there might be another entry point to the chamber, Chris stumbled up a shallow step. To the right of the step was a steep stone staircase. There were chinks of light visible at the top, slipping through the gaps between the boards of an ancient wooden door.

Slowly ascending the steps, Chris gave himself a pep talk, knowing that he would soon be by Samantha's side, but not entirely sure of exactly what he was going to do once he got there.

Gregory turned and walked up the aisle of the chapel towards its main doors. He didn't look happy about Chris's escape, *but then it did happen on his watch*, Sam thought to herself, ecstatic at the news that Chris had managed to get away from his captors. *It could all be a charade for my sake, it would hardly be the first time today*. She mulled this idea over suspiciously, but concluded that Phil, who was currently rubbing a hand over his shaved head, was exhibiting real frustration; Chris was definitely out there somewhere. Sam only hoped that he hadn't decided to do anything stupid like stick around to save her, and had just gone straight off to get help. As soon as she had finished the thought, she knew that there was no chance that he could bear to do that if it involved leaving her here.

The backhand hit from Phil came out of nowhere. 'Are you even listening to me, you stupid bitch?' Sam took a moment afterwards to collect her thoughts back from the white light that had flashed before her eyes. Her vision temporarily blurred, and she even thought she'd seen movement in a doorway behind Phil for a second.

Her sight returned without much delay. *He's anxious and losing control*, she thought, licking blood from her lips. *Good.*

Sam suddenly felt cocky, despite the bruise she could feel forming. 'There's no need for name-calling.'

Phil smiled, seeming genuinely amused for a moment, perhaps at the ridiculousness of this meek, petite thing actually having the balls to make light of the situation she was in. Then he sighed, and the amusement rapidly turned to irritation. 'You've caused me *so* much fucking trouble.' He paused, staring off into the distance for a moment before continuing, 'I'm above all this you know. I have far better things to be doing with my time than running around after the likes of you.' He began to pace, more talking to himself than anyone else. It sounded a little like he was trying to convince himself of his worth to Bradford Dixon. Sam began to wonder if he had momentarily forgotten that she was there.

Her thoughts were short-lived. She was distracted from them by definite movement from behind the pacing Phil. It came from the doorway that Lacey had stumbled through a few hours ago. *Perhaps there really are others being held here at the same time as me.*

A figure was crouched cautiously just behind the doorway, Sam could just see the shape of their jeans tucked up flush with the doorframe. As Phil continued to pace, Sam said nothing, pretending to be listening to his speech about everything that had gone wrong for him in the last two weeks, but unable to feign any sympathy for his experiences.

The figure slowly emerged and raised a finger to his lips before briefly blowing a kiss in Sam's direction. Her heart leapt at the sight of Chris, whilst a part of her was internally chastising him for his choice. He ducked away again as Phil turned to pace back in that direction.

Phil's rant momentum was abruptly broken by the now-familiar ringing of his phone. He checked the caller ID, 'about bloody time,' he mumbled gruffly. 'Mr. Dixon, are you able to talk freely?' Phil took his conversation to a far corner of the chapel's main hall for a limited amount more privacy.

Chris made his move. He darted out of the doorway and over towards Phil who had his back to him. Suddenly, one of the chapel's main doors was thrust open, and Lacey burst in, mouthing off at the top of her lungs. 'Where the fuck is Ethan? Gregory said that you told him to find…' her sentence trailed off as she saw Chris ready to lunge at Phil, who was in the process of turning in Lacey's direction.

The next few seconds played out in slow motion for Sam, whilst she screamed Chris's name for what felt like an eternity.

Chris's advance was interrupted by Lacey's entrance, and he turned his body slightly towards the source of the intrusion. By the time Sam looked over towards the woman, Lacey already had her hand wrapped around the handle of her knife. With the same expert skills that Sam had seen her demonstrate earlier that day, Lacey flicked her wrist and somehow managed to power that blade with something out of this world, driving it through the empty space down the centre aisle of the tired pews and straight towards Chris.

The angle of Chris's moving body meant that by

the time the blade reached him, he had offered up the front of his thigh as a nice, big target for the steel to embed itself into. The athlete had been lunging in Phil's direction with such force that when the blow of the knife brought him crashing to the floor, he careened into the front pews head first.

As the echoes of Sam's scream finally began to fade, an odd calmness befell the building, like everything had been leading up to this moment for the stones that rested in its walls. The eyes of faces in its stained-glass windows all stared down at the unmoving figure of Chris.

CHAPTER FORTY

Lacey was the first one to move. She sauntered up the aisle.

'I'll call you back, sir… No, it should only be a minor setback,' Phil informed Brad, watching as Lacey reached Chris's still frame.

'Don't you touch him you fucking psycho!' screamed Sam, tears pouring down her face.

'…No, I promise it won't interfere with the timetable for the next attack.' Phil ended his call abruptly.

Lacey turned to smile at Sam as she bent down over Chris, keeping eye contact with her, and slowly licked the paling man's face. She slid the palm of her right hand along his waist, over the hip, and down his thigh to where the knife had buried itself to the hilt in his flesh. With far more ceremony than was required, she pulled the blade out, and Chris's jeans immediately darkened as the blood flowed freely from his wound.

If my hands weren't tied… Sam gritted her teeth as she wrestled against her restraints, trying to launch herself at Lacey. The desire to choke the breath from this poor excuse for a human consumed her. 'I should have killed you earlier!'

'Yeah? Well you didn't. You should have, but you couldn't. Because you are *weak*. And look where it got you,' she used the toe of her flip flop to nudge Chris's leg.

'I said don't fucking touch him!' screamed Sam. Focussing her attention on her boyfriend's unmoving frame, the fight drained from her and her body collapsed as far as her tied wrists would allow her to fall.

Chris's face was growing visibly paler still as she watched, and the blood loss was clearly significant, with a glossy patch of burgundy liquid covering the top half of his jeans leg as well as pooling on the floor beneath the limb. The only thing slowing his blood's advance across the floor was the gaps between the wooden floorboards, through which it enthusiastically flowed.

Phil was reinforcing the knots in the twine around Sam's wrists when Gregory joined them in the chapel. Sam watched in a semi-catatonic state as he stood at Chris's feet before grabbing both of the unconscious man's ankles and dragging his bulk away towards the doors.

From her position, Sam couldn't tell if Chris was breathing normally, shallowly, or not at all. Lacey followed along behind Gregory, leaving Phil and Sam alone once more.

Phil followed her line of sight and seemed to deduce that she was captivated by the blood pool that had been concentrated beneath Chris's wounded thigh. Some blood had clearly disappeared down between the gaps in the floorboards. What remained on the surface had already started to thicken, but clearly some had already soaked into dry knots and cracks as the wood thirstily absorbed the hydration that it had been so desperately lacking in recent decades.

'Told you,' Phil said like a kid in the playground. After a silent pause and no reaction from Sam, he continued. He pulled her hair away from her ear and whispered into it. 'The blood soaks *deep* into the wood.'

Sam shivered involuntarily at his breath against her neck, *I hope he leaves soon, I don't know how much longer I can hold it together.* She began wishing it was her that had been attacked instead of Chris. *Hang on... "attacked".* Something that Phil had said after Chris had fallen foul of Lacey's knife now came to her, 'The terrorist attacks in the city. That was you!'

Phil straightened up and backed away, observing her with what seemed like amusement as she ignored him and worked through the indicators.

'They said on the news that David Steele was wanted for questioning about the attacks, but they also said he was a known crook, so I just figured he'd done something petty for Bradford.' She looked up at Phil. *You kept asking me who else knew about what I'd* heard, *not what I* saw. Understanding dawned on her, 'This isn't about the murder. It never was. It was always about what the murder was covering up. Bradford Dixon was the one who ordered the attack on our city.'

Phil grinned.

'And he's planning more!'

'We've found a mobile phone in a sports bag here, Inspector.'

Jane wasn't sure whether or not she was relieved that they hadn't found her friend locked into the boot of Chris's car.

'Anything of significance on it?'

'There's a number of missed calls from a "Jane Holt" on the lock screen, but the device is pin code protected, so we can't do much else with it here. There is a blue band across the top of the screen, which I'm informed by my younger, and significantly more tech-savvy, partner is usually an indication of the fact that the phone's GPS feature is currently in use.'

Jane touched Ami's elbow to get her attention, 'What app does it say is using the phone's location?'

Ami relayed the question to Jones at the scene. There was a fumbling noise as the officer on the other end of the comms system checked the phone's lock screen once more. 'Something called "Circuit Tracker".'

'Oh my god!' Jane leapt out of her chair with excitement. 'The skate-a-thon!'

'Excuse me?' Ami looked at her, completely bemused.

'Sam has an app on her phone that she uses to track her distance when she does endurance skating.' Words tumbled from Jane's mouth as she began gesticulating. 'She would have turned it on for the skate-a-thon, and must have forgotten to turn it off. It might not help us at all, but if it's still running on her phone, then we can find out everywhere that it has been since yesterday afternoon.'

Ami caught on, 'And hence everywhere the car has been. Do you know the pin code for Sam's phone so we can access the location logs?'

'No.' Jane sat back down, dejected, then her face

lit up once more, 'But I do know the password she uses for just about everything.'

Ami rolled her eyes.

'I know, I have told her she needs to vary it.'

The Inspector slid a laptop across the table. 'Well, what are you waiting for, let's hope she's ignored your advice.'

Ami made them another tea whilst Jane attempted to access Sam's Circuit Tracker account via the app's website. By the time the drink was in front of her, there was a road map on the laptop's screen, with a squiggly green line over the top of a number of the roads, representing the movements of Sam's phone. 'Here's the start, at the park for the skate-a-thon,' Jane pointed out an area where the green line ran in a closed loop, darker than in other places as it had layered over itself with each lap of the circuit that the skaters had undertaken. 'This is Sam's house,' Jane indicated, pointing to an area with a yellow circle. 'The yellow dot shows an area where the phone was stationary for more than five consecutive minutes,' she read aloud from the map's key.

'Officer Jones to base, come in please.'

'We're here, Jones, go ahead.'

'We've been approached by a dog walker; says he saw a young man near the vehicle this time yesterday. Apparently, he was holding a dog lead and told our witness that he had spent the last hour wandering around, looking for his lost dog. The witness says that the man stuck out as not being right.'

'Not right? In what way?'

'He used the guy's footwear as an example. Seems anyone that walks their dogs around here comes with some form of hardcore waterproof boots on, and he wore pretty pristine trainers, completely impractical for the footpaths here so he likely doesn't know the area, and certainly hadn't been wandering around it for hours. I've seen the terrain myself and I get what he's saying.'

'Can you get a description from him.'

'Already done,' the sound of pages being turned could be heard through the comms system, 'average height; slim build; short, dark hair; dark goatee; hoop earring in left ear lobe; and a stud in the blobby bit at the front.'

Ami smiled at the officer's ignorance, 'The tragus?' she prompted.

There was some murmuring. 'Younger colleague says "yes". Also wearing a plain black t-shirt and khaki combat trousers, and the aforementioned clean white trainers, so not much to go on with the clothing I'm afraid.'

'It's more than enough to compare to our existing description. Thank-you.'

'We'll be here another half an hour finishing up, let me know if you need anything doing in that time, Inspector.'

Ami thanked the officer and signed off. 'Let's take a look at that abduction file, shall we?' She compared the notes she'd just scribbled down to Belle and Thora's description in the file. 'It certainly looks like it's the same guy, Jane. The question is, if he ulti-mately did manage to get to Sam, where is she now?'

CHAPTER FORTY-ONE

'You really didn't know?' Phil was staring at Sam, incredulous.

'But all those people injured, the damage to the city and its communities,' Sam was shaking her head. 'What could be worth that? After everything that Brad has done to help build it up, how could he possibly just—' understanding flooded her. 'The contract. Awarded to help protect our city against something like this ever happening again. It was to fast-track the uptake of his "CONNECTED:" service, wasn't it?'

'In a nutshell. And once the money's in and all of the features are activated, there won't be anything that we can't do.'

He paused ominously, observing her. 'You see now why it's so important that we know who else you've spoken to,' he sighed, 'and now that you know for sure, we're definitely going to have to kill you.' An expression somewhere between a smile and a sneer appeared on his face as Sam attempted to compute all this new information. Phil was getting into his stride, *he obviously doesn't get much chance to hear himself speak, always in Bradford's shadow.* 'Seeing as that's cleared up, I don't mind, and in fact take great pleasure in telling you that that won't be the last attack either. There's a lot of money to be made out of paranoia.'

Sam stopped listening, the enormity of what she had managed to get mixed up in now consuming her thoughts.

'I don't know why it didn't occur to me sooner,' Phil piped up, and Sam realised he had been quiet for a minute preceding this. 'It clicked when I saw your concern over Christopher, bleeding away there. You're clearly a compassionate kind of gal, you don't like others to come to harm or feel pain if it can be avoided.'

Sam stared straight ahead, unblinking.

'So, you had the foresight to plan a strategy to protect yourself, a reaction to you going missing for too long maybe or turning up somewhere dead. Well done you. Now it obviously only covers you, and not your friends and family, else the information would have been released when we killed that other roller-girl that we accidentally picked up. So, we can pretty much start picking off your nearest and dearest, one by one, until you talk to us.'

Sam lifted her head and looked straight at Phil as he laid his thoughts out. 'Christopher is clearly gonna be of no fucking use to us now, but your friend Jane, well I can get her picked up no problem. She's at the police station right now, under the watchful eye of a friend of mine. He can easily insist that she allows him to give her a lift home... for her safety, of course.'

Sam desperately tried to keep her features neutral. *Jane! How is she even on his radar?*

Phil was still speaking. 'We tend to do our best work starting late evening, that way the last of the dog walkers have been and gone, and we get this place all to ourselves to make as much noise as we need to, or as much noise as our guests need to, which is obviously the more common case. My colleague at the police station can probably get Jane here at around dusk so that we can make a start straight away.'

Sam winced, turning her head away from Phil. *If I come clean, then it will just be me. All of my friends will be safe.* Sam mustered up the courage to speak the truth.

'It's bogus,' she muttered.

'What is?'

'My "plan", the insurance, the information to be released on my death or disappearance. I made it up to buy Chris and I some time.'

'Nice try,' Phil stated. 'Compassionate little lady, trying to save your friends. You'd say anything not to drag them into all this shit, wouldn't you, Miss Kiss?'

Sam whipped her head back round to face him. 'No, it is, I made it all up.'

'Cut the act, Samantha,' irritation edged Phil's words. 'I know that you have some sort of evidence linked to what you saw or heard in the alley that night, my police source has already confirmed it.'

Sam was confused, 'what evidence?'

'Quit playing games with me. Hand it over now, and this is where it stops. You will die, yes, but just you… and Honey Trap, and the bartender, and Christopher…' he counted on his fingers then held his hands up and wiggled the digits at her.

Sam struggled to understand why he wouldn't

listen to her, and how best to convince him of the truth. She found herself longing for Jane, they always bounced ideas off each other, then, conflicted, she chastised herself for wishing that Jane were already here, in this mess with her. 'Honestly, I don't have a clue what you're talking about! I made up the idea of insurance, I thought I could bluff it, I swear!'

'It no longer matters if your plan was real or not, what matters is that evidence exists, that we need.'

'I'm telling the truth! I don't know anything about any evidence!'

Phil ignored her. 'Jane is at the police station right now and will be due to leave for home any minute. All I need to do is make one phone call to my friend and then in a couple of hours' time, we can all have a nice little chat together.'

Sam's catatonia threatened to return at the thought of being made to watch Phil do whatever it was that he was planning to do to Jane.

'You feel it, don't you? The spectrum of emotion, the adrenaline coming and going. You should thank me, not everyone experiences something as intense as this in their lifetime.'

'You're a fucking psycho.'

'Why thank-you, m'lady. Ah, Ethan,' Phil addressed the youth who had just come in, 'bring in our large tattooed gentleman to keep Miss Kiss company for a bit, I have a call to make.' He made to leave, 'and bring me the fucking friend.'

Ethan followed him out of the doors, smirking.

Sam thought of the man who she had bumped into during the charade of her teased escape. *I knew it! I knew he was one of them.* One of the large wooden doors at the front of the chapel banged open and Ethan entered backwards, dragging something large into the room with him. As he arrived at the front rows, near Sam, he dropped his burden, the body of a large man with a shaved head and a multitude of tattoos over all of his exposed skin. 'New grounds-keeper it seems,' he said by way of explanation, 'this one is your fault too apparently.' With a sideways smile at her shocked expression, he left her alone with the man's body, its expressionless eyes staring through Sam from either side of a bullet's entry wound in the middle of his forehead.

CHAPTER FORTY-TWO

Ami scanned the rest of the marked-up map on Sam's Circuit Tracker account. There were two more yellow circles showing that the phone had been stationary, one where the field team were currently looking over Chris's abandoned car for clues, and another about fifteen miles away from that. She pointed it out to Jane. 'Is this place of any significance to Samantha or Chris?'

Jane thought hard for a moment. 'Not that I'm aware of, where is it?' On further inspection they concluded that the circle was on a country road next to a stately home. ' "Higglesley Hall", I've never heard Sammy mention it.'

'Well it's not open to the public, so I have no idea what they'd be doing there. I'll get the guys to check it out whilst they're out in the field.' She contacted the team to give them the go ahead to cautiously investigate the coordinates, and then she and Jane began looking into the detail of Higglesley Hall. Jane was scanning the area using Google Earth's satellite view feature. 'There's a building in the grounds near to the yellow circle,' she told Ami.

'Maybe there's access to the grounds next to it, that could be why the car stopped there. Oh, I've found something that mentions a chapel. Lady Gilby was the previous occupant of the main house,' she read from her screen, 'and when she died, ownership passed to her son. He wasn't interested in the heritage of the building, so moved abroad and sold the house on to some historical preservation organisation, who have yet to do anything with the place.'

Jane peered over Ami's shoulder at the laptop screen as she read this out. 'Look,' she pointed to the next section, 'it says here that he retained ownership of a small chapel on the grounds, as it's where his family is buried.'

'I'll run a full search of all records and documents for the chapel and house, see if anything useful pops up. Our team on the ground is going to send out a couple of guys to check out the location, and I'll send another small team from here to visit the residence of our fake dog walker, Ethan Madson.' Ami turned to face Jane, 'I'm pretty sure that we can take it from here now, love. I think it's time that you got some rest and you can trust us to track down Samantha.'

'I understand, I'm just so pleased that you took me seriously, thank-you.'

'Well, this has gone far beyond coincidence and speculation. You go home, get some rest, and I'll let you know as soon as we hear anything.'

Jane hugged the kindly Inspector and was shown back out to the main corridor by another officer whilst Ami arranged the raid on Ethan's address. She suddenly felt drained and sat down on a bench next to a water cooler to gather her thoughts.

The hoarse-voiced Detective Sergeant didn't know

for sure yet, but he suspected that he was very seriously ill. His deep, guttural coughs had been getting more and more frequent these past couple of months, and occasionally even brought blood up along with the air from his damaged lungs. Yet still, here he was, outside the building's back door in their designated smoking area, savouring his twelfth cigarette of the day. He'd stare at it in contempt occasionally but was still unable to just put it out and step away.

Phil's lackey had instructed him an hour ago to take the missing girl's friend to some stately home somewhere in the countryside, for God knows what reason, but over the years the policeman had come to learn that Phil was not a man that you questioned, so he didn't, and they paid him handsomely. It meant that he had been able to set up a decent future for his family before he died and left them.

The woman, Jane, had been with that chubby female Inspector all day, he hadn't managed to create a single opportunity to get her away. How on earth he was going to manage this one without giving himself away as crooked, he wasn't exactly sure.

Sighing, which brought on another bout of barely controllable coughing, he pushed open the door and went back inside. As he passed the supply room, he noticed a few guys kitting up. 'What's happening?' he asked. 'Something kicking off?'

'That missing girl whose mate has been here all day,' responded one of the guys.

'Did they manage to get a trace on the phone?'

'I dunno. They got an ID on a bloke who was seen dumping the car, and it's a match to a description we had on file.'

'So, us lucky lot,' chimed in another as he checked over his taser, 'get to go check out his last known address.' He then mimed smashing a battering ram against a door before grinning from ear to ear. *This one clearly loves his job. Good for him.*

'Whereabouts is it?' he casually asked the team.

'Some inner-city flat.'

As long as it's not a stately home, then my task is still on point.

He headed up to the incident room to check on the friend.

After half an hour with the groundskeeper's ripening body, Sam had been shoved back into the cubby. Phil's voice floated around in her head, replaying the words that he had spoken to her as he bundled her back into the dark hole; "the body count just keeps on rising, Miss Kiss. Tick tock, tick tock."

She was relieved to be in here and finally out of sight of her captors. The tears flowed freely as she allowed herself to truly feel the events of the last few hours. She grieved for Honey and mourned the lives that her friend could no longer touch with her com-passion. Sam gave herself over to the anguish she felt over Chris's incapacitation, but would not allow herself to act as though he were truly gone.

There's been so much violence, and so many unne-cessary casualties, just because I was too scared to accept the fact that my days were numbered from the second I stepped out into that alley. If I had just gone along with what they wanted, played their stupid game instead of trying to invent rules to suit me. Then... well... Chris would have been long dead, as would I... But that's where it would have ended. I feel so sorry for all that has happened as things have escalated, spiralling completely beyond my control.

Sam's splutters suddenly lessened.

But have they really? Is it truly out of my hands?

She heard Honey's voice then; "Stop saying you're sorry! Step up, attack that shit and disappear on out of here…"

Something happened to Sam physically as she thought about the words. She spoke them aloud to herself; 'Stop apologising. Step up. Attack that shit and disappear.' She had been hunched in a tiny ball against the wall of her makeshift prison, but now she began to uncurl, shoulders pushing back, chin lifting up. An oddly harmonious combination of calmness and aggression fell over Sam as she bum-shuffled her way to the cubby's door to examine the material with her hands. *What's the worst that can happen if I'm heard bashing against this door? Phil comes and knocks me out? He tortures me? Well that's on the cards already anyway, after torturing my friends in front of me.* The aggression began to produce a slow burning sensation, emanating from deep within her, fuelling her. *Nope, it's all no worse than sitting around here doing nothing but moping and waiting. I have to get out and find Chris, he could be okay. And I've got to somehow alert Jane to the fact that she's been targeted before Phil's guy brings her here.*

Sam felt her way around the small space. There wasn't a lot of room to work with, but if she squatted low, she could probably deliver a decent body check to the door. They had practiced a similar move a few weeks ago at roller derby, designed to allow you to shoulder check an opposing player in the hip, keeping yourself so low that they would be unlikely to be able to either retaliate or hold their stance.

Now's the time to see how well that lesson went in.

Honey's voice came to her again: "Make the first

hit really count. Mentally prepare yourself, you want to be where they are, you NEED it, like you need air." *Well if ever that were true, it was now.* Sam closed her eyes and focussed.

It took five solid hits in this manner to get the lock's strike plate to splinter away from the door frame. Shuffling towards the opening of the cubby, she used the edge of the strike plate to calmly and efficiently saw away at the twine that bound her wrists. It fell away from her skin and she tucked it into the waistband of her leggings. *Weapon. I need a weapon.* She looked around her, nearly everything was fixed to the floor or walls. Her eyes settled on a broken window, and she took off a sock to wrap around her hand, protecting it from the edges of the piece of glass that she wiggled free of the lead frame.

'What exactly do you think you're up to?' came Ethan's voice from behind her.

CHAPTER FORTY-THREE

Sam turned to face Ethan but didn't have a chance to adjust her grip on the glass in her hand before he hit her hard in the stomach. The blow caused her to drop to the floor and the shard skittered from her hand as she doubled over, gripping her mid-section at the point of impact.

'You know it was me that essentially killed your friend. I mean, I wasn't the one that got to slit her pretty throat, but I brought her here, and helped with the other stuff too of course. She was a fighter I can tell you. Bled out right in this very room. In fact, right around here somewhere.' He inhaled deeply. 'Can you smell it?'

Sam was attempting to compartmentalise her thoughts as she slowly recovered from her winding. She blocked out enough of Ethan's words to skim over the fate of her friend but allowed his arrogance and taunting tone in in waves, using them to fuel her growing anger.

'Why are you lot all so fucking theatrical?' she fired at him.

Ethan laughed in response, as next to him, Sam

spotted a utility belt around the waist of the grounds-keeper's corpse, still lying where Ethan had dumped it an hour ago. She turned onto her belly and began a commando crawl towards the belt.

'Where are you off to now? There's nowhere to go you stupid little girl.' He aimed a punch at her head which Sam rolled to avoid, silently thanking Belle for her obsession with them practising rolls so that they could get to their feet again quickly if knocked over.

Ethan howled in pain. He had punched straight down towards the chapel floor and been greeted by a fistful of stone when Sam's head had no longer been where he had expected it to be. 'BITCH!' he spat, and advanced towards her once more. She had reached the groundskeeper's body, and quickly found what she needed from the belt.

'I've arranged to bring your friend here too, you know. Maybe Phil will let me be the one to kill her this time.'

With all her strength, Sam drove the groundskeep-er's utility knife down with both hands into the top of Ethan's foot, near to the ankle. The sound that came out of him now was such a high-pitched shriek that it was almost inaudible, his face contorted in a silent scream not unlike Munch's representation in his painting.

Sam stood quickly before Ethan regained any com-posure and elbowed him hard in the back of the neck as he bent over to retrieve the blade from his dam-aged foot. He stumbled and moaned but was still conscious. She aimed a hard heel kick to the man's temple. That did it. He crumpled to the floor, silent.

Panting and exhilarated, Sam rolled Ethan's inert body into the cubby. She went back to pick up the utility knife from where Ethan had dropped it. Bend-ing down, something small caught her eye underneath the front pews, glinting in the late afternoon sunlight. Sam pulled it out to examine it and realised with a jolt that it was one of Honey's signature glittery hairbands.

Sam stood, quiet and statuesque for a few minutes, slowly getting more and more riled up about the gall of these people and how their disrespect knew no bounds. The part of her brain responsible for rational thought now submitted to a primal survival instinct coupled with a strong desire for revenge, both of which had well and truly kicked in, kicked ass, and taken over the running of things up there.

With resolve, Sam put on Honey's headband.

'Fuck this,' she said out loud, and marched out of the chapel.

'It's Jane, isn't it?' a soft voiced asked, cutting through Jane's cyclical thoughts as she stared through a framed photo on the opposite wall of local businessman, Bradford Dixon, seemingly with the police Superintendent. She looked up into the face of a young, friendly-looking male officer and nodded.

'Can I offer you a lift home? I understand it's been a difficult and somewhat intense day for you?'

Jane took a deep breath and counted to three, concentrating hard on not allowing the tears to break forth. She exhaled. 'I'm okay. Bus is fine.' She rose somewhat shakily to her feet, and the young officer reached an arm out ready to steady her if needed.

'My squad car is even closer than the bus stop, and you look like you could do with some company.' His brow furrowed in a genuine concern. 'In fact, I insist,' he said, his face breaking into a smile.

'Jane, I'm glad you're still here,' Ami called urgently from down the corridor, 'the guys have picked up some heat signatures at Higglesley Hall, not acting like regular ground staff. Back-up is going out to join the team already in the field then they'll move in.' She looked questioningly at the young officer standing next to Jane.

'I was offering Jane a lift home,' he explained.

'Jane, the guys feel like having you there could be useful, to help them identify Samantha amidst the other people. She might also appreciate a friendly face.' Ami looked then to the officer, 'She would need a police escort, are you available, Trent?' Ami asked.

'Absolutely,' Trent said, then, looking at Jane, 'assuming you are okay with that?'

Jane nodded.

'Okay, good luck. I'll be monitoring from here.' Ami returned to the incident room.

Shit, don't tell me I've missed her. The hoarse-voiced man sprinted to the foyer, wheezing as he approached. After a panicked look around, he returned to the incident room where the woman Inspector was sitting. 'Where is she?' he barked.

'Excuse me?' she offered indignantly.

'Sorry, skipper. The girl, that missing girl's friend.'

'Oh, we got a lead, Trent's taken her to Higglesley Hall to meet the field team there. Since when do you care anyway? Didn't you—'

He didn't hear what she said next, the panic threatening to engulf him. He stomped off outside, calling Phil's number repeatedly as he made his way to where he had parked his car. Every phone call was going straight to voicemail.

'Bloody mobile reception!' he muttered. *I've got to*

warn Phil. If they're caught and I'm exposed, then I'll lose everything! There was no choice here, he was going to have to go to the hall himself.

Jane was settled into the passenger seat of Trent's squad car, staring out of her window and biting her lip as they whipped past other vehicles on the dual carriageway.

Trent was the one to break the silence of the last ten minutes. 'I'm guessing you've had a pretty rough time of it so far today?'

Jane nodded automatically in response then realised that he would have been watching the road, so wouldn't have seen her gesture. 'Yes,' she said.

'How long has your friend been missing?'

'At l-least a full day.'

'It'll be okay, you know. We'll find her.'

Jane turned to look at him, seeing genuine care in his features. 'Thank-you.'

Another few minutes went by then Trent spoke again. 'Let's talk about something, take your mind off things. I see you like Batman,' he pointed to her bag bearing the batman logo that was nestled next to her feet. 'Movies are a passion of mine, did you like the Dark Knight Batman Trilogy?'

'I love those films. But prefer my superhero movies a bit lighter.'

'But toning those films as dark as he did was a stroke of genius by Nolan, everyone tried to emulate it after him. How can you possibly not prefer the darker-themed superhero movies?'

'It's not that I don't enjoy them, it's just that I prefer the traditional views of superheroes saving the day from wacky villains whilst dressed in bright colours.' Jane felt her words, and consequently her thoughts, flowing surprisingly freely with Trent, he was just so comfortable to be around.

'Okay, fine. So where do the Avengers films fall with you then, cos they're kinda in-between the dark and the wacky.'

'I'm a big Joss Whedon fan, so I love how he set the tone for those movies. They're awesome.'

Trent's tone then altered almost imperceptibly when he spoke next, dialling down the chatter and turning slightly more serious. 'There's a new one out in a couple of weeks.' He stopped at that, letting the hidden meaning permeate the air around them, and an exciting kind of tension developed within the confines of the police car.

Jane's heart did a little flip at the realisation of what Trent was implying. She hadn't ever really been on a date before, not a proper one, only with friends who afterwards just remained friends. Her heart then started doing a few more flips, before the familiar constriction began to develop in her throat. 'I… when… if… maybe…' her cheeks flushed as Jane realised how silly she sounded, blurting out words that wouldn't string together properly.

'I'm sorry,' said Trent, misinterpreting the situation, 'I didn't mean to put you on the spot. Forget I said anything.'

Inside, Jane was screaming at herself to tell him it was fine, it didn't matter, that it wasn't what he'd said, it was her stupid condition that had caused her not to acknowledge his invitation properly. All that came out was one single word; 'anxiety.'

Jane turned back to the window, tears forming in her eyes, furious with herself for allowing her condition to own her so completely.

Don't fall apart now, Sammy's gonna need you.

CHAPTER FORTY-FOUR

Cautiously treading her way away from the chapel under cover of trees, Sam heard a woman's voice and she instantly stopped moving. Holding her breath, she crept in the direction of the sound, being careful to step only on the soft, mossy areas of ground so as not to bring attention to herself. As she got closer, recognition hit her - *Lacey!*

Lacey was talking on the phone and held a half-smoked cigarette in one hand. Sam couldn't make out the words, but the woman was speaking in an agitated fashion, repeatedly taking enormous drags of her cigarette mid-sentence. Sam could feel her blood beginning to move around her body a little quicker at the sight of her betrayer, and a sudden, primal urge to use aggression to ensure her survival was all that she could focus on. Gently fingering the handle of the utility knife in her hand, Sam stooped low and adjusted her grip, wrapping her fingers tightly around it with her index finger snug against the ridge that acted as a small hilt.

Lacey was speaking animatedly, so didn't hear Sam's approach until she was just a few feet away.

Swinging around to see who was there, Lacey's eyes instantly scanned at head height, giving Sam an extra second or two before the other woman fully processed what was happening. It was all Sam needed. She drove the knife deep into Lacey's thigh, and without hesitation, pushed her over so she was on the floor in seconds, the winding of her landing cutting short the cry that had emerged as the knife scratched her bone.

Knowing full well that she still would not stoop to the level of these people and actually intentionally end someone's life, Sam opted instead for incapacitating Lacey so that at least she would be out of the game for now. She took aim at the plaster over where she had hit the woman's head with a rock mere hours ago, and delivered a hefty kick to the temple as she had done with Ethan, and Lacey instantly lay still.

After hanging up on Lacey's call, Sam dragged the woman's limp form into some thick bushes where the sunlight was non-existent. She tied her up with the twine she had kept and caught sight of the knife sticking out of her belt against the small of her back. She took the weapon and hurled it over the wall.

Despite Sam's earlier decision to let Lacey live potentially having cost Chris his life, she still could not bring herself to end one. *I'm not ready to cross that line. You get a fighting chance, but quite frankly I don't give a shit what happens to you now and if you live or die.* With this thought in mind, Sam grabbed hold of the knife that was protruding from Lacey's thigh and tugged hard. It was securely vacuumed into the flesh and Sam needed to use a firm grip with both hands to finally get it to release with a sickening squelch.

She watched the glossy red liquid pulsing out of

Lacey's limb, much as it had from Chris's earlier, although Lacey's bare skin allowed for a much clearer view than Chris's slowly bloodying jeans leg. Mesmerised, Sam remained for a few more seconds before shaking herself back to reality. *Gregory's likely to be close. I'd best find somewhere to hide and wait for him.*

She didn't have to wait long.

Gregory casually lit a cigarette, shielding the fragile flame against the slight breeze that swished its way through the tree canopy overhead. Wandering over near to the bushes where Sam was crouching down out of sight, he moved his head back and forth, slowly scanning the area, looking for something. 'Lace? Where are you, baby?'

Sam placed her fingers on the ground to steady herself then lifted silently to a standing position. Gregory was tall, and she had to reach her arms high up to slip them over his shoulders unnoticed. As quickly as she could, she got herself into a position where the blade of the knife that had cut Lacey was held firmly against Gregory's throat, one hand on the hilt, and the other over his other shoulder and securing the tip against the other side, preventing him from spinning around out of the hold.

'You fucking bitch, I'll skin you—'

'Keep talking Romeo, no-one's listening. Now kneel.'

Gregory did what he was told, cursing under his breath throughout the manoeuvre. Sam then noticed the gun protruding from the waistband of his tracksuit bottoms. She quickly took it and, releasing him from the knife, took a step back. Her captor turned towards her, and Sam chambered a round in the weapon. 'I know how to use this, so let's skip that conversation,' she reassured him.

'What exactly do you—'

'Shut the fuck up. You see that tree over there?'

Gregory looked to where she indicated.

'Tie your hands together around one of the lower boughs.'

He looked at her and sighed his displeasure. There was a hint of mocking to the expression that he wore.

'Tie myself with what?'

'Some of the twine in your pocket that I saw you passing to Phil earlier. You do it first, then I'll come check that it's tight enough.'

He didn't move.

Sam held her own expression firm and clicked the safety off the gun that she held.

Gregory's mocking expression fell away to be replaced by one of mild panic.

'Do it,' she affirmed.

Gregory obliged whilst Sam watched him carefully. Once he appeared to be secure, she approached cautiously, keeping the gun away from the man as she got close. She tested his restraints, tightening them a bit for good measure. Her captive winced. As she came around to the side of him, he aimed a head butt down at her. Her roller derby reflexes kicked in and she dropped low to avoid the impact. Angry, and not prepared to be their victim anymore, Sam flung her arm around in a backhand circle as she raised herself back up and caught Gregory on the cheek with the butt of the gun. The "clunk" sound as the gun met with the man's face seemed to echo satisfyingly around the little wooded area where they stood.

'I am done playing games with you guys,' Sam spat through gritted teeth as Gregory worked his jaw to make sure nothing was broken. *Time to break the bad news, asshole.* 'You were here looking for Lacey?' she gestured to where the sole of the bleeding woman's foot was just visible through the undergrowth. 'Well you've found her.'

The cocky facade dropped. 'Is she alive?'

Sam said nothing.

'Is. She. ALIVE?' he screeched at her, twisting his body to try and get a better view of his motionless girlfriend. 'Lacey? Baby?' His eyes welled up.

'It's the uncertainty that affects you the most isn't it? The not knowing. Well now you know how it fucking feels.'

'What you on about?'

'Chris. Where is he?'

'Like I'm telling you that.' As Gregory spoke, his eyes inadvertently flicked in the direction of a small barn-like building that Sam hadn't noticed before, its walls weathered and camouflaged. 'You already did,' she said, and hurried through the building's doors.

Chris was lying on the floor just inside. Sam had never imagined a person's skin could ever look so white. She kneeled down next to him and took his hand in hers. His eyelids flickered. Sam's heart skipped, 'Chris? Can you hear me?'

'S-Samantha?'

'Yes, it's me! I'm here for you.'

'S-sorry. Should have… g-gone for h-help. Couldn't… leave you.'

'Shhh,' Sam reassured him, 'it's okay, I get it,' she glanced around, 'listen, I'm gonna get us out of this.'

'I'll never let you get out,' Gregory spat through his tears. 'What have you done to Lacey?'

'Nothing I regret,' Sam retorted, not bothering to look in his direction.

'Don't be so sure,' Gregory said, still sniffling, but his tone of voice was off this time. There was an underlying confidence that hadn't been there before, alerting Sam to the faint shadow that was approaching her where she was still squatting on the ground. She calculated her timing and forced herself to stay low until the last second, feigning checking Chris for a pulse. Taking a deep breath, she popped up suddenly, rolling her body upwards and forcefully driving the back of her shoulder into the solid sternum of the stealthy newcomer. Taken by surprise, the man staggered backwards but managed to remain upright. Sam knew he would advance again within seconds, so made her decision quickly. She raised the hand that held the gun and shot him centre mass.

The shot reverberated around the nearby trees, and Sam stood motionless, gun hand outstretched but now pointing slightly upward as a result of the recoil. With huge effort, she distanced herself from what she had just done. *I can't afford to break down now, I have to get help to Chris.*

'Dear, oh dear. Now you've gone and done it,' said Gregory, the edge of confidence present in his voice had switched up a notch and was now overwhelming.

Confused, Sam looked down at the body lying splayed on its back on the floor just ahead of her. The man's jacket had fallen open as he had landed, and attached to his belt, sparkling in the moving rays of sunlight through the trees, was a police shield.

CHAPTER FORTY-FIVE

In a daze, Sam stood. The captive Gregory was heckling her as she stared, unmoving. His words were indistinct to Sam as she processed the prone figure on the ground in front of her. The image of his expression before he fell backwards played before Sam again, the briefest look of comprehension in his eyes.

She tore her gaze away and wordlessly began to walk away from the grim scene, Gregory still yapping away at her like a terrier tied up outside a corner shop.

She stuck to the shadows of the lightly wooded area that ran along the perimeter wall, her mind drifting back to the unwelcome topic of the fact that she had just shot a police officer, *What will it mean? What will happen to me? Can I even live with the guilt?*

Her increasingly more dramatic thoughts were abruptly interrupted by Phil's voice, calling her out. 'I heard a gunshot Miss Kiss, I take it you've been busy? I went to see you at the chapel but guess what I found when I got there. Let's just say what was in the hole isn't as pretty as you!'

She couldn't quite tell where his voice was coming from at first, and shrank back into the shrubbery, motionless, to try and orientate herself to the man's position. He soon came into view, then stood looking down at his hands as he fiddled with a gold ring casually, not bothering to look around for Sam. 'Are we playing a game, Sammy? Ready or not, here I come.'

Sam put her fears aside, drawing on her anger at what had happened to Chris. Phil looked as though he was unarmed, reliant either on sheer cockiness, or the fact that he thought he had Gregory and Lacey as backup. *You're on your own this time.* Sam inhaled deeply, puffing her chest out, *—and only Jane gets to call me Sammy.*

She stepped out into the open.

Phil looked up nonchalantly, as though he was not at all surprised to see Sam's dishevelled figure appearing before him. She stuck a determined, unshakable look on her face, which caused his bolshy stature to falter slightly as his eyes took in the gun hanging casually at her side, her finger lying comfortably alongside the trigger and guard. He faltered for less than a second before he was standing tall again, chest puffed out.

'So, you acquired some firepower. I'm, what, fifteen metres away? What will you do if you miss, or if there's no more bullets?'

'I won't miss,' mumbled Sam, lifting the gun and taking aim at Phil.

'It takes a lot of balls to live with taking a life, Sam. I'd know.'

Sam blocked his psychology out of her thoughts. *Well, now I've already done it once, I can damn well do it again for this asshole.* She squeezed the trigger gently, being as precise as she could with her aim and limited experience.

The gun's trigger gave under the pressure of Sam's finger, and nestled back against the rear side of the trigger guard with a gentle click. There was no recoil this time. No sound reverberating around the trees. No body falling to the ground with a thump.

Phil's initial shock that Sam had actually pulled the trigger dissolved quickly. He stopped fiddling with his rings and looked up at her with a sly smile. He began to take fast, deliberate steps towards Sam, as she stood still, stunned, the gun now hanging limply from her finger. Phil's pace quickened, rapidly closing the space between them. Sam was rooted to the spot, days of extreme emotional stress and uncertainty threatened to take their toll, and her blood-short body was close to giving in.

Not now, Sam thought to herself, *right now, you fight*.

Phil came in close, arms outstretched ready to grab at her. *He still wants me alive!* She ducked and twirled away from his grasp. Digging her toes down into the floor, she launched herself forwards to sprint away from him, but he stuck a leg out and tripped her.

Sam's knees hit the floor first, sending a shockwave up her spine and jarring her back. As the rest of her exhausted body fell to the floor, she heard Gregory shout suddenly, 'Phil! In the trees!'

It was the last thing she was aware of before her head cracked awkwardly against the floor.

The ground was shaking. As Sam lay on her back, she sensed that the movement was actually more of a rhythmical rocking than a shake. She could also hear a low rumbling, constant background noise. *I'm in a vehicle*, she realised. *Oh, God, no, please don't let them be taking me somewhere else. I've got to get out, now.*

Sam kept her eyes closed, feigning unconsciousness and did her best to calm herself. Following an internal count of three, she moved to jump up from her position, only to find that she was bound down tightly. Panicking, she thrashed her arms and legs about, hoping desperately for some kind of weak point in her latest restraints to burst open.

'Bloody hell, Sammy! Calm down.'

Jane. That bastard really did send for her. 'Jane, we have to get out of here, you don't know these people and what they're capable of. Can you get free?' Sam continued to struggle, looking down the length of her body as she felt a tight band across her chest.

Someone placed their hands on Sam's shoulders, as Jane spoke again, 'Sammy, calm down. You're safe. The police found you unconscious. You're in an ambulance now on your way to the hospital to get checked out.'

Sam said nothing for a few seconds, taking this in.

'Sammy?'

She looked across at her friend, who was sitting unrestrained except for a standard vehicle safety harness. She had reached for and was holding Sam's hand. 'You... I... really? We're really okay?'

'We're really okay,' Jane smiled, giving Sam's hand a reassuring squeeze.

'The police came?'

'Yeah, well you'd forgotten to turn that GPS logging app off again.' Jane leaned in, 'I overheard the police saying that a few of the bad guys had been left gift-wrapped for them, was that you, Thunder?'

Sam thought back, trying to recall the events that Jane might be referring to. She opened her mouth to say that she wasn't sure, and then the memories crashed back to her consciousness. *The police came. They saved me. Oh, God.* 'Jane, I did something terrible… I shot one of them.' The words came out in-between sobs, Sam wrestling with the enormity of what she was responsible for.

'Good for you, cos they were gonna do a hell of a lot worse to you if you hadn't.'

'Not one of *them*… one of the cops! I shot a cop, Jane!' Sam wailed. She turned her head away from her friend in shame and anguish.

'No, no! Well, technically yes, I suppose, but he was *their* cop. He shut down your attempted abduction investigation and cut me off when I tried to report you missing.'

Sam quietened down and slowly turned her tear-stained face back towards her friend, who was still holding her hand tightly. 'That only goes so far in easing the guilt. I still killed someone Jane.'

'Good god, no! You didn't kill him.'

Sam was stunned, 'But I hit him in the chest. He went straight down.'

'You hit him in his body armour.'

The relief flowed wet and salty from Sam's eyes.

'We're two minutes out.' The voice came from the front of the vehicle, *the driver*.

'Roger that.'

Sam looked up to see who had responded, and for the first time noticed the man sitting behind where her head lay, monitoring a lot of complicated-looking machines and dials.

'Don't worry, sweetie,' he smiled, 'you're gonna

be fine. We just need to check you over, and you need to rest.'

The thought suddenly hit her like a bus, 'Chris! Is he okay?' she blurted out.

Jane paused before answering in a quiet voice. 'I don't know, Sammy. They found him in a bad way and took him straight to the emergency room.' She leaned in, cradling her best friend's hand closer to her chest. 'They weren't sure if he was going to make it.'

'We're here. Get her ready to move,' the woman's voice from the driver's seat cut through the emptiness that Jane's words had left behind.

'There's something else, something important,' Sam fought to drag the memory to the front of her mind. 'It was something big, I need to tell the police…' her voice trailed off. *Dammit, what was it?*

The doors to the rear of the ambulance opened, and the paramedics prepared to move Sam.

'I remember!' Sam gasped, the action causing her chest to hurt.

'Just give her a minute, she's going again,' the paramedic said.

But I know about the attacks! Before Sam's brain could successfully process the message to tell her body to speak, she slipped once more into the depths of unconsciousness.

CHAPTER FORTY-SIX

The faint sounds of bickering voices were the first things that Sam heard as she woke from a deep and much needed sleep. She yawned silently and looked around her. She was faced with the unmistakable stark walls of a hospital. At the foot of her bed sat Jane, watching a repeat of some daytime chat show where a shockingly young mother had just slapped her daughter's middle-aged boyfriend round the face, drawing a cheer from the watching audience.

'I thought you'd stopped watching that rubbish,' she teased Jane.

'Sammy! You're awake!' Jane rushed to Sam's side and hugged her tight. 'I'll go get a nurse.'

Supporting her weight on her arms, Sam pulled herself up, the starched bed sheets crinkling as she moved. She took a proper look around. There didn't appear to be any police or security guards posted outside the door of her very generic hospital room.

She guessed that she was being cared for in a low-risk, recovery area of the hospital, concluding that her health was therefore not in any immediate danger.

Tentatively, she lifted her arms up. An intravenous

drip was connected to a catheter in the back of her left hand, and she swore as the needle tugged beneath her skin. In truth, she was relieved that the catheter had prevented her from stretching any further, she had already felt the discomfort in her muscles, strained from being held immobile and then the sudden exertion of her escape.

Another yawn came, and Sam debated just lying down again and going back to sleep. *It would give my body a bit more time to heal*, she attempted to convince herself. As the lazy side of Sam's brain was beginning to win the argument, she heard the sound of purposeful footsteps clacking on the linoleum floor, and a burly-looking nurse filled the doorway. She came directly over to Sam and began to check her vitals. Over the woman's shoulder, Sam saw Jane follow her in.

'Right, Samantha is it?' the nurse asked.

Sam nodded.

'Well, everything seems to be okay. Your heart rate, breathing, all that business is pretty much in the normal zone. You'll have a couple of nasty bruises on your face, but no broken bones and the swelling already seems to be on its way down. We'll need to get the results of some blood tests back, which I expect will show that you are in need of a nice, big meal, nothing more.'

Sam smiled at the nurse. The woman was an intimidating presence with a bulky appearance, but she had kind eyes and a gentle touch. 'Now, even assuming the bloods come back okay, we still won't be able to let you go until you've had something to drink, a proper meal to eat, and been to the toilet,' the nurse struck the items off on her fingers as she spoke. She scribbled something on the chart that hung from the foot of Sam's bed. 'Okay, that's all recorded,' she looked up directly at Sam 'how do you feel?'

'Not too bad. Like I could sleep for a week, but other than that I think I'm okay.'

'There's some police who have been waiting here for a short while that insist they need to speak to you as soon as you're up to it. They want to catch you as soon as possible whilst everything is fresh in your mind, but your well-being is my only concern. Are you up to it?'

Sam nodded.

Jane threw her a questioning look.

'Really, I'm feeling okay.'

The nurse glanced at the machine that was monitoring Sam's heart rate. 'Medically, I am happy to give you permission to go ahead with the interview, but if you don't feel up to it emotionally yet, which would be completely understandable after what you've been through, then I can send them away,' she looked at Sam expectantly, hands on her ample hips.

'I'm grateful for your concern, but I want to do all that I can to help the police on this. I feel like I've left it long enough already,' Sam added sheepishly.

The nurse nodded her understanding, 'Okay, well I'll give you a few minutes to freshen up, and I'll bring you something to eat. Then after that I'll escort them through.' She left the room, closing the door behind her.

When she returned a few minutes later, she was armed with a tray of food for Sam. 'Here you go love, I'm told it's awful, but it'll do you some good and tick one of those boxes I need to be able to discharge you.'

Sam prodded at a rubbery roast potato with her plastic fork. Jane wrinkled her nose as Sam lifted the potato and tore the thick skin that had formed on the gravy.

'Okay, you need to fill me in on everything while I eat this, to take my mind off the task.'

Jane told Sam how she had tried to report Sam missing. 'I spoke to this guy who shut me down. Course that turned out to be one of the bad guys. Anyway, I was pining a bit, so I listened to the voice-mail you left me on the night of your bout and I heard something that ended up proving you must have been near the murder that night. There wasn't much, but it was enough to get me taken more seriously.'

She continued, whilst Sam wrestled to chew through a piece of beef. 'Eventually, two raids were ordered, one to your abductor's address, and one to Higglesley Hall.'

Sam gave up and swallowed her beef half-chewed, 'Higglesley Hall?'

'That's where you were found, in the grounds.'

Sam saw Jane blush momentarily, before grabbing one of Sam's potatoes to nibble on. 'That distraction tactic will not work with your oldest friend,' she grinned, 'what are you not telling me about?'

'Okay, so there was this cute young officer who gave me a lift out to the Hall, you know, as a friendly face for when we recovered you. He asked me out actually, but I went full-SM and couldn't say "yes",' she looked down into her lap.

Sam was about to say something, this was huge news from her friend, but Jane carried on.

'So, I guess the bad cop got there first, not real-ising that the field team had also been sent to the same location, and they came in and found you soon after.' She pulled a face as she swallowed the tasteless, rubbery mush.

'And then you arrived, with the cute young officer?' Sam gave Jane a knowing smile.

'Trent, yes. Anyway,' Jane hurried on, 'when we got there, the tactical guys were rounding up anyone they could find. Sounded like you'd been keeping yourself busy, as they commented that the people they found generally seemed to be either restrained or unconscious,' she smiled slyly at Sam who felt her cheeks go a little red. 'Then some paramedics brought you past and I hopped in the ambulance with you. The rest, you know.'

'So there really was evidence then,' Sam mused. 'Phil, the main bad guy, said something about the police having some evidence I'd handed over, which really confused me because I'd been bluffing about that exact fact, so I figured he was just calling me on it or something!' Sam set aside her tray and settled down into the bed as Jane snatched the untouched bowl of jelly up.

There was a sudden knock on the door. It opened before Sam had a chance to respond, and a woman entered the room with a man following her. 'Good evening, Miss...' the woman glanced down at the paperwork she was carrying.

'Just Samantha is fine.'

'Samantha.'

She looked to her colleague, and then to Jane, 'Are you family?'

Jane swallowed her mouthful of jelly but remained silent.

'She's my best friend,' Sam responded on her behalf.

'I'm sorry, but you may only have family present for this interview if you wish, not friends.'

Jane's face broke into a small scowl.

'It's okay, Jane,' reassured Sam, 'I'm fine, really.'

Jane came to the bed where Sam was now sitting up on top of the covers, and gave her friend a hug before leaving the room, giving the police a hostile look as she went.

CHAPTER FORTY-SEVEN

The man waited for the door to close fully behind Jane before speaking. 'Samantha, I'm truly sorry to ask you to relive the events of the last couple of days, but we need to speak to you about your ordeal.'

He doesn't look sorry at all. 'Okay,' Sam let out a long, low sigh. 'Where to begin?' she asked out loud, but more to herself than for her stoic audience.

The man consulted his file, which was much thicker than the paperwork that the woman held.

He's the one running the show. She came in and spoke first to put me at ease. Well, bigger fool you, I'm past being manipulated.

'We've been told that there's a possibility that you may have witnessed the murder behind the Tin Whistle pub. Is that true?'

'Yes. I did.'

'Let's begin there then, shall we? Assuming that this was the first trouble that you encountered?'

'Yes, it all started with that.' *So many people died, just because I happened to step outside.*

'Okay, why don't you start by telling us the things you know for sure; what you were doing there, and what you saw.'

Sam explained how she'd gone outside to call Jane, and described the facts of David's murder at the hands of Phil. The pair exchanged short glances when she detailed David's knife to the chest and the slit throat, *that information must have been deliberately kept out of the media.* Sam knew that her spot-on description had just given her story the credence it needed for them to take everything that came afterwards seriously.

She told them she had thought that she'd managed to slip back into the pub unseen, 'What happened to Honey soon after proves otherwise though.'

'Don't worry about that, her murder is being looked into separately, as no leads have turned up any links as yet.'

'Don't worry about it?' Sam raged, 'no leads? I'm *giving* you a lead, it's *not* separate. They told me themselves that they were responsible, frequently. They used it as a warning to me, telling me her death was all my fault. I lent her my shirt you know, and they went after her thinking she was me. One of the men relished telling me that he was there when Phil slit her throat.' Another glance between the officers that Sam caught out of the corner of her eye, *another detail kept out of the media.*

The male officer gave his partner a look, and she reached forward to rest what was clearly supposed to be a reassuring hand on Sam's knee, but her reluctance was clear. She removed it quickly before Sam had a chance to do so with force. 'We'll make sure that the investigating officers are aware of the link, they'll come to speak to you separately.'

Something doesn't feel right here. A young woman has been murdered and I'm telling them exactly who by. Why don't they even seem to care?

'Please continue, Samantha, what did you do after you left the alley?'

Sam didn't feel much like co-operating; she didn't feel like there was any point. She'd humour them and get them out of here then find someone competent to speak to who would listen to her and get justice for Honey. 'We went home. I discovered that the men I'd seen in the alley the night before were Bradford Dixon and his bodyguard.' She stared awkwardly down at the sheets for a moment, then lifted her gaze defiantly. 'I tried to report what I'd seen but decided against it after seeing him with your police Superintendent.'

The police officers didn't flinch at the mention of Dixon's name, *as if they already knew.* 'Just to confirm, this is Bradford Dixon, the local businessman?'

Corrupt police or not, this is what I was afraid of. 'Yes, the one that was reported as having won a big defence contract in the wake of the recent terror attacks.' *The attacks!* Sam's brain scrambled for the right words to tell them precisely what she'd overheard in the alley, that David Steele being under suspicion was endangering Bradford, and Phil's full confession to her that the attacks wouldn't be the last.

She observed the woman tapping her pen on her notes, looking bored, and the man take out his phone and type out a quick message, pocketing it again once it was sent. 'Okay, well we'll come back to that identification.'

Sam narrowed her eyes. *Come back to it? But surely that's exactly what you're here to find out?* her mistrust of the pair grew.

'So you didn't report the crime you had witnessed, and then what happened next?'

Sam noted the dig and ignored it, 'Well, nothing happened at first, at least not to me. Then they took Honey, and when they realised that she wasn't me, that's when they came for me at the park.'

'And that was this man?' the policewoman held up a mugshot of Ethan.

'Yes, that's him. Do you have him?'

'We sent a team to pick him up at his house, but he wasn't there. The force is on the lookout for him. Can you please tell us about your experience at the park?'

Now sure that all of this was pointless, Sam detailed only briefly how she had been threatened by Ethan, being sure to mention Honey's noted absence at the event, and Ethan's reference to her. She told of how Phil had later invaded her home as she was waiting for Chris to arrive. Throughout, neither officer took notes.

'And then you and Christopher were taken to the Hall's chapel where you were found earlier this evening?'

'Yes, how is Chris? I only know that he was brought here in a bad way.'

'I'm afraid we don't have any information on his condition.'

There's a surprise. Reluctantly, Sam put Chris to the back of her mind and briefly summarised her experience at the chapel. When she was finished, the man thanked her. 'I know this is hard, but we do need to go back over some specifics.'

'We'll be as quick as we can,' smiled the woman, finally warming up in her awkward role.

'So, you are sure you recognised one of the men in the alley as Bradford Dixon.'

'One hundred percent,' answered Sam, frustrated. 'The other man from the alley, Phil, is usually with him at public appearances, you can check footage. Also, David called him "Brad" when he was begging just before he was stabbed in the chest.' She delivered the last line straight-faced and matter-of-fact, a show of conviction to her story and a reminder to her audience of the horror that she had borne witness to.

'We get that you are tired and that this is hard,' he glanced down at his papers, 'but, Miss Beaven, the problem is this; we have already spoken to Mr. Dixon. You see, Christopher came-to in the ambulance long enough to blurt out a couple of things, one being that Mr. Dixon was responsible for the death of David Steele, the other being that you saw it happen. Now, we know that you witnessed David Steele's death as you have details that were not made public, and we believe you completely about what you think you saw. Unfortunately, when we spoke to Mr. Dixon about his whereabouts at that time, he had an alibi.'

'I suppose you mean Janice,' Sam replied indignantly. 'He told someone on the phone that that's who he was with.'

There was that glance again. 'He made a call?'

'He took a call, yes.'

'I don't suppose you know who it may have been from.'

'No, sorry.'

'Well, we can look into Mr. Dixon's call records for that evening, and hopefully they will help clear up any confusion.'

The bastards still think I'm wrong. 'One way or another?'

'Yes, one way or another,' the man smiled.

His partner took over, 'You said there was a groundskeeper who was killed?'

'That's right.'

'We've not come across a body yet that I'm aware,' she looked up from her file and smiled at Sam, 'but we'll take another look, of course.'

'Of course,' Sam could feel the anger pushing her heart rate up and was pleased that the burly nurse had disconnected the machine that she was hooked up to that had been beeping for each pulse. 'Have you checked the chapel interior for blood?'

'Forensics have been over the scene, yes,' the man smiled.

'I think we have what we need for now,' the woman stated, closing her empty notebook with a satisfied clunk. The pair stood to leave.

Sam was incredulous that this appeared to be the end of their interest in her. *I guess they're not relishing the prospect of going after a pillar of the local community for conspiracy to commit murder.* She suddenly realised that the pair had told her absolutely nothing. 'Wait, what happened to Phil? Did you catch him?'

They both turned to look at her, blank expressions on their faces.

'The man that murdered David Steele and Sarah Honey, then held me captive for two days?' she clarified.

They still didn't quite seem to know how to answer, like Sam was asking them what was on the hospital menu for dinner that night.

'He was there when I blacked out near the chapel,' she told them, exasperated, 'it was him that threw me to the ground.'

'He must be in the wind at the moment, we didn't pick up anyone called Phil,' the woman advised.

'So, Bradford is still out there living his life, and

no one knows where Phil is either?'

'I'm sure this Phil will have left the area and won't be returning too soon, there'll be too much heat. Now, we may need to contact you again to clarify—'

'I suggest that you leave.' Sam felt heat in her face as the blood rushed to her head, fuelling her anger at the incompetence of the pair before her. 'Now. Until you show me who I can trust by bringing Dixon in for questioning, I'm not giving you a damn thing more.'

There was an awkward silence whilst the pair seemed to want to look anywhere but directly at Sam.

'You're not giving me a reason to give you anything. Now if there's nothing else, you could start with catching Phil,' she folded her arms across her chest with finality.

'We wish you a speedy recovery,' the man said to her. With that, they were gone.

CHAPTER FORTY-EIGHT

Sam watched the police officers' backs as they re-treated out of her room. She was thinking about Phil and the fact that he was still out there somewhere, maybe not even that far away.

Jane entered a few seconds later. 'They had a shocking bedside manner.'

Sam looked at Jane, confused, and wondering how much of their interview she had witnessed.

'It's one of the few perks of staying quiet so much, I hear a lot. That and the fact I was just outside, straining to hear.'

They never even bothered introducing themselves. I don't know their names, and they didn't leave cards or anything. A paranoia slowly began to reach out its conspiratorial fingers within Sam. 'What if they aren't even police, Jane?'

'Well, I recognise one of them from the station—'

'Doesn't mean they're not working for the other side still.'

'That's what I was going to say next; they were speaking to each other as they got into the lift, saying that it looked like you were "sticking strong to the

Dixon story", whatever that means.'

'It means I don't know who to trust with what I know.'

They were both quiet for a few moments before Jane broke the silence, 'What happens now then? I heard that Phil, the main guy, got away?'

'Yeah, they weren't terribly forthcoming with anything really, so I'm not too sure. Hopefully someone will be in touch to let me know soon. I can't believe that I just get discharged from here and go home and that's the end of it, there's dangerous people still out there, doing horrible things, that have a personal issue with me... and there's something else.'

Jane looked at Sam expectantly, detecting the subtle change of tone in her voice.

'The people that took me... were also responsible for the terrorist attacks in the city.'

Jane said nothing, but her wide eyes and general expression on her face spoke volumes.

'They alluded to it in the alley when I saw them kill that guy, David Steele. They took me because they thought I knew that already, thought I'd under-stood it from what I'd heard them say at the time, and kept me alive because they wanted to know who else I'd told. I worked it out eventually, and then Phil confessed to me too.'

Jane continued to stare, open-mouthed.

'And they're planning more.'

'You have to tell someone, Sammy!'

'I know, but who? I'll do it as soon as I get out of here, but to people I feel I can trust. I know that Bradford Dixon has the local police in his pocket, and not just the little guys, I even saw him having a heated conversation with the Superintendent when I went to report what I'd seen.'

Understanding filled Jane's features, '*That's* why you left the station so quickly! The Inspector I was with pulled up the CCTV from that day and we saw you leave soon after you'd arrived. You looked like you'd had some sort of shock.'

Sam allowed her clenched muscles to let go a little. 'So not all local police are as unhelpful as that pair that were just here?'

'No,' smiled Jane, 'if they were, I'd have left the station that day and never have found you!'

'Found me? That was you?'

'Yep,' Jane answered proudly. 'I saw Chris's phone —'

'Chris! I need to find out how he is.'

Jane sat down in the chair beside Sam's bed and took her hand. 'I asked about him when I was outside earlier. He's in surgery, and apparently it's quite complex. He's lost a lot of blood, and a couple of key arteries have been severed at what they tell me is an awkward angle. I think the key thing is that they are doing their best and will let you know when there's any news.'

Jane saw Sam's slightly panicked impulse reaction, 'Let's not dwell on it right now, okay? There's nothing we can do. For now, let's just chat, and be normal, and forget about it all for an hour or so, because you need some rest.'

'Okay,' Sam agreed reluctantly, then smirked at her friend, 'tell me all about Trent.'

Sam's blood results still hadn't come through, so she had been told that she would have to stay in the hospital overnight and would hopefully be discharged the next morning.

She was about to start flicking through a movie magazine that Jane had picked up for her in the hospital shop when she heard a soft tapping at the door.

'Come in,' she called.

A smartly-dressed man and woman entered Sam's room. They were trying to act casually, but there was a sort of urgency and excitement in the way that they exchanged looks with each other whilst the woman held the door for the man to follow her through.

Sam eyed them with a mix of suspicion and intrigue as the air in the room changed, like something big was about to happen. She got the distinct impression that this pair felt they needed to play their roles just right, as the woman slowly approached the chair where Sam was sitting.

'Samantha?'

'Just "Sam" is fine, can I help you?'

'We certainly hope so. I'm Helen, this is Mark,' she gestured to the man with her who raised a hand in a friendly wave. 'We're with the National Crime Agency, and I know that you've already been through this today, but we were really hoping that you would be prepared to speak once again about what you have witnessed.'

Sam gave the pair a cursory assessment. No pursed lips, no hard stares, no resentment. They had already been a lot friendlier than the local cops had been. She noted the male and female combo again, and idly wondered if this was a psychological ploy to make her feel more at ease or if women were finally being better represented in such positions. 'I want to help however I can, but the police that visited earlier didn't leave me feeling like there had been much point. What exactly is the angle on it for you guys? I got the impression from the locals that they were just dealing with the Steele murder.'

Mark was the one to reply. 'We've come to talk specifically about Bradford Dixon. We want to know everything you heard, particularly with regard to bombings, future plans or deals, anything you can tell us that might help prevent future attacks like the one a couple of weeks ago, and anything to help us get Dixon.'

'We took this part of the investigation over when Dixon's name came through to our system in relation to your case.' Helen explained. 'We've been watching him for a while.' She gestured to the visitor chairs, 'May we sit down?'

Sam nodded and the two NCA officers pulled the chairs round to face Sam in her big armchair so that they could all see each other comfortably.

Helen started. 'We have a confidential informant who was working closely with David Steele on the attacks, sadly not closely enough to be trusted with information that could have helped us to prevent them,' she added with what appeared to be sincere regret, 'although they did manage to prevent Pendleton Tower going up at the same time.'

Mark took over, 'We found out that Steele was grooming terrorists for hire, but although our CI was told by Steele that the cause was bogus, he hadn't managed to find the identity of whoever he was taking orders from.'

Sam thought back to what she had heard in the alley, 'David Steele told Bradford that no-one else knew about his involvement in David's "last endeavour". I guess he was referring to the attacks, wasn't he?'

'We think so. We suspected Dixon,' Helen had recovered from her earlier sadness, her voice business-like again, 'as he fit the profile from the snippets of info that we got; a well-respected businessman; enjoying success; giving back to the community; in touch with his roots. Also, air travel records showed that he had visited each of the other countries that had been hit within two months of their attacks.'

'Unfortunately, for all it's quite damning in terms of finger-pointing, legally it's only circumstantial. Just because he happened to visit those countries doesn't prove a thing, he'll claim it's pure coincidence, and we have nothing to say back to that.' Both agents looked directly at Sam then.

'Until now. Until me.'

CHAPTER FORTY-NINE

Sam had warmed to the pair of NCA officers, it certainly appeared that their intentions regarding Bradford Dixon answering for his crimes were genuine.

'No pressure, but you can break this case wide open for us, Sam,' Helen smiled a crooked smile at her that did little to hide her desperation for Sam's co-operation.

'Surely it's just the word of some random person against an absolute pillar of the community?'

'Not at all, it's far more than that,' Mark explained. 'It's clear that you really were in the alley that night, your detail of the murder scene is precise, and you are aware of details that weren't provided to the media; they're undeniably first-hand. Secondly, forensics have studied the voicemail you left on your friend Jane's phone, and confirmed that Steele's voice from our CI's wired recordings is a definite match, proving that you were close enough to David Steele on the night of his murder for his voice to be picked up by your phone. You're a very credible witness.'

There were a few seconds of silence, broken by

Helen, 'How about you tell us everything that you know, everything you heard Dixon's guys say, on the night of Steele's murder and over the last few days and we take it from there?'

Sam looked at the two interviewers, looking back at her expectantly. *These two have already offered up way more information than they've got from me, and they look just as keen to now sit back and listen. They're the real deal.* She took a sip of water, wondering how the hell she had managed to get mixed up in all of this.

'Why don't you start with telling us exactly what you saw and heard behind the Tin Whistle. I know you've already made a statement about this, but I'd like to hear you tell it personally.'

She obliged, leaving out no detail and attempting to recall as precisely as possible the wording used when speaking about the terrorist attacks. Recounting the story naturally led her on to all the other events, concluding with her face-off with Phil that had left her unconscious. 'I assume from what was said that the whole thing was kept pretty need-to-know within the ranks of Bradford's organisation, that it's probably only Phil that knows the real truth, about Brad being behind it all.' Sam looked to the two agents for more information, 'I hear he got away?'

'He did. But we also doubt he would have been much use to us, he's too loyal to Dixon.'

'It's our understanding that he owes some sort of personal debt to Dixon, so he's unlikely to drop him in anything.'

Sam's demeanour had changed when they had begun to discuss Phil, and it didn't go unnoticed by Helen. 'We can keep you safe, Sam. I'm not going to lie to you, you already have a target on your back, and Phil *is* out there still, but we can take care of you.'

'It just feels so… insurmountable. How can I convince anyone that Bradford "darling" Dixon could ever have done that to his own precious city?'

Mark leaned forwards, 'We have enough evidence to build a case for the murder, which will show the people a new side to their hometown hero. Dixon was confirmed to have taken a call within two minutes of your voicemail being left for Jane, and the caller has since been interviewed. Their statement agreed with your description of events in that Dixon told them that he was with Janice at the time. When you mentioned Janice to the police earlier, they ran a check on Dixon's mobile phone location history. It's not possible to get a precise historical location, but we can find out what cell his phone was in by what tower it was connected to… it wasn't Janice's.'

'And it was in the cell where the Tin Whistle is located. That's enough to possibly place him at the scene, and certainly discredits his alibi. When Janice was told this, she folded, asking for witness protection, so now he has no alibi.'

'Although lying about an alibi is suspicious, it's still not the proverbial smoking gun,' said Mark.

Helen directed her gaze straight into Sam's eyes. 'Your statement about the murder is enough for us to bring him in, plus what you've been privy to about the terrorist attack means we can probably hold him for as long as we need to to build a stronger case.'

Sam let out a long, slow breath as she attempted to process all that information, and more importantly, where she fit into it all, and how safe it was going to be. Helen clearly knew the look; 'We could possibly get him on the murder without your name being mentioned,' the crooked smile reappeared, and Sam knew what it was leading up to, *there's a "but" coming*... 'But, with your testimony, we just might be able to get him for the terrorist attacks too.'

Sam suddenly picked up on something that she kept hearing. 'You keep saying "attacks", plural?'

'Ours isn't the first country to suffer this,' Mark explained. 'There's been three other attacks that we believe were actually just a scare tactic to get governments to sign defence deals with Brad's businesses around the world. The first two were in the Middle East and Africa. Mass killings in those areas don't tend to make the news over here, sadly that's just the way of the world.'

'There's been rumblings of similar attacks to come in other European cities, but with your help we can work to prevent that from happening by getting him behind bars before he can fully set anything up.'

Sam let out a long breath as she mulled everything over. It was a lot to take in, and she couldn't work through just how it might affect her, but she couldn't sit back and do nothing. The NCA needed her to help them prevent further attacks. She felt that she trusted Helen and Mark to keep her safe, they seemed to have a genuine care for her well-being, as well as for their own agenda.

'What would you need from me?'

'We need you to testify in a private hearing, stating what you witnessed.' The two agents had visibly relaxed and Mark had taken the lead with explaining the procedures. 'This would instantly get us warrants to access more info on Dixon, travel records, bank accounts, etcetera. Following that, testify in court to his part in the murder of David Steele.'

'That would be a charge of conspiracy to commit

murder,' chimed in Helen.

'We would need to keep you in protective custody in the meantime. For all the murder is a local case, we will handle your security, as we need you, and a successful conviction, for our case and for the bigger picture.'

'When you say "in custody", you don't mean…'

'Not in a cell, no,' smiled Mark, anticipating Sam's question from the worried look on her face. 'We would take you to a safe house, and you wouldn't be able to tell anyone the location.'

'Only us and a few other trusted officers that would be assigned as your protection detail would know where you are.'

Sam looked sheepishly down at her fingernails as she fiddled with her hospital wristband. 'No offence, but Phil said they owned the police.'

'That's why we want to oversee your protection directly, that takes it out of the hands of the locals who may have been best buddies with Dixon at school.'

Aside from the chance to put all of this behind her, it wasn't the most appealing offer she'd ever had. 'But if Bradford goes to jail, won't people come after me, you know, as revenge or something?'

'I don't have a good answer to that, Sam,' Mark replied candidly.

CHAPTER FIFTY

Helen saw the worried look on Sam's face, 'We will obviously attempt to track down Phil and any other accomplices who may have been involved. We will do everything we can to keep you safe. In all honesty, you'll be better off with us anyway whilst Phil is out there, at least whilst the current crimes are all so fresh.

'I'll draw up the paperwork so we're ready to move as soon as you are,' Helen said. 'If you would like to send your friend, Jane, to your house to get some of your things and bring them here for you for when you leave, we can make sure that she has an escort.' She took Sam's phone from the top of her bedside unit and held it out to her.

'I suppose I'd better call work and let them know I won't be around for a while too.'

'We can do that for you,' said Helen, getting her pen ready, 'where do you work?'

'Besides the Tin Whistle, also at a care home near where I live, Oakwood Residences.'

Helen began writing the name down and then suddenly paused. 'Were you aware that Phil has a relative who is a resident there?'

Sam's eyes widened with shock. 'No! Who?'

'An uncle, Alf something.'

'Alf,' Sam repeated, staring into space and picturing all the games of chess they'd had together. 'That must be how they tracked me down at home. I'd been wondering about that. Phil told me that a co-worker from the pub had led them to me, but he didn't know where I lived. He must have told them that I worked at Oakwood.'

'So, they know where you live. But you have us now,' Helen flashed her a reassuring smile. 'If you'll excuse me, I must go, I need to make arrangements for your stay with us.'

'Helen? There's one more thing. The police that visited earlier said that forensics had been over the chapel. Did they find evidence of other people at all?'

The woman looked at her with curiosity, 'Forensics have been over the scene, yes. They only catalogued the blood found as a result of injuries sustained by yourself, Chris, and your abductors. What are you thinking, exactly?'

Sam fiddled with a loose thread on her hospital gown. 'They said that they had been using the site for interrogations for years. Phil made a comment about the blood soaking into the wood, even when they tried to clean it up, and also about burying bodies in the graveyard. He might have just been trying to get inside my head,' she looked into Helen's face, seeing genuine sympathy there, 'but maybe you could look for DNA matches there for missing people or something? At least put some families straight on the disappearances of their loved ones... maybe,' she trailed off.

Helen approached her and put out her hand for Sam to shake. 'We will, Samantha,' she promised, then she left the room to make arrangements.

Mark took up a position outside of her hospital room door, tasking himself with her protection until someone arrived to escort her onwards, as well as giving her some privacy whilst she filled in Jane and rattled off a list of what to pack.

There was a knock at the door of Sam's temporary bedroom, followed by Jane's voice, 'Sammy, are you decent? I've brought pizza!'

Sam threw down the book that she had been reading and bounded over to open the door for her best friend. An armed police officer stood next to Jane with a takeaway pizza box. 'I have duly checked the food for contraband, and I deem it safe for our little princess.' He winked at her and turned to retreat back downstairs.

Sam opened the pizza box and smiled, shaking her head as she discovered a slice missing. 'Thanks Charlie, you do keep me safe!' she shouted after him and he muttered a "no worries" over his shoulder.

She turned her attention to her friend. 'Oh my gosh I've missed you!' she flung her arms around Jane.

'It's only been just over a week,' Jane laughed.

'But you try living in a safe house for that time. I thought it would be quite cool and exciting, but after the tenth hour in a row of watching TV episodes back-to-back and reading my fourth novel, it's all gotten a bit old and boring.'

'Your company seems nice though, the guy that escorted me up especially, he's really friendly.'

'Charlie? Yeah, he's a sweetheart. They all are really, they're fantastic, but I still only want to spend so many hours a day with them, you know. Anyway, thanks so much for coming to visit, I know it's a faff having to have the escort here and all that, but I really appreciate it.'

'No worries. It did take three times longer to get here than I think it should have, with all the manoeuvres my driver was pulling off to try to ensure that we didn't have anyone following us. But I guess that's just to be expected when your best friend is living in a safe house pending trial.'

'It's not a trial as such, just a more formal procedure than me just giving a written statement.'

'Whatever, it's still brave.'

Sam looked at her friend, 'What else am I gonna do, Jane? The man that took me is still out there, and he's going to be coming for me one way or another. I may as well try to do some good whilst I wait.'

Jane opened her mouth to respond, then closed it again. 'Let's forget all that and eat.'

They both tucked in to the pizza, Sam wrapping the gooey cheese around her fingers and starting to feel like normal again, eating takeaway with her best friend. 'So, have you got anything to tell me? What's going on in the outside world? They prefer for me not to watch the news in case I'm influenced by anything before I testify.'

'Nothing much going on in the wider world really, but I do have some news for you on a more personal level.'

'Oh yeah?' Sam sat to attention.

'I've applied for uni, down South.'

'Jane, that's fantastic! What made you decide to go for it?'

'Well, I've been to a couple of roller derby practices this last week, and—'

'Hang on… what?'

'Yeah, I know!' she laughed. 'I've found myself really opening up, and I'm okay talking to the girls for some reason, maybe something to do with them all being relative strangers to me, and they just don't put any pressure on, I don't know. Anyway, the experience of that made me think that maybe I could handle university, in another town, where there's no expectations from people, and speaking to them feels less… monumental. If I just take it one step at a time… you know?' She fiddled with a piece of ham that was attempting to slide off her slice of pizza in a waterfall of cheese. 'And I confess that after your recent ordeal, there may also have been an element of "life's too short" in my decision.'

'That's rather fair enough really. How is the skating going then?'

'Really well, Belle says I have a natural talent for it, so I guess we'll see where that takes me.'

'What are your chances of getting in? To uni, I mean.'

'Pretty good actually,' Jane replied through a mouthful of tomatoey dough. 'I have a family friend who is a teacher that deals with the university admissions within their school. The word from her is that apparently my A-level results, A-A-B, should get me in to most places with an unconditional offer before this year's A-level results are even released.

'I mean, it's just applying for now,' she took another bite of pizza, 'I don't have to actually attend if I change my mind. Baby steps, right?'

CHAPTER FIFTY-ONE

The women chatted some more as they ate, Jane also telling Sam that she had been out with Trent a couple of times.

After a short period of silence, Sam brought up something that had been bothering her. 'You remember Travis, the bartender I worked with at the pub?'

Jane nodded, 'The one that pointed the bad guys in your direction? How could I forget?'

Sam looked uncomfortable. 'I heard from the officers today that his death's been ruled as the product of an overdose. He suffocated, but apparently it's quite normal for the body to basically forget to breath when you've taken cocaine with alcohol.'

'So?' Jane licked her fingers.

'So I know he was killed on Phil's orders, but there's absolutely no evidence to back me up.'

'Okay, well I guess the bad guys just get away with this one, heaven knows, he deserved whatever he got.'

'He was a friend, and I want to go to his funeral, but I'm not allowed out at all for any reason.'

'You want to go to his funeral?' Jane said,

shocked.

'Jane, he *died* because of me.'

'No, Sammy. *You* nearly died because of *him*. You owe him nothing.'

'If it wasn't him, they'd have found another way. They were relentless.' Sam looked down, Phil's leering face appearing vividly in her mind.

Jane spoke more softly then, seeing the pain in her friend's expression. 'Stay here, Sammy. Stay safe.'

They spent the rest of Jane's visit discussing university life, with Jane telling Sam about all of the different societies that she was considering joining. She also told her that the women at Stormy City had all been asking after her, and that they were considering some sort of special drill at practice to mark her return. 'Thora suggested dodgeball on skates, but I'm not sure it was a very popular choice,' she laughed, and Sam chuckled too at the image now in her head. Jane checked her watch, 'I'm sorry, Sammy, I have to go. I have a date with Trent.'

'Don't you be sorry about that! Go. Have a great time.'

Soon after Jane had left the safe house, Jim, one of the police officers who was staying there, called upstairs to Sam. 'I've got a call for you, Sam.'

She went down to get the phone from him, and caught a glimpse of Charlie, slouched down on the sofa, remote control in hand, flicking through the TV channels.

'It's your mum,' Jim explained holding out his mobile phone, 'the switchboard put her through to my phone.'

Sam took the phone and held it up to her ear as she went back up the stairs. 'Mum?'

'Hi, sweetie! Oh my gosh it's so good to hear your

voice. You sound okay, are you okay? How are you doing?'

Sam smiled at the familiar voice. The barrage of words was very much typical of Sam's mother, but her tone and delivery were slightly more panicked than was usual. 'Hi, Mum. Are you home now? They told me you were cutting your cruise short and flying back at the next stop. I felt bad; you didn't have to do that.'

'Like hell we didn't. Our only child gets abducted by industrial terrorists, who plan to torture her for information then kill her; and you think we wouldn't come back?'

'Well, when you put it that dramatically,' Sam chuckled, 'but I'm okay, I'm safe now, I'm even under armed protection.'

'Oh, excellent,' her father chimed in, the phone obviously on loudspeaker his end, 'we'll just go back and re-join the cruise then, after all, I think they still have our luggage. See you in a month.'

'Okay, point taken. Have they said when I can see you?' Sam asked eagerly.

'Not until after the trial or hearing or whatever it is. But we've been told that's only in a couple of days?'

'Yeah, Thursday. I guess that makes sense, they're only trying to keep me safe. After all, it would be a bit rubbish if after all of this, someone followed you here or something.'

'Quite. Utterly rubbish, but extremely sensible. Speaking of which, or the opposite in fact, what's this I hear about you having pink hair now?'

Sam chatted casually with her parents for the next twenty minutes, discussing their trip and plans to redecorate areas of the house when they returned. For the first time in weeks, Sam forgot all about what she'd been through, and everything felt normal and right with the world.

Once they had all said their goodbyes and Sam had promised to contact them as soon as she was allowed to see them, she left the room to return Jim's phone. On the way past the dresser she grabbed the pizza box which contained a single slice that she and Jane had left for Charlie.

She bounded down the stairs, invigorated by the contact she'd had with some familiar people, and her first with the outside world in well over a week. As she descended, she caught the tail-end of a conversation about the vintage wallpaper. 'Surely you hate it too?'

'Look, the boss likes it. If you look in from outside, it looks like a little old lady's house, it's nondescript.'

'The boss likes it cos she's bloody old!'

The two police officers were both laughing about Jim's comment when Sam entered the lounge area of the open plan ground floor. She saw Charlie hurriedly reach for the remote control to change the TV channel at her appearance. A program was on talking about how Dixon Defences had announced 500 new jobs in the city to help support the demand for its new "CONNECTED:" service. Bradford's stupid face was suddenly replaced by that of Harvey "Two-Face" Dent, the Batman villain, and Sam couldn't help but smirk to herself at the irony.

She tossed the phone to Jim, who was slouched in an armchair looking like he was settling in to nod off. 'Cheers,' he mumbled, somehow still having the wits about him to catch it.

'It could do with a charge now,' Sam warned him.

'Honestly, never lend your phone to a teenager,' he jested.

'Teenager? I keep telling you, I'm twenty-three.'

'Yep, same thing.'

Shaking her head and smiling at the grumpy policeman, she held the pizza box out to Charlie, who had settled on watching a crime drama, of all things.

'You absolute star,' he exclaimed, opening the box, 'marry me.'

'Come on, Charlie, we've already discussed how your wife would feel about that,' she retorted.

'Relieved, I suspect,' piped up Jim, raising himself out of the armchair and stretching. He plugged his phone in to charge at a socket next to the stairs, whilst Sam got herself a glass of water from the kitchenette.

'I'll pretend I didn't hear that. Are you turning in now, love?' Charlie asked over his shoulder.

'Yeah, all that teenage gossiping has worn me out.'

Jim smiled at her as he crossed the room back towards the window.

'Can I get you guys a beer before I go up?' Sam headed towards the stairs.

'You tease, we're on duty!'

'Which is more than I can say for some people,' Jim chipped in from behind the curtain where he had been checking on the unmarked police car parked outside. 'Looks like Lee's coming to take a leak again, you need to stop offering him so many bloody coffees, Charlie.'

'Hey, we've all been there. It's tough work staying awake on the night shift in a parked car. The very least I can do is get him coffee.'

Seconds later there was a knock at the door and Jim went to answer it.

'Alright, Lee?' Jim asked as he pulled the door open. 'You know—' he didn't get to finish the comment before a wall-shaking bang resounded throughout the building, and he was knocked off his feet by the door being catapulted open into him.

CHAPTER FIFTY-TWO

Smoke grenades were hurled into the house through the wide-open door, instantly clouding the entrance area and rendering both the attackers, and Jim in his position on the floor, invisible. Sam heard a gunshot and saw a flash light up the smoke. The sound of a body hitting the floor reached her, followed by another, more muted shot.

Sam looked at Charlie, who had leapt off the sofa and was standing to her side, slightly closer to the action at the front door than she was. His gun was drawn and aimed at the fog advancing towards them. 'I can't risk hitting Jim,' he muttered, more to himself than to the paralysed Sam.

They stood there, frozen. A few seconds passed before a silhouette could be seen emerging from the cloud. He was about Jim's build. Sam wasn't familiar with the policeman's gait to assess the figure on that, but the gas mask that slowly took form on his face suggested that whoever it was, it was foe.

Too late, Charlie realised the same thing, but the incoming bullet had already entered his shoulder. He fell down backwards onto the floor, hitting his head on the skirting board as he landed.

Sam didn't hesitate. She grabbed Charlie's gun from where it had dropped to the floor, and yanked Jim's phone loose from its charger. Scrambling up the stairs, she heard a scuffle behind her, followed by another muted gun shot.

Using the time wisely to help her get ahead, she didn't pause to look back or wonder what was happening below her. Survival was what mattered most now. Nothing else.

Hitting light switches off as she passed them, Sam turned the corridor around her into a black hole before running into her room. She looked around frantically for a place to hide. She'd remembered something she'd once seen or heard about having an elevated position over your enemy being an advantage. Settling for the dresser situated behind the door, she clambered up on top of it, Jim's phone still in one hand, Charlie's gun in the other.

Attempting to calm herself in her hiding spot, she breathed slowly and deeply, waiting. Slowly, and with a hand that barely shook, she reached up over the top of the bedroom door which was slightly ajar and aimed the gun down towards the doorway. With the other hand she woke Jim's phone and began to call emergency services with it.

She was distracted from speaking to the operator who answered her call as she caught a glimpse of one of the intruders as he cautiously entered a room across the corridor. He had taken the gas mask off, so the smoke was obviously only intended as a distraction for their entry into the house rather than a way of forcing anyone out. *Perhaps none of us are supposed to make it out.*

Sam's enforced calm demeanour faltered as the

man left the room opposite, turning so that his face came into view.

'Come out, come out, wherever you are,' Phil chanted. 'You know I'll find you, Miss Kiss. You could just save me the time, I'm a very busy man, you know.' He stepped away from the other room. 'You know the boss has some really big plans that you are going to royally fuck up if we let you carry on with this ridiculous game you're playing.'

Who said anything about a game? Sam thought of Honey, and a tear formed. She thought of Travis, of the tattooed groundskeeper, and the twenty-seven other people whose DNA had been gathered from within the chapel floorboards by forensics teams. She took a deep breath, and she thought of Chris.

Phil's head appeared in the doorway beneath her. Sam tightened her grip on the gun. Silent, steady, patient, she waited for him to fully come into view, not wanting to get anything wrong.

'Uncle Alf always said you gave in easily, letting him beat you at chess. Where's the challenge for an old man in that?' he said as he entered the room. He made his way quietly and deliberately over to the bed and crouched to check beneath it. Exhaling slowly, Sam began to squeeze the gun's trigger whilst Phil was bent low over the bedroom carpet. She did it gently at first, ensuring as accurate an aim as she could, and then gradually applying more pressure.

Jim's mobile phone bleeped a loud and urgent "low battery" alert, milliseconds before the bullet intended for the centre of Phil's back exited Charlie's gun. Phil whipped his head around at the sound of the phone and instinctively hit the ground and rolled to one side, the bullet skimming the top of his ear. Looking to the source of the sound he recognised that it was Sam that had shot at him.

He did his best to regain some form of composure, and to stand up and confront her, one hand pressed firmly against his ear and blood oozing out from between his fingers, snaking its way down the contours of his forearm.

'Hi asshole, you found me.'

With his good hand, Phil pulled his gun up to point at Sam. He was too slow. She was already pulling the trigger three more times, flying metal penetrating straight into his head.

It's been long enough now, Sam told herself as she stared at the lifeless body of her one-time tormentor. *He's not going to be getting back up like in the movies.* A small amount of blood had pooled on the floor beneath Phil's head, and Sam had seen enough episodes of CSI to know that head wounds should normally bleed a lot, but that dead bodies don't tend to bleed at all. Phil was gone for good.

She was sitting atop the dresser still, her legs dangling down in front of the drawers. Charlie's gun swung loosely from her finger, still accessible if it was needed. She looked down at the shiny metal object and suddenly remembered its owner.

Charlie was lying where she had seen him hit the ground, the rise and fall of his chest told her that he was still alive. Jim lay on the floor of the kitchenette, two large, burgundy stains visible on his sweatshirt. His chest was not moving. The same went for an intruder that lay near the front door, his gas mask still on. *He and Jim must have shot at each other in the fog, that's the first two shots that I heard.* She looked again forlornly at Charlie, splayed out on the ground. *And you must have taken the third shot, the one that bought me time to run upstairs*. Shaking off her grief, Sam managed to tilt Charlie up enough to see that there was no exit wound on his back. She ran to the kitchenette, doing her best not to trip over the dead intruder, and grabbed a tea towel. Immediately returning to Charlie she applied pressure to the wound on his front, as the welcome sound of sirens approached.

'Armed police! Drop your weapons and come out slowly with your hands in the air!'

'It's clear,' Sam yelled back, 'they're all dead, but I need a medic for an officer here who's been shot. Please hurry.'

Armed police entered the door in formation, fanning out around the room. Clocking Sam, two of them broke off to attend to her and Charlie, whilst the others moved from room to room and shouts of 'Clear!' came loud and strong in different voices.

'The uniformed officer parked outside, Lee?' Sam questioned the rescuer nearest to her.

'He's dead, I'm afraid.'

Sam's head fell onto her chest at the news.

'Single shot, instant,' the man assured her.

'It doesn't make it any better.'

'No. No, I don't imagine it does. Let's get a stretcher in here now,' he barked into his radio, 'this man is breathing, and we need to stabilise him.'

Sam stepped back to let the new arrivals do their job, watching dumbly as Charlie was wheeled out, still unconscious.

She was still there hours later when forensics had been and gone. The dead intruder's gas mask had been removed and Sam was asked if she could identify the young man whose vacant eyes lay beneath it, but she didn't recognise him, *just another in Bradford and Phil's long line of thugs for hire.*

Hours of repeating the evenings events, in detail, through the night into the dawn had exhausted her, but she managed to stand and move across the living area when Phil's body was brought down the stairs lying on a stretcher.

'I know this is a strange ask, but can I just have a moment please?' she asked the people that were removing the intruder.

'It's actually not that unusual. Bag open or closed?'

'Open, please,' Sam replied, unflinching at the morbid question.

The man undid the thick plastic, exposing Phil's bloodied face, parts of his mangled ear hanging on in desperation. He stepped back, but remained close by, as Sam stepped up to the body.

'You said you'd find me. But I don't think you had quite accounted for what you had helped me to become. You've helped me find my aggression, and now that I know it's there, I will use it, wisely. It's the only thing I will ever be thankful to you for. As for everything else… fuck you.'

CHAPTER FIFTY-THREE

Sam looked around uneasily as she disembarked the bus, studying the man on the bench nearby as he read his newspaper, and the youth leaning against a lamp-post at the street corner breathing in the vapour from an e-cigarette. She suspected that this paranoid habit would be with her for life now, or at least as long as the whereabouts of Bradford Dixon and his cronies were still unknown. The city's "CONNECTED:" installation had conveniently failed to track them down, despite months of effort. It did scare her, on a daily basis, but Sam was done with being made a victim and so was refusing to live her life in hiding.

Her phone dinged; it was a message from Jane. "See you soon, I know you're gonna do great today, so don't sweat it! Xxx". Feeling no less nervous, she crossed the road and headed towards the entrance to the sprawling leisure centre. There was another youth, this one in a leather jacket, smoking, standing just outside the entrance doors - staring at her.

He looked away when she made eye contact. Sam's heart rate picked up as she continued on her approach to the doors, altering her trajectory slightly to try and put a decent amount of space between herself and the youth. He glanced up at her again then reached into his jacket. Sam froze.

He pulled out a mobile phone, gave her a strange look as she stood rigid, staring, then pressed the screen a few times before holding the phone up to his ear.

Sam felt ridiculous. She hurried away into the building as the youth began speaking in a foreign language, *probably about the crazy weirdo he just saw outside.*

She distracted herself by bringing her thoughts back to what lay ahead; *This is it, I've made the roster for a game, and now I have to deliver.* She let out a long sigh and then busied herself with checking for the third time that her mouthguard was in her kit bag.

It was the biggest turnout that Stormy City had ever had at one of their home games. In fact, it was the biggest turnout that Sam had ever seen at a roller derby game in general. Local interest in the sport had increased dramatically following its mentions in the news reports on Honey's death.

'Sam!' an excited Cazz came running over to her. 'First game! Are you excited? Nervous?'

'All of the above.'

'You'll be fine, you've been rostered for a reason,' Cazz reassured her.

'Thanks, Cazz.' Sam replied, meaning it.

'Good luck!' Cazz returned to her position behind Stormy City's merchandise stand where Nikki's wife was attempting to lay out the T-shirts in order of size one-handed, rocking their two-month-old baby in her other arm.

Sam caught sight of some of the skaters from the

opposing team, the Coastal Rollers, and gave them a friendly wave. With the exception of a couple of stony-faced women, those that saw her returned the gesture. The two leagues had scrimmaged against each other a few months prior as a way of introducing Jane to the league that she would be joining when she went to university, so most of them were now familiar faces.

She spotted Belle stashing some bottles of water at one of the bench areas and went over to her. 'This is our side then?'

'It is indeed. You feeling ready?'

'Ready as I'll ever be.'

'You'll be fine, you've trained hard and worked tirelessly on what you knew your weaknesses were.' She straightened up and checked her watch. 'Anyway, you'd best kit up, warm-up is in twenty minutes.'

Sam kitted up with the rest of the team. Her nerves continued to come and go in small waves, calming momentarily as she watched Belle drawing Sam's player number over the scar that Lacey's blade had left on her upper arm. The familiar sounds of velcro fastenings and hockey tape being unreeled put Sam at ease momentarily.

She pulled a stick of lip balm out of her bag and applied it liberally. The fruity scent of artificial watermelon flavour filled her nostrils, reminding her of her favourite chewy sweets to have at the cinema. For a moment she was transported away from the excitement and anticipation around her, remembering when she and Honey had gone to watch a twelve-hour marathon of the film adaptations of a series of young adult novels.

The urgent sound of a hockey-stop near her

brought her back to the present. 'Okay, lads,' Belle's voice boomed over the cacophony of sounds around them. 'Get your asses on-track now for a quick individual warm-up. I'll be calling you in two minutes for our team warm-up, so go out and remind yourself of what this floor feels like to skate on.' She got on-track herself and repeatedly practiced sprinting forwards and stopping, before sprinting forwards again with urgency.

Sam took a hearty swig of her drink before getting to her feet and joining her coach on-track.

Her's nerves disappeared completely during the team's skate-out, she was too full of pride to worry about anything as she heard the announcer call her name and she waved at the audience as she did a lap of the track. As she returned to her team's bench, Sam looked over at the Coastal Rollers' bench area and saw Jane waving enthusiastically at someone in the audience. Following her line of sight, Sam spotted a young man that she didn't recognise wearing a Coastal Rollers shirt. He was seated with a large group of Coastal supporters and waving back with a smile on his face.

Another man waving frantically in the audience caught her eye. *Charlie! I didn't actually believe him when he said he was going to come and watch.* Sam waved back cheerfully, pleased to see that he was no longer wearing the sling that he had had on the last time that they had met for lunch.

Just then, she was brought back to herself by someone affectionately touching her arm. 'Hey babe, how are you feeling?'

She turned to the source of the voice and was filled with warmth and reassurance. Chris stood smiling at her and she was hit again by how much she loved him, just like she had been the first time that she had seen him after his surgery when she had been completely overwhelmed, realising just how much he meant to her.

'I just wanted to wish you luck on your debut. Managed to get some of the boys to come along too,' he gestured to a group of lads sitting on the trackside mats that Sam recognised as being Chris's teammates from football.

She grinned at him appreciatively. 'Thanks for supporting the game, and for officiating,' she gestured to the "NSO" printed on the chest of his shirt.

'I'm not just supporting the game, although I do have an appreciation for it now,' he leaned in toward her, 'I'm supporting *you*. Not that you need it, you're officially the strongest person I know.'

She beamed, 'I'll take that.'

He viewed her lovingly for a moment, 'Skate like lightning… Thunder Kiss,' he kissed her. 'Right, I have to go and be impartial now,' he turned to go as Sam directed her attention towards the track where the Coastal Rollers had started their skate-out.

'Oh, and Samantha,' Chris's eyes met hers as she looked back over her shoulder. They were steeped with sincerity.

She stared back, waiting.

'If any of them hurt you too badly…'

Damn you, Chris. There you go again. Why did you have to go and ruin a perfect moment by bringing back the protective streak. Have you learnt nothing about me?

His serious tone wavered. '…Hurt 'em back for me.'

It took Sam as long to register Chris's words as it did for the seriousness in his facial expression to drop, replaced instantaneously with a huge grin before he turned and began a slow jog away.

Sam spotted Jane stepping out onto the track with the Coastal Rollers for their skate-out. Jane hadn't selected a skate name when Sam last spoke to her, so Sam listened intently as the announcer read out each of the opposing team's players' names and numbers in turn, craning to see the back of her friend's orange shirt as she passed. Unfortunately the players were doing their laps in a tight formation and Sam couldn't see yet.

When it was Jane's turn her tall figure popped up from within the tight, low pack of skaters, and her shirt finally came into view. Sam squealed with delight as the announcer introduced her friend who was now owning her condition; 'Making her debut here today with the Coastal Rollers, it's Speechless!'

When the Rollers finished their skate-out Jane came over to Stormy City's bench rather than her own and gently collided into a hug with Sam.

'Chris is really proud of you, before the game has even started!'

'You gleaned that from body language? You're getting better.'

'No, he told me earlier.'

'You two have been speaking?' Sam grinned, 'that's a big step.'

'Yeah, I mean we've hardly been meeting to chat over coffee, it's really been e-mail communication, but it's helped to start a relationship, and I managed a brief conversation when I saw him earlier. Admittedly he did most of the talking, but one step at a time, right?'

'You've been… e-mailing?'

'Oh yeah.'

'Er… what about.'
'Well *that*, would be telling.'

CHAPTER FIFTY-FOUR

Sam couldn't for the life of her think what her previously incommunicable friend and boyfriend might possibly have had to discuss. She spotted the guy in the Coastal Rollers top from earlier trying to get Jane's attention again. 'Your fan club appears to need you.'

'What?' Jane looked in the direction of Sam's gaze and saw the man waving. 'Oh, that's Dean,' she waved back at him.

'So, where's Trent?'

'Yeah… that didn't really work out.'

'Okay,' Sam laughed, 'well I guess you can introduce me to Dean at the afterparty then.'

'Yeah, he's a good one, he knows he has to help me sometimes, but doesn't speak for me automatically, you know? Trent was always doing that, I think because he met me during an SM flare-up, he always thought of me in that way.'

'I can see how that would happen.' Sam sighed. 'It sounds like we have a lot to catch up on.'

'Yeah, I'm sorry I've not been in touch more, uni has kept me busy, and I have a pretty hectic social life too.'

'I doubt that,' muttered River from the bench.

'Seems that some things still don't change though,' Jane commented quietly.

'Spot-on there,' Sam threw a glare at River who was obliviously inspecting her nails.

'But yeah, I feel more confident in myself now, and the mutism hasn't been much of an issue at uni actually, new town, new people and all that. A bit of a fresh start and no expectations from people, I guess. This morning has been great, with so many familiar faces, and knowing people on both teams, I feel pretty relaxed actually! Which is new,' she added, smiling. 'I still doubt I'll be the main communicator on-track, it's one of the reasons I prefer jamming.'

'Jane, people love you for who you are, not whether or not you speak up on-track… this *is* who you are.'

Jane smiled sheepishly.

'You jamming today?'

'I am indeed, but don't tell my team that I told you that!'

'You'd best get to your bench, looks like your coach wants to give you all a pep-talk. Good luck!'

'To you too.'

Sam huddled in with her own team who were just going over the tactics one last time. She glanced over her shoulder towards the crowd and saw her Mum and Dad who instantly started waving frantically when they saw that she was looking in their direction. Her mother raised a camera and began taking what would probably amount to an astronomical number of photos by the end of the game. "It's what parents are for", she would inevitably say.

Following a final chat with the other referees, the

head ref gestured to the announcer that all the pre-game procedures had been completed. The announcer then signalled for the music to be cut so that he could be heard clearly.

'Ladies, gentlemen, boys, girls, humans of all varieties! Lend me your ears! Thanks for coming down to support your nearest and dearest! Hands up if you have no idea what Roller Derby is? That's fine! Sit back, enjoy the action and watch the one with a star on their head for starters! We welcome and enjoy the opportunity to convert you, and convert you we will!'

A cheer went up from all the skaters and a good portion of the attentive audience, Sam's enthusiastic parents included.

'But before we begin, please give us a moment of your time. Last year, tragedy struck Stormy City. Honey Trap was an enormous part of the league, there aren't many of you here who haven't met her; on-track, intimidated by her fierce competitive nature; or off track, touched by her kindness. Like me, you were probably in awe of her ability to live life for the moment.

'For those who aren't aware, Honey Trap was taken from us, killed tragically in her prime. We've been reassured that Honey did not go quietly into the night. The fight and spirit that each and every one of us admired her for was evident to the bitter end.' He had known Honey well himself and faltered at the last few words, his voice breaking into squeaks.

After taking a moment to recover, he held his head back up and continued, 'Almost all of the Stormy City Team that stand here before you now came through intakes that were run by Honey, and it is testament to her patience, encouragement, and determination to help everyone see the best in themselves that they are on this roster today.

'As recognition of this, a bee has been appropriately incorporated into the logo for Stormy City in her memory so that she will always be a part of the league, and with the team on their travels.'

Another cheer and more clapping followed from the spectators as Sam absent-mindedly slid her fingers over the bee on her own chest.

When the noise had sufficiently subsided, the announcer raised a hand and spoke once more. 'Before we start today's games, I would like to invite you all to join me in observing a minute of silence to mark the passing of Honey, and to spend some time remembering her for the force of nature that she was, both on and off-track.'

He signalled the start of the silence to the head referee by lowering the microphone and clasping his hands together, head bowed. The referee did one long whistle blow, and then all seven referees took a knee to observe the silence.

Sam hung her head low, a series of images of a smiling Honey flashing through her head. Always smiling, always encouraging.

After a few seconds she lifted her head and looked up at the solemn crowd around her. *This isn't fitting for Honey; it doesn't represent her and her life at all.* Without really thinking, Sam suddenly began to awkwardly clap her wrist-guarded hands together in applause. The announcer's head snapped up in her direction and her teammates looked at her in confusion. She continued nevertheless and saw the sudden understanding in the announcer's expression as he placed the microphone gently on the floor. He nodded at her and then began clapping himself. It wasn't long before the whole hall was united, clapping and even cheering the minute away until the head ref blew his whistle sharply four times.

'For Honey everybody!' shouted the announcer. 'Game on!'

The crowd clapped one last time as he sprinted out from the inside of the track and over to where the P.A. system was set up. The music started up again, a rousing dance tune.

'You heard the man; for Honey, let's take this!' shouted the team captain, Jynx.

Sam realised then that Honey didn't just belong to her, but to everyone, and was determined to do her proud today.

The head ref blew his whistle.

'Quick!' Belle yelled, 'get the first line-up on-track.'

Sam stayed at her team's bench as five of her team-mates leapt away towards the jam line, marked out with black and yellow diagonally-striped tape on the ground. Sam knew that she was on the second line-up, so she had to stay ready.

The first whistle blew, and the two jammers began their individual fights through the pack. They both managed to get out of the pack on the opposite side of the oval to where Sam was sitting at the team bench. Only a few seconds separated them.

As the blockers in the pack reformed in preparation for the jammers' next approach, the audience behind them were suddenly visible to Sam. Then she saw him. Only fleetingly, as the man was busy moving between other audience members. Then he was gone, and she was no longer sure of herself.

Was that really Bradford Dixon? It didn't look exactly like him, but I've only ever seen him wearing a suit, I don't know what he'd look like in anything else. This man had on a knitted jumper and a baseball cap; she hadn't had time to take in anything more than that before he'd disappeared from view. She tried to shake the feeling off, *Bradford never does his own dirty work anyway, he's hardly likely to turn up here.*

The four whistles came that signified the end of the first jam and Jynx clapped her hand on the back of Sam's shoulder, 'we're up.'
Sam bounced to her feet and hustled onto the track as the previous line-up rolled red-faced past them towards the bench, exchanging the odd high five on the way.

It wasn't until she'd taken up her position behind the jam line, the other jammer just a foot to the side of her, that the nerves fully hit. The row of Coastal blockers directly in front of her, the music pumping out of the speakers at the end of the hall, the din of her friends and family in the crowd shouting her name, the announcer naming her and the opposition jammer, "Betty Badass". It all caused a sort of aural claustrophobia inside Sam's head. She took a deep breath in, held it, let it out slowly.

'Five seconds,' came the call from the jam timer. It acted as a sort of trigger for Sam. The din dropped away, and a sense of focus came over her. Her muscles tensed almost imperceptibly as she braced to pounce forwards. She held her breath. The whistle sounded.

She and Betty lunged forwards together. As Sam smashed into the seam where two blockers' shoulders met, she heard the announcer; '…and Betty slips straight through a gap in the Stormy wall made by her assisting blocker.'

Sam eyed the gap, but it closed as quickly as it had appeared. '…But no joy there for Thunder Kiss. She's hopping across the track to try another seam, and I think I see a shoulder in-between those ribs, wiggling hard.'

Sam pushed her toe-stops hard against the floor as she wiggled, and enough space opened up for her to slide a hip-bone in between the two blockers.

'No lead jammer as yet, with both teams efficiently holding back the jammers.'

The crowd were cheering on both teams, and Sam tried to absorb some of their energy. Using her hip, she hit hard into the thigh of one of the blockers that had her pinned. The blocker's knee gave way and she slid to the floor. '…And Thunder Kiss leaps over the Coastal blocker's legs…'

Sam moved to the inside of the track where there was a small gap to get past her own blockers who were keeping the frustrated Coastal jammer at bay. Jynx didn't flinch as Sam grabbed her around the waist to steady herself and slipped through between Jynx and the track boundary tape, pushing off her friend to help propel herself forwards around the track.

'…and she's away out of the pack!'

CHAPTER FIFTY-FIVE

With no more obstacles in front of her, Sam dug in the edges of her wheels and powered forwards, at the same time the welcome sound of two short whistle blasts came from her jam referee declaring her lead jammer and causing a huge cheer to rise up from her bench and the audience.

'The Coastal Rollers now switching tactics to play offence and trying to help their jammer get past that Stormy wall.'

'Make some holes!' on Betty's orders the visitors attempted to play offensively, hitting the home team's blockers to try to help get Betty past them and on her way to scoring some points.

A few short seconds later, Sam found herself already approaching the back of the pack of skaters, ready to lap them and buoyed by her success at fighting through the pack first out of the two jammers.

They had not been prepared for just how quickly Sam had come around again, and so not a single one was paying her any attention as she approached.

'Woah! Thunder Kiss *sails* past the whole pack! Four points, as easily as that Stormy City have evened the score.'

She skated on round the track, barely believing her luck. On her next approach, they were ready for her.

'Jammer coming!' cried one of the blockers.

It still wasn't enough.

Sam hopped from one foot to the other, making it impossible for the opposition to predict which direction she was going to take, and she easily glided past the two blockers who were trying to prevent her from scoring, despite them seeing her coming this time.

'Betty Badass is still stuck behind the Stormy City blockers. She's got to get this initial lap completed as soon as possible. There will be no points for Betty 'til that's done!'

Sam kept going. Each time she approached the pack, the visiting team's blockers seemed more flustered, and less prepared for her.

Finally, Betty broke free and began to follow Sam around the track. Sam's bench coach signalled to her to get through this one last scoring pass and then call the jam off before their opposition could score. She pushed on, ready to hit the orange blocker wall hard. With no jammer of their own in the pack to distract them this time, they were prepared for her. 'She's coming in hard. Brace! Hold it.'

Sam bounced off their wall and landed sprawled half on the track, and half off, over the inside boundary. Glancing backwards, Sam could see Betty approaching the pack. She could also hear her own coach screaming at her; 'Call it! Call it!'

Still on the floor, Sam tapped her hands on her hips to call off the jam. Breathing heavily, she peeled herself off the floor once the final whistles had sounded. The twenty-four-point jam that she had just secured would be great for team morale, though Sam still considered most of the points to be luck.

She ran her fingers gingerly across the friction burn she now had on her thigh where it had contacted the floor and winced. 'Nice rink rash,' Nikki admired as Sam returned to the bench, 'and nice work too, 24 to 4 now,' she gestured to the scoreboard.

A few jams later, Sam sat nervously at the bench, pulling at the loose edges of one of the stickers on her helmet.

'You've chipped your nail varnish, Sam. Give it a rest,' instructed River.

Sam examined her purple glittery nails, painted to match her team's uniform. River was right. Sam settled instead for pulling at the mesh of the fishnet tights that she was wearing as her silent tribute to Honey. Stormy City still held the lead now, but by a much smaller margin than before, with the Coastal Rollers having slowly closed the gap created by Sam's high-scoring performance.

River was jamming for the next line-up, a position that Sam knew she wasn't really comfortable in, but the team's bench coach believed in throwing in some unknown playing styles to keep the opposition on their toes, and this was River's turn.

She was fumbling her way through a pair of opposition blockers when Jane came to join her Coastal teammates holding River. Finding herself surrounded, River panicked and flung her shoulder up and back wildly, the whole of her upper body following through. She pulled off a beautiful can-opener onto Jane who was positioned behind her. Cantget, who was sitting on the bench next to Sam winced and involuntarily clutched her ribs. The sudden force into Jane's sternum took her off her feet and she fell hard to the floor straight onto her rear.

'Stopped block!' shouted some of the Coastal Rollers' supporters from the crowd, spotting River's illegal move. The pack referee nearest to River had noticed too and was already blowing his whistle. 'Purple, three, nine,' he called out, confirming her penalty.

River looked furious. She raised her hands, shrugging at the referee in an indignant, questioning gesture as she took herself off the track and headed to the penalty box. Sam watched the referee approach the box to speak to the penalty timer, the announcer following close behind. He raised his mic as the ref moved away from the penalty box and play continued. 'Clarification there from the referee that River Bruise will be serving a full minute in the penalty box; thirty seconds for a stopped block, and another thirty for insubordination; you can't give the refs attitude when they're just doing their job, that's what the allocated Official Reviews that each team have are for.'

'Okay, with our jammer in the box they're gonna pick up some extra points from us now,' Stormy's bench coach was explaining. 'We need to try and claw them back on the next jam. River is going to come back on-track angry, sloppy, and uncontrolled, and quite likely to land herself right back in the box. Sam, are you okay to jam this next one?'

'I am, but surely River will still be in the penalty box as a jammer when it starts, so we can't field a different jammer anyway?'

'True, but we can put you out there as pivot and get River to do a star pass when she's back on. Hang at the back of the pack, and then when she comes back on-track behind the pack, you'll be there, ready to take the jammer helmet cover from her unobstructed.'

'Ah, that makes sense,' Sam donned the striped pivot helmet cover and got to her feet as the four whistles signalling the end of the current jam were heard. As Sam passed the penalty box on her way to the jam line she saw River still visibly fuming. Their bench coach caught her attention, pointing to their own head and making a small gesture to indicate removing the jammer helmet cover. River nodded very slightly in no direction in particular, "message received".

Sam was nervous about receiving her first star pass, but she helped her other blockers to stop the Coastal jammer from getting past for the first twenty seconds or so of the jam. When River was standing with only a few seconds left to serve of her penalty, Sam did as her coach had suggested and dropped back.

Then it happened again.

She glanced in the direction of the crowd and her eyes met those of a clean-shaven youth. *He feels unbelievably familiar*, she stared for a few seconds. He didn't react to her obvious attention, as Sam tried to process what Ethan would look like if he didn't have his prominent goatee.

Sam's world was then literally turned onto its side.

CHAPTER FIFTY-SIX

Sam's lapse in concentration on the game had allowed an opposing blocker to connect hard with the side of her thigh, taking her legs out from beneath her.

'Ooofff! She'll be feeling that hit for days!' the announcer exclaimed, 'oh, and like she's been shot out of a cannon, River Bruise is out of the penalty box, no holding back! Giving it everything to catch the pack now.'

River removed her helmet cover only when she was almost on top of her teammates. Sam leapt back to her feet just in time for her jammer's approach, when she deftly slid the cover across into Sam's outstretched hand. Sam didn't bother to place the cover onto her head until she had skated past all of the Coastal Roller blockers, who were looking all around to try to locate a skater with a star on her helmet.

'Thunder Kiss is first out of the pack, but ineligible to be lead jammer after taking a star pass. After this initial pass, she can come around again and start scoring points.'

Fighting to get past the blockers on each pass Sam was working so hard that she could taste the sweat gathering on her upper lip. Stormy's blockers managed to hold the other jammer for almost the full two minutes before she made it out of the pack. After earning herself lead jammer status, she immediately called off the jam to stop Stormy City from getting any more points.

The score now stood at 65-72. Collectively, Sam and the other players on her line-up had closed the points gap that had opened up whilst River had been steaming away in the penalty box.

The jam over, Sam looked back to the audience, but she couldn't see the clean-shaven version of Ethan anymore. *It's game day nerves,* she told herself sternly. *Stop trying to turn this into something you can physically fight off.*

When the first half of the game ended, the Stormy City players all returned to their bench for a team talk on how things were going. Jynx commented on how closely matched the two teams were; '—we can genuinely win this one, but only if we keep our eye on the ball, well, the jammer,' she smiled at her own joke.

Sam was still breathing heavily, having just come off-track. The once freshly-laundered scent of elbow and knee pads had now been swallowed up by the more familiar smell of sweat-soaked derby pads.

The team's bench coach came over to Sam. 'You're doing great, but there's still room for more aggression from you. I look at you on-track and you skate how Honey did. We can't replace her in our lives, but on-track... you have her skills, you just need to find her confidence. You are holding something back out there, Sam. Find that trigger that you need, show me that inner strength and focus, like nothing fucking matters except you being where you want to be on the track.'

Sam nodded her understanding, unsure of what to say. Coach was right, they couldn't replace Honey, but Sam could honour her as best she could by taking control of her fears.

'Thora, you're bleeding,' Jynx pointed to her lip. 'Sort it out before we're on again.'

The second half started with a pile-up on the first whistle involving both jammers and at least half of the other skaters on the track. A couple of penalties were called immediately, but once the jam had concluded the referees called an Official Timeout to allow them to work out exactly what had occurred, and if anyone else needed to be penalised.

Belle took the opportunity to have a quick chat with the whole team. 'Play is starting to get increasingly penalty-heavy as we're all getting tired, them included,' she gestured to the other team bench. 'I don't want avoidable penalty calls thanks to flailing limbs, so let's reign it back in and leave those mistakes to the other team to make. We can't afford to risk continuing play like this, at 75-72 the scores are just too close…' she trailed off, suddenly looking a little alarmed as her gaze fixed itself between the heads of two of the skaters, staring off in the direction of the audience.

A couple of people followed her eyeline but didn't seem to see anything out of the ordinary. 'Belle, you still with us?' Cantget asked, 'what's up?'

This brought Belle back, 'Yeah, I'm fine… sorry,' she shook off whatever it was that had interrupted her. 'Everyone take a couple of deep breaths, let out the panic and chaos as you exhale, and bring that focus back to your game.'

Sam took a moment to close her eyes and attempt to centre herself, but it was futile amidst the slurping of sports drinks and swift blast of asthma inhalers that came from various directions around her.

She was on next as a blocker and rolled casually up to the jam line with the rest of her line-up, determined to continue to play clean, being one of the few players that day that had not yet paid a visit to the sin bin.

The officials were still conferring, so she relaxed her stance, realising that this timeout might take some time. A familiar voice came from behind her, 'Looking good out there today, Thunder Kiss.' She turned to see Jane, the star-adorned jammer cover on her helmet.

'Looking good yourself. I've noticed you directing your team on a couple of occasions, nice to see you showing that SM who's boss, Speechless.'

Sam saw her mother waving frantically at her again from the crowd and she gave her a thumbs up in return. Her eyes scanned past the audience to the main entrance where a desk had been set up to take spectator's entrance fees. There was a couple by the desk, the man was paying for tickets, and the woman was staring straight at Sam.

CHAPTER FIFTY-SEVEN

Sam didn't recognise either of the two people, and the woman soon averted her gaze, but she shivered anyway.

'Are you okay?' Jane asked quietly from behind her.

'Yeah, I just…' she sighed. 'I know it's stupid,' Sam turned to face her friend momentarily, 'but I keep thinking I've seen Bradford Dixon here, or one of his lackeys, and just now that couple over at the entrance desk,' she gestured with a nod of her head, 'something doesn't feel right about them either, they look out of place, and they're paying to come in having missed the entire first half? It just… dammit, it's probably just my brain's way of coping with game-day nerves. I'm seeing things.'

'Sammy, not all people who come to roller derby games are part of the community, a lot come to support friends and family in their first game,' she gestured in the direction of Sam's parents. 'They might have just got stuck in traffic, and although on the surface it might not be worth paying to get in just to watch one half of the game, maybe they have someone here that they don't want to let down, so they did it anyway.'

Sam glanced at the pair again, picking their way across the rows of seats that had been arranged across the length of the hall, getting as close to the track as they could without sitting on the front matting. Jane's points were valid, and they were trying to get good seats trackside so were probably a player's family. Sam relaxed a little as she got comfortable with the thought. 'So, stop being so paranoid?'

'Basically, yeah. That said, they are still out there, so if you really think you've seen them, then I believe you.'

'That's just it… I'm really not that sure.'

The sound of a whistle blew away her concerns as the referees wrapped up their conference in the centre and reassumed their positions trackside.

'Here we go then,' Jane took up her chosen position behind the jam line, a few feet back and close to the inside track boundary.

Sam smirked, turning to face Jane so that she could easily track her lateral movements. 'I make no apologies for anything that might be about to happen.'

'It's about bloody time,' jibed Jynx good-naturedly. She had her back to Jane and was next to Sam, their hands on each other's shoulders, each ready to guide the other or help brace against an impact if needs be. The whistle blew and Jane launched herself sideways and straight into the link between Jynx and the blocker on the other side of her, who was not fully ready for the impact. Jane passed through easily, reached out and swung off the hips of one of her own blockers and was subsequently declared lead jammer.

Sam was so proud of Jane as she heard her calling short orders to her Coastal teammates for offensive help as she came around to lap the pack. She had come a long way in the last year. They both had.

The end of the game was soon upon them. Both teams had given it their absolute all for the second half, and the scores were now even, each team with 134 points.

The next line-up rolled on-track to play what was highly likely to be the final jam of the game. Jynx addressed those left at the bench, Sam included. 'Okay, there's a minute-twenty left on the game clock, so this is bound to be the last jam. Let's cheer our hearts out for the girls out there.'

'We only need one point to win this,' exclaimed Thora.

'One point more than they get you mean, we need to stop them scoring too,' River responded negatively.

'Have faith, River,' smiled Sam, *I'm trying to*. She absent-mindedly scanned the crowd whilst waiting for the jam start whistle. No-one's presence jerked her back to reality this time. *Backs up the "it's all in my head" theory.*

The whistle blew and the skaters set off in a scrum of orange and purple; protective pads; and pushing and shouting. Cantget was jamming for the home side and somehow seemed to appear from underneath the mass of bodies. The players at the bench all cheered her as she accelerated around the bend whilst on the other team, Betty Badass was still fighting her way out of the pack. Betty managed to break free just a few seconds behind Cantget and set about chasing her down.

The Stormy blockers reacted by forcing their way

to the front of the pack, just as Cantget reached the back. She slipped through a seam between two ribcages and scored three points. Not concerning herself with the other orange shirt further ahead, she called off the jam before Betty could make use of her first scoring pass.

The jam ended three to nothing, giving Stormy City the lead overall, 137-134.

'That's it then?' queried Thora, 'there's less than thirty seconds left on the game clock, so that was the last jam. We've won!'

Sam whipped her head round to the score and timer board. Thora was right, there was only twenty-seven seconds left, the head ref must be about to blow the final whistle any second now.

'They'd be mad not to call a timeout though,' chimed in Jynx. 'Oh, there you go.'

Sam looked to the visitors' bench, where all the players were jumping up and down, either waving their arms to get the referees' attention or making a "T" shape with their hands.

'The Coastal Rollers are calling a timeout,' informed the announcer excitedly. 'Folks, you do not get this every day. Stormy City are now up by only three points after starting the last jam neck and neck with the Rollers. Normally, with less than thirty seconds left on the game clock, we would be finishing the game here at this score, but as there's time left on the game clock, however little, then if either team calls a timeout here for any reason, another jam will be played. This is about to get intense. Let's break it down, Strategy Challenge time!

'If Stormy City get lead jammer, they can stop the jam before either team score and keep their current three-point advantage. Buuuuuuuut! Our visiting team, the Coastal Rollers, need to get four points in this jam to win overall,' he held up four fingers on one hand. 'To do that, they need to make sure that Stormy City do not get lead! The Rollers then also need to complete a full, four-point scoring pass through the pack before the jam ends, and you can be sure that Stormy are not going to want to let them! I cannot wait to see how this is going to play out!' he finished sincerely. 'It's all down to which jammer gets lead.'

CHAPTER FIFTY-EIGHT

Matt, the Stormy City line-up manager and Jynx's husband, spoke next. 'Okay everybody, there's going to be one last jam, but, like, *really* the last one this time. So, let's get this final line-up sorted.' He glanced down at Cantget, who was sitting on the floor massaging her ankle. 'You're our best jammer, how tired are you feeling? Has the adrenaline kicked in?'

She looked up sadly. 'I'd love to, but I did something to my ankle when I pushed through the wall during the last one.'

Matt didn't hesitate in moving his gaze elsewhere. There wasn't enough time to dither over things. 'Sam, I want you jamming.' It wasn't a request.

Sam had relaxed into the game as things had progressed, *but this is different, the pressure on this jam is immense*, it was literally win or lose.

Her bench coach must have sensed her panic. They grabbed her by both shoulders and turned Sam to look them directly in the eyes. 'Listen. All you have to do is get through.' They held an index finger up. 'Once. That's it. Get lead and call off the jam. Nothing more. No points. No laps. We just need to keep the score as it is, and we win.'

Sam exhaled slowly.

'They,' the coach nodded their head towards the Coastal Rollers' bench where the players were currently all in a huddle, 'need to get lead so that we can't call it off - our blockers will worry about preventing that - and then they also need to get at least one scoring pass to keep themselves in the game, all whilst holding you back. Our goal is infinitely more achievable than theirs.

'Once through, and call it. Okay? Nice and zen, just get it done. Matt chose you to do this because we know that you can. Now YOU just need to believe it too.'

Sam bit her lip then nodded resolutely. *I can believe it. I've trained hard for months. I know I can achieve this. I just need focus.*

Matt's voice broke Sam back out of her little bubble. 'Sam, listen. I'm gonna put Belle and River on with you to block, you choose who you want as your pivot and other blockers, people you work well with.'

The timeout was coming to an end, and both teams were readying to re-enter the track for the last time.

'Thora and Jynx, you're blocking,' Sam said decisively, 'Belle, you're pivot. Let's finish this.' She glanced once more at her coach as she donned the jammer helmet cover. 'Once through, call it,' they mouthed to Sam, and gave her a thumbs up before retreating to their chosen spot as close to the edge of the track as the referees would allow them to get.

'What do you need from us, Sam?' asked Belle calmly as they collectively approached the track boundary.

'Just give me some room. Hold their jammer tight

but give me space to pass you guys.' *I don't want anything to slow me down.*

Belle and the others hustled to the jam line before the other team and wordlessly took up their positions on the back line. This placement gave them the best chance of catching and holding the opposition jammer.

Jane came on as a blocker for the Coastal Rollers and smiled reassuringly at Sam before putting on her game face. She, like Sam, clearly felt that any more encouragement would be inappropriate with such a tense score separation hanging over them.

Sam sensed the Coastal Rollers' jammer drop back a couple of feet behind her, probably planning to follow Sam's chosen path through the Stormy City blockers when they made a gap for her.

The announcer was introducing the teams. 'Jamming for the Coastal Rollers we have Hit 'n' Run, and for Stormy City it's Thunder Kiss. She's had a great game today, but can she give the home team one last quality performance today? Time will tell, people.'

Sam risked a glance around, thinking that seeing her parents might take her mind off the pressure that she was putting herself under. But instead she became painfully aware of the tension and anticipation in the room. The stereo was playing loud music, but the audience were still and silent, some on the edge of their seats, and some that had given up on seats altogether, standing biting their nails.

A group of the Story City supporters were whispering to each other, looking austere. Cazz noticed Sam looking over at them. She cupped her hands around her mouth and screamed, 'Bring the thunder, Sam!'

This set off a chant from the rest of the supporters, and within seconds 'BRING. THE. THUN-DER!' was the only thing that Sam could hear. Sam expected to feel ready to crumble under the pressure, but for some reason the chanting grounded her instead.

A feeling of complete invincibility began to creep over her. She could almost physically feel it spreading itself around her body, enveloping the areas of her brain that were still in panic mode. She heard the chanting now as if through a fog and it helped her to focus. No expectations in the voices, the words acted purely as a reminder to her; don't hold back, don't apologise, push on through, go in hard.

Suddenly, it hit her. She could absolutely do this. It wasn't life and death, she'd already been there and felt that, and now she understood what Honey had known; giving it your all on the track was nothing, you weren't going to die from it, so what was there to be scared of? What reason to hold back? 'None,' the answer floated through her head in Honey's voice.

Sam blocked everything out and fixated on something she'd once heard Honey say; *"No apologies, no holding back, no reason not to give it my all."* She lowered her body into a squat. Tensed her quads. Readied her feet, and waited.

CHAPTER FIFTY-NINE

'Five seconds!' The call came through the fog, clearing it instantaneously. The crowd stopped chanting and fell silent once more.

Sam's eyes flicked upwards, surveying the scene before her in an instant. Her blockers were established on the back line. The Coastal Rollers were in front, practically sitting on the laps of the home team. Her blockers had nowhere to go. Except backwards.

Sam counted down the remaining seconds in her head.

Four…

Digging deep, she searched for that confidence and drive that she now knew she had within her. She turned her head slightly to find the other jammer, about three feet back, over her right shoulder.

Three…

Finding the forcefulness she knew she would need, she applied pressure to the outside edges of her skates, ready to move.

Two…

She suddenly launched herself backwards. Away from the jam line with its two walls of blockers.

Away past the other jammer, who seemed confused as to what Sam was doing. She stopped about twenty feet behind the jam line.

One…

Sam had never been great with the confines of a scrum start. Back here, it felt like she had all the space in the world. Transferring her weight onto her toe-stops she leaned forwards as the jam start whistle sounded. She then began to push forward on them like a sprinter in a hundred-metre race, barrelling back towards the jam line.

Hit 'n' Run was still distracted from Sam's sudden backwards movement and was not prepared for the Stormy City blockers. They instantly dropped back behind the jam line and engulfed the jammer. Belle was the closest blocker to the inside of the track, and she pushed her fellow blockers and Hit 'n' Run, who was caught up in between some of them, towards the outside, leaving some of the width clear for Sam as she had requested, just as she shot past them.

Sam's attention was fully on the Coastal blockers in front of her. Jane and another woman had their backs to her, and a stout blocker called Hefty Lefty was in front of them. Hefty was facing Sam and instructing the other blockers which side of the track she was heading towards.

No apologies, no holding back, no reason not to give it my all, Sam ran her new mantra through her head as she veered sharply to the right.

'To the outside!' barked Hefty Lefty, who was watching Sam's movements carefully.

Sam prepared herself. She dug her right foot into the floor and bounced back off it to change her direction.

'Inside! INSIDE!' Hefty shouted in a panic, but it

was too late. Sam smashed into the link between Jane and the other blocker in the same way that she had thrown her whole bodyweight at the door of the cubby she had been held captive in all those months ago. The unfortunate Coastal blocker that took the brunt of Sam's hit collapsed straight down to her knees and fell away. *One down.*

'Thunder Kiss now attempting to slip through the space she's just made, but Speechless and Hefty Lefty move in swiftly to protect that inside line… Thunder Kiss switches direction and does not hold back, PLOUGHING that shoulder into Lefty's chest! A skater's front is a biiiig legal target area to offer a jammer.'

Sam had ducked down low before hitting Lefty with her shoulder, then followed through with the full strength of her body, moving slightly upwards just before the impact. That combined with the force of her approach lifted Lefty off her feet and down onto her rear. The move had put Sam in front of Jane now, *that first blocker I hit down will be back on her feet about now.* Now she had to keep going forwards to make sure they didn't swallow her back into their wall.

The lead jammer whistles had not been blown yet, so Sam knew she still had work to do. *Where is their fourth blocker?*

As she looked ahead down the straight, she saw River in front of her. Her teammate had broken forwards and was braced to assist. Sam grabbed River's outstretched hand as she approached, and River powerfully whipped her forwards. As she let go of her teammate, Sam realised where the fourth Coastal blocker was.

'Thunder Kiss now faces Betty Badass playing a

last line of defence.'

With her back to Sam and looking over one shoulder to track her, Betty was covering the inside line of the track, right by the apex of its curve. *I'm going too fast from River's whip. If I hit her now, I'm going straight down, or worse, to the penalty box, then it'll be game over for Stormy City.*

'Speechless is giving chase.'

From somewhere behind Sam sounded a satisfying thud.

'A beautiful hip check on River Bruise from Speechless; taking her by surprise, off the track, and onto the floor!'

A part of Sam cheered her best friend's revenge move along with the audience, but she didn't have time to consider it fully. She had a choice to make.

Sam surveyed Betty Badass, the biggest and strongest of the Coastal Rollers. The blocker was on edge, waiting to see which direction Sam would favour.

Sam jerked her shoulders towards the outside of the track and Betty responded by committing her body weight in that direction. Leaning her hips and shoulders away from the inside ready to move into Sam's path, Betty left her feet in position right by the inside line, leaving Sam no room to pass.

At this point, Sam was almost on top of the blocker. It was now or never.

Steeling herself, Sam launched up off one foot and then the other, leaping over the blocker's lower leg where she had kept it guarding the inside line.

Time slowed.

Sam's heart beat a crazy rhythm in time with the music as she knew she'd finally pulled off the apex jump that had so far eluded her.

It felt graceful now, in those frozen moments that she soared through the air, but she was prepared for a messy landing afterwards, *as long as it's in-bounds, I don't care what it looks like!*

One foot landed first with the other trailing behind. Both of them hit the floor just a couple of inches away from the boundary tape, but on the right side of it.

The crowd erupted.

Supporters and skaters on both teams cheered Sam's move as the rest of her body followed her feet towards the gym floor. Her momentum brought her crashing down into a barrel roll along the track as the referee blew two short blasts on his whistle.

The announcer's excited voice pierced through Sam's thoughts of disbelief, 'Oh-ho! And with that amazing jump, Thunder Kiss is lead jammer!' From her position on the floor, Sam fumbled to tap her hips and end the jam.

Her sideways view of her teammates revealed that they had kept Hit 'n' Run contained. The refs blew the four whistles that indicated the end of the jam, shortly followed by the game wrap-up whistle.

Sam had done it. Stormy City had won.

Still on the ground, she rolled onto her back and stared at the ceiling for a few seconds, grinning. *I did it.*

She let the feeling sink in for a moment, then, turning her gaze sideways, she looked for her parents in the crowd. The elation disappeared instantly. She rolled over and jumped to her feet, desperately scanning the smiling faces.

'Hey, you were *awesome*!' Chris came over, beaming. 'Wait. What is it? What's wrong?'

'He's here.'

'Who's—'

'Dixon. He's here. I saw him earlier, but I just didn't know for sure, I thought it was me imagining things, my nerves, you know? But I've just seen him again, and others. He's here.'

CHAPTER SIXTY

'Sam?' Belle came over to where Sam and Chris stood as all around them skaters were hugging players from the opposing team and thanking each other for the game. 'Look, I don't want to worry you, but earlier I thought I saw the guy that tried to take you at knifepoint during the skate-a-thon. I didn't say anything at the time, cos I wasn't a hundred percent, but I've just seen him again and now I'm pretty certain.'

Sam was shaken, but her demeanour remained calm. She had known that this would happen, that she would have to face up against them someday. She breathed out slowly. 'Thanks, Belle. I'm pretty sure you're right, I've seen him too. Clean shaven now?'

'Yes. That's what threw me the first time I think, I just wasn't sure.'

'I need my phone. I've got the number for the NCA officer that's heading up Dixon's manhunt, she needs to be told immediately. Keep a close eye on them if you can, we can't let them leave if we can help it.'

'Be careful,' said Chris, 'you don't want to have to

go up against these guys alone.'

'Relax, I won't be alone; you guys are here,' Sam smiled at him reassuringly.

'Maybe I should—'

'Should what?'

'Never mind.' He looked directly into her eyes, 'I trust you.'

She leaned across and kissed him on the forehead as Belle looked on, her face full of concern.

'I'm only going to the changing rooms. I'll come back to make the call. Just… try not to let them leave the building in the meantime.'

Avoiding the audience members who were approaching the track-edge ready for their high-fives, Sam manoeuvred her way to the women's changing room and went straight for her kit bag. She rummaged around beneath her Stormy City hoody and her hand closed around her phone. Straightening up, she heard a click as the door to the changing room was locked.

'We haven't yet had the opportunity to meet, Thunder Kiss,' came the voice from behind her.

Heart in her throat, Sam spun around.

There he stood, the same height as her only because she still had her skates on - Bradford Dixon.

He leaned forward and ripped the phone from her hand, 'I'll be having that, we don't want any pesky voicemail issues like last time, do we?' he said, and switched it fully off.

He looked around the room at the scattered hoodies, spare helmets, and kit bags strewn around and seemed to conclude that they were alone. Sam couldn't help the tell-tale shocked expression that spread across her face, letting him know that she had not been prepared for his intrusion.

'Don't think about screaming. I have people outside that will end the lives of your loved ones faster than you can take a breath.'

Sam was fixed to the spot. Even the freshly lubricated bearings in her wheels seemed to be frozen when she would usually be fighting their attempts to roll on the slightly sloping tiled floor.

'So. Samantha,' he looked her up and down and sighed. 'You have caused me... *so* much trouble. Where do I even start to make you understand? Of course, I can't actually make you understand as easily as I once could, now that you killed my best man!'

Sam managed to regain enough control over her senses to start scanning the room for opportunities. Bradford saw her examining the door that he currently separated her from. 'Oh, be my guest,' he gestured past him, 'but really, you needn't bother running, there's no point. You know I have the power and the money to find you anywhere in the world that you might try to crawl away and hide.'

'I don't do that anymore,' Sam swallowed, finding her voice.

'What, running?'

'Crawl away and hide. It's not who I am.'

'Oh, I'm well aware. Because thanks to you, that's who I bloody am, isn't it?' he raised his voice slightly, but kept it low enough to still be drowned out by the music in the main hall outside. 'It's *me* that's been hiding in the shadows for months. *Me* that's had to run any time that I thought someone might have discovered where I was,' he moved in closer, 'because as soon as they get me home, they're gonna bring you out, aren't they? You,' he sneered, 'the only person in the entire fucking world that can link me to those "terrorist attacks",' he drew double quotes in the air with his fingers on the last two words.

Sam said nothing, letting Bradford talk, the sound of his own voice bloating his self-importance, like it had the night he ordered David Steele's murder. In the meantime, she needed to get it together and think of a plan. For now, all she had was to keep him talking and buy some time.

'But without you, the authorities have nothing on me. So I could resurface, come home. Maybe as the victim of a failed ransom. Yes, I like that. I could escape after "months of imprisonment", just in time to foil another attack by the people who took me, the perpetrators of the last attacks on the city, and they needed me to allow them access to the Connected network to hide their activities.'

'That's what you did,' it made sense to Sam now, 'you programmed the system to ignore you, *that's* why they couldn't find you with your own state-of-the-art product.'

'I admit it wasn't a great advert, but I wasn't expecting to have to use that feature. Another thing to add to the list titled, "Samantha's Fucking Fault",' he spat. 'But when I come back, I can help them find everyone else involved in the attacks and prove its worth once more.'

'Sell out everyone you've worked with, you mean?'

'Why not? What are they to me? They'll be useful for the other attacks I have planned in cities that are still sitting around with their thumbs up their arses, trying to decide whether to invest in Connected or not. After I achieve the desired uptake, I can sell the morons out and start profiting once more for all the bloody effort I put into marketing that software. Of course, that brings us back full circle to you, doesn't it Samantha? I can't do any of that whilst you're still wandering around.'

'You call what you did "marketing"? You're completely deluded, you know that?'

'I'm a fucking fugitive! At least until I tracked you down, I was.'

'How did you find me?'

'Connected, obviously. I might not show up in searches on the software, but my backend access still works. I mean, it was risky, but I couldn't get you at home as that's under surveillance, I needed to know where else you would be likely to be.'

'I'm flattered. All this for little old me.'

'Well, I do have a personal interest in your downfall. You disposed of my best and most trusted man. I needed him to coordinate the next attacks and leave me with some deniability.'

'And he killed one of my best friends,' Sam almost whispered through gritted teeth.

'Ah, yes, Miss Honey. That was unfortunate, an unnecessary accident, you can hardly hold it against us.'

Sam began to slowly seethe at his attitude.

Bradford inspected his nails, and suddenly the magnolia changing room walls faded away, and Sam was back in the alley behind the Tin Whistle, watching this maniac prepare to end Steele's life with a simple nod.

'I'm not the sort of man to get my hands dirty usually Samantha, I prefer to leave that to others, like Phil. But you've left me little choice, having disposed of him, a fact that has annoyed me so much that I'm prepared to deal with *you* personally.'

CHAPTER SIXTY-ONE

Bradford was casually leaning against the wall by the changing room door now. Sam considered making a run for it, she had to do something at least to prevent more attacks and loss of innocent life, even if not to protect her own.

'So… what do you want from me, exactly?'

'I need you to not be able to contest my story. I know you've made a statement already, but I can easily find ways to discredit you, especially if you're not able to defend yourself.'

'Fine,' she gulped, 'kill me then.'

'Not so fast, princess. I also need you to suffer… because of the hassle you have put me through, consider it an interest payment. So, I want you to tell the NCA yourself that you made up everything about me, so that you could blackmail me.'

Sam stared at him, open-mouthed. *He can't be serious.*

'I want you to tell everyone how Phil was the mastermind of the attacks, and that I knew nothing about it. That he was planning to frame me and use his shares in Dixon Defences to take control of the Connected project.'

'Charming. You'll even sell out your right-hand-man after he's gone.'

Bradford sighed contentedly, 'He was always so loyal, he'd be proud to still be of service to me even after his death.'

'You know they were on to you before I was ever on the scene.'

'But they didn't have anything on me.'

Hands empty of any weapon, Sam couldn't see anything that she could use. She decided a swift kick with her skates on was worth a try, and discretely shifted her weight, putting one toe-stop down to steady herself then poised to kick out with the other foot. 'If you think I'm agreeing to that then—'

'Oh, but you will. Remember I told you that I have people outside with your friends and family?' he took his phone out of his pocket and showed her the messaging screen. Just two words were displayed in what appeared to be a message ready to send to multiple recipients. It read "kill them".

Bradford studied Sam's face as she felt her blood drain out of it. 'All I have to do is hit "send". So, you'll agree to pretty much anything I tell you to.'

Sam's muscles felt frozen in place again, tensed, ready to pounce, but knowing she couldn't.

'I'm enjoying this now! That look on your face is starting to make all those months of moving around from place to place worth it!'

She hung her head, the feelings of defeat creeping in, winding their fingers around her heart and squeezing. Her gaze settled near to Jane's kit bag, on a shirt with her friend's name, "Speechless", on it, and she realised that she would lose regardless; either her friends and family were killed because she didn't cooperate, or millions of innocents were killed because she did.

Then she spotted something else near Jane's kit bag, and it fuelled her.

'Just so I'm clear, you blew up five buildings in the city, ordered the murder of the man who helped you arrange it, killed my friend, kidnapped me, sent your thugs to try and kill me at an NCA safe house, and now you want me to pretend none of it was you, so that you can blow up another load of buildings in another load of cities, all to sell more software and make more money, even though you already own half of this city?'

'That's about the upshot of it, yes. I mean, let's be clear, your friend's murder and your kidnapping were actually nothing to do with me, but the rest of the stuff… yeah. I've poured millions into the Connected product suite, and if I have to blow a few people up to get some return on it, then fine.'

Sam held her look of disbelief for a few seconds longer, before suddenly melting it into a smile that she just couldn't contain.

Bradford looked uneasy, 'What? What is it?'

'You may have power, and you may have money… but you also have an unfortunate tendency to collect witnesses every time that you get close to getting those perfectly manicured nails dirty. I, on the other hand, I have friends.' Sam was enjoying the power shift, her relief allowing her to fall into theatrics, 'In fact I have this one friend in particular, she's got a lot of experience with being quiet and going unnoticed. Speechless?'

Bradford's mouth fell open as Jane's tall frame unfolded from the floor where she had been half tucked under the bench.

'Dropped my mouthguard,' she held it up, covered in bits of fluff. In her other hand was her mobile phone, which she then put to her ear and listened for a moment.

Bradford had still not moved, other than gaping from one woman to the next and back again, clearly trying to comprehend where exactly Jane had come from, all the derby gear lying around acting as camouflage for her.

Jane nodded to no one in particular, then pulled the phone away from her ear. 'Detective Inspector Tanaka says they have enough, thanks,' she smiled at Sam.

At that moment, Bradford knew his world had just collapsed around him. The look of shock turned to one of sheer malice, and an evil smile erupted on his face as he raised his own phone, and hit the "send" button on his pre-composed message.

CHAPTER SIXTY-TWO

With nothing left to lose, Sam launched herself past Bradford, knocking him roughly to the ground. She reached for the door and tussled with the lock, her heartbeat pounding in her ears, terrified of what she might find on the other side. Jane was directly behind her, having rushed past Bradford sprawled on the floor. The door gave way, and Sam stumbled through straight into a handsome, middle-aged woman on the other side.

She gently manoeuvred a confused Sam out of her way and stepped forward of her protectively.

'Mr. Dixon, I have reason to believe that you are in there. Please come out slowly with your hands in the air.'

A couple of uniformed police officers suddenly appeared next to them, a little out of breath.

'Just in time, boys,' the woman flashed some form of identification to them, 'get your cuffs ready and your dancing shoes on, because this one will warrant some celebration.'

Bradford appeared in the changing room doorway, hands in the air, his expression that of a beaten man.

One of the uniformed officers stepped forward to physically restrain him, whilst the woman informed him of his rights.

Suddenly remembering why she had bolted through the door in the first place, Sam turned around to face the hall, and almost tripped over a leg on the floor by her skate. A clean-shaven Ethan was lying on the floor, defeated, with Bella and Thora sitting on top of him.

'Hey, Sam, so… meet my Mum, Chief Superintendent At-The-Brawl,' Belle gestured to the woman who was now holding Bradford firmly by the elbow. 'She always comes to watch my games.' Her eyes followed Sam's gaze to Ethan's prone figure beneath them. 'Oh, he was guarding the door, a couple of girls came to complain that he wouldn't let them in to get to their stuff.'

'We intervened,' said Thora unnecessarily, beaming.

'Hey, Mum, I think he has a knife on him, I can feel something digging into my butt cheek.'

Thora sniggered.

'I hope so, honey, then we can charge him with carrying,' she instructed one of the uniformed officers to pat Ethan down.

'Skipper,' the young officer nodded an eager acknowledgement.

Jane came up behind Sam, putting a reassuring arm over her shoulders. 'They're all okay, Sammy.'

It was Sam that was speechless right now as she took in what had been going on around her.

Thora pointed over to a solid wall of rollergirls, practiced at not letting people escape through the gaps between their bodies. They were surrounding a group of three men and a woman who were busy being detained by another two police officers. 'They were sooo easy to flush out,' said Thora, 'they were all too busy watching you, so none of them had actually been watching the gameplay.'

Cazz had appeared behind them, 'So Thora decides they look out of place, and she goes and asks them which team they thought had the best ball control...' she burst out laughing.

'Yeah, it was a dead giveaway when they actually tried to think of a viable answer!' Thora collapsed into hearty giggles with Ethan still under her, grunting in discomfort.

'Samantha!' Chris came jogging over, 'I was by the main entrance, but pretty sure the police have everyone now.' He looked over her shoulder to where Belle's mother was standing holding a handcuffed Bradford Dixon by the upper arm. He nodded in their direction, 'Your doing?'

'Well, mostly Jane's actually! I just kept him talking,' she exchanged grins with her friend. She noticed that Chris seemed unable to take his eyes off his former employer. 'Dixon Defences stock will fall rather dramatically when word gets out, I imagine. Probably good that you changed jobs when you did.'

'It still feels weird, you know. Like a betrayal. I looked up to him so much when I was younger,' he continued to watch Bradford as the uniformed officers led him away out of the building. 'Still,' he suddenly seemed to be snapped out of his reverie, 'onwards to bigger and better things, am I right?'
Chris placed a gentle hand on each of Sam's shoulders, and turned her away from all the commotion going on around them. 'You know, some of the main things I love about you; your devout loyalty to those you care about; your perseverance; and your

take-no-shit attitude,' his voice softened as he looked directly into her eyes, 'I get it now, I realise that derby gave you all of that,' he laughed softly, 'and that it's not all hot pants and glitter.'

Sam smiled as Chris carried on.

'I know I can be over-protective, but I just care so much for you that it's automatic, and it's hard for me to reign it in. I also realise that you *can* think for yourself, I don't own you, and you're not mine to take care of how I see fit,' he paused and exhaled deeply. 'So, I know that you said you still don't feel any different about relationship commitment, and marriage etcetera after our ordeal... but I'm gonna ask you something anyway.' Pulling a small box from behind his back, Chris got down onto one knee in front of Sam. There were some small gasps from behind her as a couple of the Stormy City skaters realised what was happening.

Sam was horrified. She did not want the commitment of marriage yet, despite her strong feelings for Chris. He *knew* this, and yet here he was, down on one knee in front of her, in front of *everyone*, about to ruin everything. He didn't seem phased by the look on Sam's face, in fact, his expression had something more akin to amusement behind it. 'Samantha Beaven,' Chris began, 'would you please do me the honour—' he slowly opened the box. Inside, glinting from all angles underneath the harsh gym hall lighting, was a highly polished silver key, '—of moving in with me.'

Shocked, confused, and not in small part, relieved, Sam managed to find her voice, 'Move in, to your place?'

Chris scratched the back of his head and over-acted being casual, 'Yeah, well my flatmate has recently moved out, so there's space at my place now.'

'Don't you think that maybe you should move in with me? My place is much nicer.'

'I was hoping you'd say that, but it wouldn't have made much sense to present you with your own key and invite myself to move in now would it?' he grinned.

Sam threw her head back and laughed.

'So, is that a "yes" then?'

'Yes! But are you sure that you'll be okay with that being all for a while?'

'Samantha,' his tone lowered in a serious fashion, 'I'm not losing you again. I'll do whatever you want, whatever it takes, to keep you in my life and close to me.'

Chris stood and Sam hugged him as her teammates all cheered the couple. 'Er, Chris… I'd best find Mum and Dad and explain to them what they just saw. I don't want Mum picking out her Mother-of-the-Bride outfit on the way home.'

She looked around the hall once more, 'It's been a really strange day.'

CHAPTER SIXTY-THREE

'Please tell me that's the last of them,' Belle said to Chris, 'I mean, I love lugging heavy boxes around as much as the next person, it's a good workout, but even I'm done now.'

Chris laughed, 'Thank-you again for your help, Belle, and there are a couple more bags, but I've got those covered.'

Belle checked her watch as Sam flung herself down on the sofa.

'I'm ravenous, are you staying for dinner, Belle?'

'No, I have to go, I've got Team West Indies training in the morning, so I want to get to bed at a reasonable time.'

They said their goodbyes, as Chris thanked the two guys from his football team that had also come to lend him a hand with the move. A minute later, the front door closed, and it was just the two of them left.

'Welcome home,' Sam said quietly to Chris, who responded with a squeezy hug where they lay entangled on the sofa.

Sam's phone dinged a message alert. 'Oh wow! It's Jane, she's been accepted onto a holiday training program at a software company. She says it leads on to a managerial position when she's finished her uni degree!'

'That's brilliant, that's what she's always wanted, isn't it?'

'It is. It's perfect.' Sam was beaming as she typed Jane a quick congratulatory message back.

'Funny how you've both ended up moving forward with your careers at the same time.'

'It's just a counselling course, it's not a new job.'

'Not yet, but I know you'll be great at it, so it won't be long,' he kissed the top of her head.

'Come on, roomie,' Chris said, snatching up his newly-cut key from the coffee table, 'let's go grab some pizza to bring home.'

'You're on!'

The two put on shoes and headed out the front door. As she passed, Sam straightened a frame on the wall that had been knocked during all the to-ing and fro-ing with boxes throughout the day. She smiled slightly, her fingers tracing across the words on the award from her first home game with Stormy City: "Awarded to Thunder Kiss, for her fearlessness (and for beating the bad guys)".

THE END

OTHER WORKS FROM
KAREN POMERANTZ

If you enjoyed Bring the Thunder, please download or sample my novelette, Trapping Honey, available from most eBook stores.
Trapping Honey is the story of Sarah Honey's abduction, and precedes the events of Bring the Thunder.

Also available is The Cost of Living, a short, creepy horror story exploring the dark side of humanity's desire to live forever.

KEEPING INFORMED

You can keep up to date with my goings on, including news of future releases, via social media by following me on Twitter and Instagram, and liking my Facebook page.

You can also follow my author pages on Amazon and Goodreads.

CREDIT WHERE CREDIT'S DUE

I want to give a huge thank-you to a few people that have helped me tremendously through the process of writing and editing this book, either with their kind words when they were needed, or their harsh ones, because sometimes that's needed too!

My Mum, Mal,
Carrie & Red Jolley,
Eve Pomerantz,
Lisa 'Pinky & The Pain' Ward,
Sarah Johnson,
Harri Clarke,
And of course, my husband, Paul.

FEEDBACK FOR THE AUTHOR

It only takes a moment to rate Bring the Thunder on Goodreads, Amazon, or your chosen eBook store. It really helps me reach more people so please consider doing this if you have the time.

If you enjoyed my debut novel, it would mean the world to me if you would write a review.

SELECTIVE MUTISM

Selective Mutism isn't as rare a disorder as you might think. There is a lack of awareness and understanding of the condition and consequently it is often overlooked as a diagnosis. It often only becomes apparent when children are first entering a social environment outside of the family home, such as starting to attend school or nursery, and is commonly mistaken for shyness in the child.

I only know of this specific anxiety disorder myself as a friend struggles with the condition. She currently attends university, and although her condition is much improved from when I first met her almost ten years ago, she still has close family members that she has never been able to utter a word to.

SM is best treated as early as possible. The ongoing effects if left unchecked can include social anxieties as well as difficulties at school, both academically (as the child may be unable to ask for help when they are struggling), and with day-to-day tasks, such as asking to be excused to go to the toilet.

Even if the symptoms of the Selective Mutism itself are successfully treated or overcome as the child gets older, the aforementioned effects can have consequences lasting well into adulthood.

It is for this reason that I chose to include an SM sufferer in my story; the more people that have even the slightest awareness of the existence of this disorder, the greater the chance that even just a few more cases are caught and able to be treated at an early stage.

If you'd like to know more, visit the websites and social media profiles of SMIRA, Selective Mutism Foundation, and Selective Mutism Association.

ROLLER DERBY NAMES

Although "Honey Trap" is a derby name of my own invention, there is at least one person that came up with it first. The name is registered to number 93 of the Valleys Roller Dolls on the International Master Roster – any likeness to my character is purely coincidental.

Stormy City is a league name of my own invention, although a similar one does exist - Storm City.
Storm City Roller Girls is a flat track derby league located in Clark County, Washington, that is committed to promoting the empowerment of women of all races, national origins, religious beliefs, sexual orientations and body types by creating positive athletic role models and a community-based sport for those of all skill levels.

* 9 7 8 1 9 1 6 0 3 6 7 1 0 *